To Donn
Mew

C000176541

THE DOLL
MAKERS

PENNY GRUBB

ACORN INDEPENDENT PRESS

Praise For The Author

I particularly enjoy the fact that these books give a real picture of life as a 21st century private investigator, rather than slipping into the hackneyed `amateur sleuth' model.
Susan Alison, author and artist, Bristol

This is Crime as it should be written, Crime set in the real world where family life and financial worries impinge. Not quite hard-boiled, not quite noir... I think Penny Grubb could just be carving herself an entire sub-genre niche.
Linda Acaster, author

Penny has a way of getting inside the heads and hearts of her characters to bring them to life. Even her villains carry characteristics that make the reader care what happens. But it is Annie who we really empathise with, in spite of her faults, irritabilities, occasional snap judgements and chaotic domestic lifestyle.
Must Mutter Literary Blog

Praise For The Doll Makers

*I just had to keep on reading and reading and reading.
How could I stop, even to sleep, when Annie was in such
straits? In fact I came, madly, near to feeling that she
needed my support and that I needed to stick by her to the
end.*
Unmissable.
R Harris, Barrister and writer

*The story holds the reader's interest from the start and
keeps a tight grip on it to the last word.*
Stuart Aken, Author and reviewer

*The Doll Makers is beautifully textured with a rich
number of threads running through the story to a real
roller coaster ending.*
Angela Dracup, Author and reviewer.
Mystery Women website

Copyright © Penny Grubb 2011

Published by Acorn Independent Press Ltd, 2011.
First published in hardback by Robert Hale Ltd in May 2010

The right of Penny Grubb to be identified as the Author of the Work
has been asserted by her in accordance with the Copyright, Designs and
Patents Act 1988.

This book is sold subject to the condition it shall not, by way of trade or
otherwise circulated in any form or by any means, electronic or otherwise without the publisher's prior consent.

Printed and bound by CPI Group (UK) Ltd, Croydon, CR0 4YY

ISBN 978-1-908318-68-8

www.acornindependentpress.com

About the Author

Penny Grubb is a novelist as well as an academic and Chair of the Authors' Licensing and Collecting Society, the largest writers' organisation in the world. Her fiction includes the crime series featuring Private Investigator, Annie Raymond.

Penny won the Crime Writers' Association's Debut Dagger for her novel, the Doll Makers, one of her Annie Raymond series. In 2010, Like False Money, another novel in the series, was nominated for the CWA John Creasey Dagger. A writer all her life, Penny penned her first story at age 4 and won her first writing competition at age 9. She has worked in a variety of jobs and seen the inside of hospitals and pathology labs across Europe. As well as her crime novels, Penny's work has been published as short fiction, non-fiction, textbooks, academic papers, articles and radio broadcasts.

Find out more at:

www.pennygrubb.com

Photograph by Weronika Dziok

Also By The Author

The Jawbone Gang

Like False Money

Both titles are now available in paperback,
published in 2011 by Acorn Independent Press

Acknowledgements

Thanks to all the family for their unconditional support, especially the Thursday trio for reading the manuscript in so many versions, and to B Dziok for his incredible talent in creating the artwork for the cover

To Ann for a friendship spanning six decades that so enriched my life.

CHAPTER ONE

The words changed on the long drive north. Annie's determination did not.

In the Ladies at Leicester Forest East, where she stopped to top up – coffee for her, water for the car – she pulled a comb through her hair and practiced what she would say. *Dad. I have bad news.* It was the antithesis of the old coming-home fantasy, where her short-cropped hair would be a little longer, her five feet two inches would be clad in a smart business suit, and she'd smile as her father said, 'I always knew you had it in you, Annie'. She'd failed his every expectation since she was eight years old, and now at twenty-eight she was about to turn his life upside down.

The early morning sun made a mobile oven of the car, and the journey became hotter and stuffier. The blower gave her tepid air and hot engine smells, before beginning a clatter like a death rattle. She clicked it off.

By the time she reached the M6, the traffic eased, allowing more space to rehearse the scenes in her head. From Lockerbie to the outskirts of Glasgow she listened to the ghosts of future conversations.

It's not me, Dad. It's Aunt Marian.

Your aunt? What's she to do with it?

Incredible that her mother and aunt had been sisters. Annie sometimes studied her own reflection for whole minutes at a time, trying to cut away her father's features and see her mother, but there was nothing she could home in on. Her mother must have been small and slight like her aunt – yet not like her at all, or her father could never have loved her. And her father wasn't over tall himself; only just made the height requirement when he joined up. But he was stolid and had a stockiness Annie could see in herself.

Though she made good time, Glasgow was well awake and bustling. The traffic demanded her concentration as she drove through and out towards the ferry docks. Cars bounced up the ramp as sea-birds screeched overhead then swooped into squabbling bundles on the water's surface. She nudged her car on to the deck and climbed out to spend the few minutes of the crossing up on the foot passengers' walkway, where she leant on the rail. The sea air rushed over her as the ferry pushed its way across the Clyde. The light changed, the clarity of early morning giving way to the haze and heat of the day. For a minute, she surrendered to the sensations of coming home, the smell of the sea, the empty mountains rising up ahead.

She remembered her aunt's voice on the phone. *A massive drugs consignment, Annie. So exciting ... lost in the hills ... your father's had a terrible time.*

She could dilute out her aunt's exaggeration, but her father had confirmed a Customs sting gone wrong. Drugs had come this way. Not the huge pantechnicon that her aunt imagined, *Drugs consignment Ltd* blazoned on the side of the lorry, but something big. She wondered if it had crossed here, on this ferry. And where had it headed, how had it been lost? A customized vehicle maybe, or customized people. As she squeezed back into her car, she looked at her fellow passengers, but surely there were no drugs mules amongst this lot.

Last lap now. Tell him and get it over with, face the consequences. No other option. He'd give her a rough ride, but he'd come through for her. Facing him would be part of the penance.

If she still had the BMW Aunt Marian had bought her, she'd almost be home. But the old Nissan coughed as she jigged it down the ramp, and she daren't take the direct route over the mountain passes.

As soon as she could, she'd swap this overheated vehicle for tracksuit and trainers, and get into the hills. Nothing cleared the mind better than forcing muscles to their limits. She'd taken to pounding up the Victorian stairways of the older stations once she'd moved to London. They were every bit as good at getting thighs and calves to screaming pitch and lungs to white heat, but lacked the challenge of the hills, hidden ravines waiting to trap the unwary who strayed from the tracks.

As Annie parked outside her father's house and shut off the engine, a movement caught her attention. A small figure carrying a covered basket scuttled down the path that led from the mountain track. A memory superimposed itself, then melted away. Annie stopped. Her mother's face shimmered just out of reach at the edge of her mind.

The girl's head shot up, maybe sensing Annie's stare. Their eyes met and Annie let out a sigh. It was only the girl from the Doll Makers delivering dolls to the shop. The girl ducked her head and scurried on.

Annie turned back to her father's house. This drugs thing had better be nothing. She didn't want to find him weighed down under his own problems, she'd brought enough new ones with her. Bag over her shoulder, she marched up the path.

The door swung open and her smile froze. It was the housekeeper, not her father, framed in the doorway. For a moment they stared their mutual dislike and then footsteps hurried up from the darkness of the hallway. 'Annie, you're early,' her father said. 'How are you?'

She sensed more than saw the tiny twitch of a knowing smirk. Mrs Latimer might be the stupidest woman alive, but animal instinct told her Annie was in trouble.

I've bad news, Dad...

She swallowed the words. 'Fine.' She greeted her father with their customary arm's-length hug and brief touching of cheeks.

Dad ... The moment slipped away.

'I've to do a couple of hours this morning,' her father said, with an apologetic nod to the jacket of his uniform as he tucked his warrant card into the pocket. 'I wasn't expecting you so early. You have a rest after your journey. We'll go down to the pub at lunchtime.'

'Aye, you've set off in the middle of the night to be here by now.' This from Mrs Latimer. 'There's nothing wrong, is there?'

'No, everything's fine.' Annie gestured towards the bag where her running shoes hung by their laces. 'I'll go out for a run. Get the journey off me.' *We'll go down to the pub at lunchtime.* Just like old times.

She turned and looked Mrs Latimer in the eye, catching a shaft of disappointment. Mrs Latimer thought she'd scented a false trail. Annie didn't allow herself to feel smug.

The afternoon found Annie lazing outside the pub, a pint of heavy in her hand, legs stretched out. The vast expanse of the loch spread in front of her, the sun glinting off small waves, the incoming tide hustling pebbles along the shore. Children raced about, their laughter and shrieks overlying the rhythmic slap-slap-slap of water against the wooden landing.

She breathed deeply, trying to relax, and lay back and listened, wanting to eavesdrop on other people's conversations if she couldn't be alone. The voices wouldn't come together. They were a blurred backdrop to the rhythmic slapping of the water, the low growl of the pebbles. The loch stretched out in front of her, dark, cold; untouched by the heat of the day.

A shout from the crowd of children down by the jetty pierced her protective shell. 'Dad! See what I've got!'

Dad ... It's bad news...

She cut her eyes towards the group, half-focused on the young boy, pulling at something he'd snagged below the quay. Freddie Pearson. She had a memory of him outside the shop playing a pseudo-gruesome tug-of-war with another child where a straw doll jerked back and forth between them and eventually ripped apart.

She turned away and saw her father, his stocky form framed in the doorway of the pub, blinking as he stepped from the gloom of the bar to the bright sunshine. She watched as he wandered over. This was the perfect opportunity. *Dad, I've bad news...*

'DAD!' Freddie Pearson's voice ripped through the summer breeze at a volume that couldn't be ignored. Annie saw Freddie's father glance over his shoulder, rolling his eyes in good-natured exasperation to his mates round the table. 'Good lad, Fred,' he shouted. 'Reel it in like I've showed you.'

Annie lifted her feet off the ground, flexing muscles that weren't used to these hills.

'Looks like the rain'll hold off.'

Her father pulled out a chair to sit beside her. He smiled.

'Dad...' She paused to swallow, her mouth suddenly dry.

As she met his gaze and started to speak, they were both jarred by a bellow from down by the water.

'DA...AD!' Freddie was seriously frustrated now, his yell so sharp that everyone turned. He'd reeled in his catch, struggled to lift the rod high enough for his father to see what swung on the end of the line. High enough for everyone to see.

Annie's mind gave a horrified lurch – a flashback to two boys laughing over a torn doll, its smile incongruous as straw spilt from its severed limb. She saw the pint-pot slip from her grasp in slow-motion, tipping as it fell, brown liquid and foam spraying in the splintering of glass. As it shattered at her feet, her eyes focused again on the children by the landing.

That was no doll on the end of Freddie's line.

Chapter Two

There was a moment of absolute quiet, then pandemonium erupted. The smashing of glass, the scraping of chairs as people scrambled to rise, shrieks losing all sense of play ... and underlying the mayhem, the steady slap-slap-slap of waves on the jetty. The loch was no longer backdrop to the benign summer's day.

Annie couldn't drag her eyes from the water's surface, knowing that under the silver glint of the waves were fathoms of cold, heavy darkness. And somewhere out there was the rest of it ... the rest of Freddie's catch.

People shouted. Someone ran screaming towards her father. She jumped up and tried to shake her mind back on track. Where were the lightning reflexes she took such pride in? She looked at the crowd round the quay, then out again over the water. The rest of it wouldn't be out there, it would be caught under the wooden structure the children fished from.

She took a deep breath, remembering that she could cope with nasty situations, and turned towards her father. Briefly she met his eye, saw realization dawn. She had to help him deal with this. Matching his step, she strode with him towards the landing, bracing herself for the worst. Whatever ... whoever ... was down there was in an advanced stage of decay for Freddie to have reeled in just part of a leg.

The frenetic panic pushed Annie aside with the rest of the crowd, as hurried calls brought in officialdom to take over the scene and lay down order in flapping tapes and specialist teams. She stayed on the periphery, and watched her father pace up and down. He spoke into his phone and joined grim-faced confabs with colleagues, or just marched back and forth as though measuring the ground, a dark crease of worry above his eyes.

She listened to the excited horror in hushed comments from the people around her. Freddie Pearson, sitting on a low wall, his father at one side, a young policewoman leaning solicitously over him, was the only one whose expression showed undisguised delight at the sudden drama. Something on her father's face stopped Annie from joining in the eager speculation, as though she was the one in the crowd with a missing relative.

But Dad, I have to talk to you... And how could she burden him with her own problems now? She remembered Aunt Marian's excited speculation about the drugs heist. How much was her aunt's exaggeration? How big the nugget of truth? And even if it were nothing, now he had this. She glanced again towards the pier, then turned away. No one needed her here. She headed for home.

By evening, the house was dark and quiet but for the padding footsteps of her old enemy. The clock on the mantelpiece gave a tinny chime announcing seven o'clock as Mrs Latimer entered the room and started straightening cushions. Funny how priorities change, Annie thought. She could manoeuvre Mrs Latimer out of her father's life now if she put her mind to it. It had once been her greatest ambition, but the need was gone. Mrs Latimer was a stupid woman who would never be more than a housekeeper to him.

'Oh why don't—?' She stopped and took a deep breath. Then she turned and began again, keeping her voice neutral, not letting the irritation show. 'Why don't you get off now? I'll see to things.'

Mrs Latimer pursed her lips. Annie watched the inner struggle. Would she stay just because she knew Annie didn't want her, or would the wish to get back to her own house triumph? Annie let out a sigh as home comforts won the day and Mrs Latimer went to get her coat.

'Make sure that you tell your father...' A peremptory stream of orders followed, designed to show who was really in charge.

Annie switched off, gazed into the middle distance and didn't move until the door slammed and she was alone.

She moved aimlessly round the house until the ring of the phone interrupted her thoughts. Her hand was outstretched for the handset before she registered the muted sound. It rang in her father's office, not in the hall. That meant Mrs Latimer had forgotten to switch it through before she left.

Annie hurried to the kitchen and flicked through the rack of keys on the wall. She was at the office door when she heard the answer-phone cut in. It took a few seconds to get the door open and for her to cross the room. She stopped within an inch of her target. Mrs Latimer's voice came through the machine.

'Just a reminder, Annie. Don't forget...'

Annie tensed in a wave of irritation. Mrs Latimer was reminding her to go into her father's office to switch the phone back so it rang in the hall. The woman had forgotten but wouldn't admit it. Why couldn't she simply say, 'I forgot. Please would you...?' The office was Mrs Latimer's domain, always had been. *I'll do that ... I'll get it ... You know your father hates anyone in the office when he's not there...*

And now the woman was giving detailed instructions on where to find the key. She'd raised her voice, obviously picturing Annie helpless the other side of the door with her ear pressed to the wood. This was too much. Annie reached out, plucked the receiver from its rest and put it straight down again with a huff of satisfaction at shutting the woman up.

This room had always been her father's sanctum, children not allowed. It was still a forbidden room, but he trusted her enough these days not to hide the key. The desk was tidy and locked. There'd been no photos on its surface for nearly twenty years. Dark wood and leather gleamed at her, just as it had all that time ago. And the same tang of furniture polish hung in the air daring any speck of dust to settle. The silvery sheen of a filing cabinet was new, but otherwise the room was as it had always been. She thought back to childhood days when she'd tried every trick to find a way in. Then, when she was eight years old, they'd laid her mother out here and the room lost even the appeal of the forbidden. It was somewhere she didn't want to be.

She was aware of a movement and saw that one of the cats had slipped in. She followed it across to the window and looked out over the garden. Musing on the past opened a vista on territory that was safe from current problems and severed limbs, but still uncomfortable.

It was almost twenty years since she'd stood in this room by the coffin. Memory conjured up the warmth of Inspector McMahon's hand as it engulfed hers. *Be a brave lass, Annie.* She tried to catch the memory that would translate the scene to the funeral at the church. Had it been at the church? Why didn't she know?

McMahon was long gone. She'd heard he worked himself into the grave over those twelve months up to his retirement, but had to give up with the killer on the loose. As memory showed her Inspector McMahon's face, she was drawn to the look she'd seen in her father's eye, down by the quay. It had been gone almost at once, overtaken by the practicalities. He'd become the efficient copper in charge of the situation. A terrible rush of *déjà vu* gripped her. It hadn't been a pleasant sight for any of them, but her father had seen more in it than an anonymous severed limb swinging from Freddie's line.

She wanted him home quickly, early, to show it wasn't anything serious. It was hardly going to be trivial, the loss of a leg, but she wanted to hear there was a rational explanation, that it was nothing sinister, that whatever he'd thought, he was wrong, that maybe she'd be able to talk to him after all.

It was a big house. Too big for him on his own. But it had been too big for years. Her mother's murder meant no more children in it. In fact, it meant the one child they had would be shipped out. Memories of her mother's death reached out and touched her from all sides. The fights with Mrs Latimer. Her father, a fleeting presence, a white-faced fury who appeared only to shout.

Behave yourself, Annie!
Annie! Be quiet!

I had to shout, Dad. It was the only way to get you out from behind that door. Why didn't you see? I needed you so much.

Where were these ghosts coming from? She'd laid them to rest years ago. She and her father had all this out. Here in this room, seven years after her mother died, when she was fifteen years old.

'*Why did you throw me out?*'

'*It wasn't like that, Annie. I didn't want you to go.*'

How strange that she should feel the pain in his voice across the years when she hadn't heard it then.

'*You wanted me out of the way so you could shag the Latimer bitch.*'

Slap.

Christ! Had she really said that to him? Is that what she'd believed? *I'm sorry, Dad. I was only fifteen. Fifteen and packed with rage.*

Involuntarily, her hand went to the side of her head, as she relived the sting of the blow that had almost knocked her off her feet. And she saw the shock in his eyes, horrified at what he'd done. Her own pain had been so sharp, so urgent, she hadn't seen his. Maybe he really had tried to do his best for her. But he'd shipped her out to live with her mother's elder sister. It had been an open wound of resentment that left Mrs Latimer victorious in Annie's real home. From the age of nine, she lived with Aunt Marian and home was just a place to visit. Had years of denying the memories obliterated them? Had she had one real conversation with her father since she was fifteen years old, and why couldn't she remember her mother's funeral?

The sun set over the loch, crimson tendrils snaking out across the water. Framed by the office window, it was a picture-postcard end to the day. An incongruous backdrop to a body in the loch and to a crumbling dream that pulled the ground from under her.

The cat twisted round on the windowsill, eyes bright, ready to explore the forbidden room. She scooped it up and tucked it under her arm.

She'd die – really die – before she saw her aunt caged in a home. If she were on her own in this, she'd keep quiet, let the flat go and hole up in the rented lock-up. She'd climb back out of this pit, like she'd climbed out of others. Oh yeah, she'd be fine. But Aunt Marian...? *I have to tell him. I can't just let it land.*

Watching out over the garden, a cat draped across her arm, Annie mulled over being wrong about a body caught up in the wooden struts of the jetty. The team her father brought in searched under and around and found no sign of it. And thinking back to the way he'd looked, the way he'd acted, she wasn't sure he'd expected them to.

It was a classically beautiful view, down the glen, out over the loch and to the mountains beyond, but Annie felt none of the peace it usually gave her. The sense of something rotten she'd brought with her pervaded the whole landscape. The smooth water was no more than a silk sheet covering a decomposing corpse.

Back in the kitchen she made sandwiches and cocoa. There was one image she could be sure of at least. Her mother had made cocoa to soothe her at the end of a long day.

The chocolatey smell of the dark powder mixed into her earlier musings and brought a memory into focus. It hadn't been her father's boss, McMahon, who'd told her to be a brave girl. It was here in the kitchen that a warm hand had engulfed hers. It must have been Aunt Marian. For a moment the memory brought warmth at the thought that it was her aunt who'd consoled her. She smiled and then shuddered as she relived the way she'd gulped out the involuntary sobs that were all that were left of full-blown hysterics.

'I want it like Mummy makes it' – sob – *'like Mummy makes it.'*

But Mummy was cold in the room down the corridor and Aunt Marian didn't know how to make it like Mummy made it.

McMahon hadn't held her hand at all; he'd dragged her off the coffin. At eight years old, she hadn't a chance against his long years on the Glasgow streets. Even so, it was pandemonium she remembered. Arms flailing, feet kicking, desperation to get to her mother. Desperation for something. Memory had fragmented over the years. The picture jumped from crowded mayhem to quiet sobs and Aunt Marian.

Why could she never see her mother's face, even in her dreams where the faces of the straw dolls took centre stage, trapping her in a dark maze? There were no photographs to remind her. None in her father's office, and none anywhere else in the house. She remembered something of the fury in which she'd taken advantage of an hour on her own a few weeks after her mother's death. She'd gone systematically from room to room gathering all the pictures, smashing the frames, ripping open the packets in the photo drawer, even taking the negatives. She'd burnt them all. Her father came home to a daughter sobbing over a heap of ash.

The click of the latch cut through her thoughts. She shook the memory out of her head and moved the pan of milk on to the stove as her father came in. 'I've done some sandwiches and I'll have a hot drink for you in a mo.'

'Thanks, Annie.' His voice held both surprise and pleasure. 'You didn't have to wait up.'

She felt a warm glow that reflected off his pleasure. Whatever had happened in the past, they were here for each other now. 'What's the story, Dad? Have you found out...?' She left the question hanging, not knowing how to ask what she really wanted. How much of you is this thing going to take? Will I have you back in time to come to Aunt Marian's?

'They've taken it off to the morgue. We'll know more when they've had a proper look.'

'But could it be an accident? Whoever it ... uh ... belongs to, could they be all right?'

He toyed with the sandwiches she'd made. 'It's early days to know anything.'

She wondered if he were trying to convince himself or her. She saw no point in pretending. 'It's not all right, is it? I could tell by the way you reacted. What did you see? One leg severed below the knee doesn't automatically mean someone died, or that it wasn't an accidental death. You're acting like someone was murdered.'

'Forensics'll tell us, but it didn't look to me like a leg cut from a living body.'

She waited for him to go on, but instead he took a bite from his sandwich and stared into the middle distance.

'When I saw it ... close up I mean...' Annie spoke carefully. 'I thought it might be off a shop dummy. The skin looked like plastic. Was that because it had been in the water a long time?'

He shook his head. 'A few days. A week at the most. I'm sure of it. Forensics'll prove me right.'

'Who's saying you're wrong?'

'Oh, C-I-bloody-D are poncing in as usual, thinking they know it all. I know this coast, Annie, and I know what a body looks like when it's been in a fire. They're saying what you are. Shipping accident, leg been in the water for weeks. As if. I know these tides. I've an idea there was a complaint from down your aunt's way. I'll look it out later. Someone seen dumping trash in the loch. I'm betting that was the killer dumping the legs.'

'Legs plural?'

'Yes, I'm pretty sure both legs will have been dumped. There's probably little left of the other. It's been luck this one survived. But weeks!' He tossed his head in contempt. 'As if meat of any sort is likely to survive that long. It was still tangled in a bin bag. The other one'll have fallen out and been eaten days ago. I doubt we'll find it.'

Annie, about to speak, suddenly realized what he'd said. She felt shock prickle her skin, and spun round as though to see to something at the sink. He mustn't see her face. *I know what a body looks like when it's been in a fire.* Her mother. Twenty years ago a killer tried to burn her mother's body to hide the crime. Tried and failed. Fire scorched her legs but left the rest of her untouched. The memory of what he'd seen must have stayed with him as clearly as the day it happened. Freddie Pearson's catch had raked up the worst time in his life.

She thought of her own agenda, what she'd come here to say, how she relied on him to help her break the news to Aunt Marian. No doubts on that score now. She'd head off alone to her aunt's tomorrow, and try to find her own route through the mess.

She gulped back her cocoa. It was supposed to soothe, but it bloated her. *I want it like Mummy makes it.*

CHAPTER THREE

Annie came down the next morning to find her father already at breakfast. 'Annie.' He greeted her with a smile, but his eyes focused elsewhere.

'Are you OK, Dad?'

'Yes, fine...' His voice tailed away as he looked beyond her through the window that faced the slope down to the loch. 'Fine ... Yes, it'll be fine again today.' Annie watched his attention wander as he turned to her. 'And how's business?'

She too looked out over the garden and down the glen. The air was still. Nothing but the tide moved the water in the loch. Any other time there would have been no more than a scorching day ahead in the haze that hung over the hills. Everything looked too still, too calm, the shining perfection of the water's surface just a veneer.

He'd asked the question she needed. The opening to allow her to say, 'Business is terrible, Dad. We can't hold out much longer. If Pieternel doesn't work one of her miracles, which she won't by the way, because it's too late for that, I'll be out of a job and homeless, not to mention up to my ears in debt before the year's out. And worse than that, Aunt Marian's coming with me, because...' It was what she'd come to tell him.

'D'you know, they've barely said a word to me,' he burst out suddenly. 'New bloods in from the city. Don't know the area at all.'

It was a well-worn theme. CID muscling in, not knowing what they were doing. She supposed relations were especially fraught if a tenth of Aunt Marian's drugs tale were true.

'They'll have to come to you for local knowledge on this one, Dad.' She tried to bolster him. 'Where else will they go?'

'Try telling them that, Annie. They're still sore about that business the other month.'

'That'd be the drugs thing? What happened?'

He gave a mirthless laugh. 'They didn't even bother to get in touch until they'd made a mess of it.' As she made coffee he told her about a van being tracked from the city. 'They expected it to head for Fort William but they lost it for a couple of hours. It was found burnt out. Sheer incompetence.'

'Surely no one's trying to blame you.'

'Och, you know what they're like, Annie. It turned up down your aunt's way.' He gave her a wry smile. 'I'm sure she's told you all about it. Anyway, it's good to know you're doing well. Your aunt'll be pleased to see you.'

She held on to her smile. His mind had told him she'd given the reply he needed to hear. *Annie's fine.* For once, his wayward daughter wasn't the one bringing in the trouble.

'How are you, Aunt Marian? I'm phoning from Dad's. We've had a bit of an incident.'

'Aye, we know all about it, dear. Fancy that reporter trying to get young Freddie to pose with his fishing rod. And quite right of Mr Pearson to knock him down...'

This was news to Annie, but it didn't surprise her that her aunt's matchless grapevine had kept her up to speed. Aunt Marian loved a drama, and would want her niece on the spot to show off as an authentic link to the mystery.

'I'll be with you later today, Aunt Marian. How have things been this summer?'

Summer was a mixed blessing for Aunt Marian. She liked the warmer weather and the bustle of summer tourists that gave extra life to the place. The downside was a sitting-room full of strangers and her favourite armchair taken if she wasn't quick. But even the downside had an up side, because strangers provided a fresh audience every year.

'There's a very nice young lass staying,' Aunt Marian began. 'Her name's Charlotte Grainger.'

Uh-oh, thought Annie, on guard at once at her aunt's tone. There'd been an incident a couple of years ago involving one of the summer guests. It had brought home to Annie that her capable aunt had turned into a vulnerable old lady. She and her father had seen off the vulture, but the worry remained. As Aunt Marian grew older, would she become a target for conmen? Because no one lived comfortably in a guesthouse in a prime position without a good sum tucked away.

'She's not been very forthcoming,' Aunt Marian went on. 'But I'm drawing her out. She came and asked if I could help her. Well, she half asked, but I got it out of her. She wasn't trusting me fully, but she does now.'

Annie could see her aunt as clearly as if she were in her line of sight and not miles away. She would be hunched over the phone in the hallway, her free hand choreographing her tale. She felt a ripple of unease as she pictured the scene where this Charlotte Grainger, whoever she was, reeled in Aunt Marian with the promise of mystery and intrigue. She pushed away the thought that she was in no position to judge, whatever the woman planned.

'I'll be away up to Aunt Marian's this afternoon,' she said at lunch, looking at the window as the sharp rat-a-tat of a sudden downpour cut across her voice. Her father just nodded, but she saw Mrs Latimer's face light up.

'I'd have thought—' Mrs Latimer began and then stopped.

Annie smiled. Mrs Latimer wanted to condemn her for deserting her father at a time like this, but couldn't for fear of making Annie change her mind and stay.

'Thought what?' Annie teased.

She sensed a movement beside her. Her father had tensed. Christ, she thought suddenly, he must be fed up with this constant sniping whenever I'm home. As Mrs Latimer flounced off into the hallway and up the stairs, Annie took in a deep breath and said, 'Don't take us seriously, Dad. We'll never be best pals, but it's only sport these days. If she'd admit it to herself, she enjoys it as much as I do.' As she spoke, she wondered if it were true.

'She's a good housekeeper, Annie. I'd struggle to manage without her.'

'I know.' She smiled at him and wanted to tell him it was OK with her now. In fact, she had to tell him. Real conversation had to start somewhere. 'It's OK, Dad. I wouldn't want you to let her go. It's ... it's still hard for me. We used to row a lot when you weren't here. After Mother died. She said things I can't forgive her for...' *Don't ask me what things. Don't ever ask me...* 'I'm sorry. Really I am. But it's in the past. I know you need her. It doesn't bother me, not the way it used to. It's ... it's different now.'

Your turn. Say something. Don't let it drop. It was horribly uncomfortable, but she needed it to carry on, needed them to communicate. She might be living here soon.

Maybe he too felt the need to hold the connection between them. He cleared his throat. 'Do you remember Inspector McMahon?'

She nodded, yes. Of course she remembered him.

'They both tried to help you after ... afterwards. You never took against the inspector the way you did Mrs Latimer.'

He didn't say things about my mother. 'I was thinking about him yesterday. Trying to remember. Dad, Inspector McMahon was there in the office. But I can't remember Mother's funeral.' The words came easily. Annie wondered why she hadn't asked before. For twenty years she'd searched for the memory, but this was the first time she'd said the words aloud.

He looked at her, surprised. 'You didn't go, Annie.'

'Didn't...? But I remember ... Inspector McMahon...'

He gave her half a smile. 'You blacked his eye.'

'No!' Her first reaction was indignation. It was another of Mrs Latimer's lies. Then the memory crept back in. His arms struggling to hold her. Yes, it had been a struggle though she was only eight and he as big as he was. 'My God, yes. Why on earth...? What did I do?'

'It was our fault, Annie. You asked to see your mother. I just need to see Mummy, you said. You were so calm about it, and so firm, we thought we should let you.'

'I can sort of remember. Did I see her?'

'Yes, but it overwhelmed you. I think ... we thought ... you might just kiss her goodbye, but ... We had to get the doctor in to sedate you.'

That explained the fragmented memory. 'Dad? What did I do? I remember Inspector McMahon pulling me back, but what did I do?'

'You tried to pull your mother out of the coffin, Annie. It was understandable. You were only eight. We shouldn't have let you see her.'

'I tried to...?' She struggled with the fog that lay over her memory. *My God, did I really try to...? No. No, I didn't. I wasn't trying to drag her out. I know I wasn't, but what was I doing?*

'It was Mrs Latimer who calmed you that day, Annie.'

Her head shot up, all other thoughts stifled. 'It was Aunt Marian. I remember that bit. Here in the kitchen.'

He shook his head. 'Marian had gone ahead to the kirk. She didn't ... she doesn't know what happened that day. We told her you were too upset to come.'

Mrs Latimer? The thought of Mrs Latimer holding her hand, telling her to be brave, making her cocoa... 'I thought it was Aunt Marian,' was all she could think to say.

'Uh ... well, I know you didn't ... don't ... like her, but she tried to do her best for you. Really. So how long will you stay at your aunt's?'

The sudden change of tack came as a great relief. Annie wished she'd never taken the old memories out. 'Oh, just a few days.' She cursed the wobble in her voice as she scrambled out of the pit of real conversation and back to the solid ground of banalities.

'Will you come back by the smokehouse and pick up some salmon?'

She smiled. 'Of course I will.'

Annie nursed the car round the twists of the coast road, peering through a curtain of water, and hoped it would be fine for the return journey, because the detour to the smokehouse would take her over the mountain. The ferocity of the rain eased as she arrived at the guesthouse. The main street was deserted, but there was an air of busyness in the general debris of the summer season, too many parked cars, litter overflowing the bins. It wasn't a large community, but grew ten times its size in a good summer.

She'd intended to arrive mid-afternoon, but it was nearly six o'clock when she sneaked in through the kitchens to grab a chance to towel her hair dry before Aunt Marian saw her and insisted she have a complete change of clothes.

A furtive voice from the hallway brought her up short. A woman about her own age huddled over a cell phone. Annie stayed still in the shadows and ran her eye over the drawn features, deep-set tiredness in the worried expression, the straggly lack-lustre blonde hair showing a telltale dark tide at the roots. With nothing but gut instinct to go on, Annie knew this was Charlotte Grainger, Aunt Marian's *very nice young lass*.

It took a moment to interpret the anxious stuttering. 'Look ... I ... uh ... I was really wanting to speak to someone. I was hoping ... I don't know if I should leave a message ... only it ... it's important...'

Annie gave her a mental nudge – go on, leave a message – maybe the woman would spell out the scam she planned for Aunt Marian.

'I wouldn't want to breach client confidentiality. Uh ... I wouldn't ... You'll know who I mean. I know you have your doubts about them, but it's worse than that ... I realize I shouldn't have taken any tapes, but I was worried. I followed the path Lorraine took. There was something really odd. I think there may have been— Oh!'

The woman took the phone from her ear, gave it a bemused look, and then listened again before clicking it off and turning towards the sitting-room. Annie watched her retreat and felt far more benevolent towards her. Aunt Marian may have lost a little of her edge, but she wouldn't be outwitted by such a ditherer as that.

Annie stayed for a moment in the shadow by the stairs, looking round the familiar hallway of Mrs Watson's establishment. She hated its genteel restrictions, but it suited Aunt Marian like a hand-made glove. It was a comfortable base in familiar surroundings where she was waited on to whatever degree she wanted. And Annie was about to snatch it all from her, to remove the financial base that made it possible.

When she'd left, her father had been on the phone in the office and, as she put her head round the door to signal goodbye, had heard the words, '...week at the most. Yes, I thought so.' He'd given her a smile and a thumbs-up. So his theories on the leg had been confirmed. It hadn't been in the water long. She wondered if that also meant it had been thrown into the loch just down the road from Mrs Watson's, where she now stood looking at the blank sitting-room door.

CHAPTER FOUR

Annie knew she had to be paraded before the other guests, and slipped into the sitting-room nursing a hope there wouldn't be too many of them this year. She suppressed a groan. The room was packed.

'Annie dear! How are you? Do come and meet...'

Annie returned her aunt's grin of welcome, and noted the iron-clad curls of a new perm that framed the small familiar features. A new stab of guilt sliced through her at this reminder of the effort her aunt always made for her visits. There was a general stirring as people shuffled obediently forward or half rose from their chairs. Mrs Watson's guesthouse attracted the sort who were past energetic rambles or hill climbs. Annie wondered at their coming all this way to a renowned beauty spot to sit in a cavernous room watching TV. She smiled her polite smile and said her hellos, looking into faces she wouldn't recognize again, and listening to names she wouldn't recall. Except for one. Charlotte Grainger. She'd guessed right. Charlotte was the woman she'd overheard on the phone, and she looked just as nervy now as she had then.

'How do you do. Your aunt said ... uh ... told me about ... uh...'

Charlotte was in such a lather of indecision as to whether she should shake hands, Annie had consciously to time her move to grab the flapping fingers and squeeze them between her own.

Others, doubtless primed by her aunt, murmured about 'that nasty business', 'that lad fishing', before they turned back to their papers or the TV, their duty done. Annie supposed they were all up to their eyes in 'my niece who's a big success

23

in London, you know.' Only Charlotte, pinned by a look from Aunt Marian, stayed nearby as Annie perched on the arm of her aunt's chair.

'How's business, dear?' Aunt Marian held her head high and spoke in triumphant tones. 'I know how hard it must be to get away with all the work you have on. Still, I suppose you must have plenty of people working for you now.'

'Everything's going fine.' The words were out before Annie realized she'd spoken them, but what else could she have said? *We sacked our last employee last week.* No way. She wouldn't have sullied Aunt Marian's moment of triumph for anything. This set of guests would be gone by the time the crash came. How long would it be, left to her own devices, for Aunt Marian to realize the full implications, that Annie's imprudence would pull this comfortable retirement out from under her?

Her aunt would give up everything and live in a council bedsit to help out, Annie knew that. Her money had always been at Annie's disposal. 'I hate to think of you waiting to inherit, dear,' she'd said many times. 'So just you remember, if ever you're in need, you come straight to me.' Annie had resisted for years, but then a chance came up that looked too good to let go by.

'I don't need money, Aunt Marian. I just need to get a foothold in the business.' Aunt Marian had guaranteed the loan. And the next one ... and the one after that. Annie was certain her aunt hadn't a clue how much it all came to. And even if she did, she wouldn't know how the interest charges had hiked things up, how the missed payments had spiralled the debt out of control. Her aunt had set aside her own grief to help bring Annie up. She'd softened the blow of the bewildering loss of her mother, and now, because of the niece she'd done her best for, she would live out her life in penury. Waiting for the crash wasn't an option. She couldn't let it land on her aunt without warning. If only her father were here. He'd find a way.

Her aunt's voice cut across her thoughts. 'Do you still see anything of your old schoolfriends? Margot for instance. I know she works in London. You and she were such friends.'

Margot? What on earth made Aunt Marian pick on Margot to ask about? A wave of conflicting emotion swept through Annie as the face of her old schoolfriend came to mind. Margot who'd stood up for her at school when the others turned against her; and Margot now, supercilious, ultra-successful, with her plush suite of offices not much beyond a stone's throw from Annie's own. Not that an Olympic stone thrower could bridge the chasm between them these days. She became uncomfortably aware of her surroundings, where she perched next to her aunt in a room full of strangers. The rough moquette of the chair arm made her want to squirm. The commentary from the TV boomed out as an unnatural backdrop to a crowd posed to turn in unison at a pre-arranged signal and announce her sins out loud. She felt her fists ball as she spoke and was amazed to hear the calm tones that came from her mouth.

'No, I haven't seen Margot in months,' she said. 'She's too busy for socialising these days.'

'I always had my doubts about that girl, but she's doing well, I hear.'

Where would Aunt Marian hear anything about Margot?

'Oh, I think she's doing OK.' Annie blanked out a mental picture of the suite of offices she'd seen the one time she'd visited Margot at work. She still felt the incongruity of Margot having chosen to throw herself into the world of drugs counselling in a business that had blossomed to embrace complementary therapies of all types. There was little that Margot wouldn't dabble in, but Annie soon learnt the enthusiasm focused solely on the business side and money-making potential. Margot herself was covered by private health insurance and wouldn't have approached any of her own franchised therapists for any reason other than to collect money. She smiled at her aunt and said, 'She was renting an office not far from Harley Street the last I heard, but I haven't seen her in ages.'

'They've taken over the whole floor now,' a voice chipped in, and Annie turned to stare at Charlotte, who stood awkwardly behind her aunt's chair.

'Do you know Margot?'

'Och yes, dear, didn't you know, Charlotte works for Margot. Margot often recommends Mrs Watson's to her city friends. We've had a fair few of them over the years. I'll say this for the lass, she hasn't forgotten her roots.'

'Margot?' Annie blinked. She'd had no idea. Was Margot successful enough for finer feelings these days, and doing her bit for the local economy? Margot would hear all about it when the business went belly-up, and Annie cringed at the thought of Charlotte telling her how Aunt Marian had boasted.

'Now then, dear, how about some tea? I've asked Mrs Watson to serve it in my room. And I've asked Charlotte to join us.'

'Charlotte has a bit of a problem,' said Aunt Marian as they sat round the small table and she poured tea.

Charlotte gave a whimper and nearly dropped her cup. 'It was in confidence really.'

It was impossible not to feel something for Charlotte's plight. This was supposed to be a holiday for her, a period of relaxation, and she'd come up against the anxiety factory that was Aunt Marian. Annie knew only too well the need for tricks to divert her aunt who was always on the lookout for a sapling worry to grow to giant oak proportions. She tried to give Charlotte a reassuring smile.

'Don't worry.' Aunt Marian waved aside the protests. 'Annie's in the business. She'll sort it out for you if anyone can.'

'Really, it's very kind, but I don't know that anything needs sorting. I certainly wasn't thinking of employing a private eye.'

'Actually, I'm not a private eye,' Annie said, with a pointed look at Aunt Marian.

'Yes, you are, dear,' Aunt Marian said placidly. 'Charlotte knows all about it.'

Annie took a couple of deep breaths and pushed her chair back from the table, resisting an urge to get up and pace the room. 'I was a partner in a PI firm in Yorkshire for a while,' she told Charlotte. 'But I sold my interest and bought into a London business.' *More fool me.* 'We investigate insurance fraud. At least that's where we specialize. We very rarely take on anything else. And we don't do the cloak and dagger stuff.' This time next month, she added to herself, we won't be doing anything at all.

Her cloak and dagger comment was said with a sharp look towards Aunt Marian, who gave her a benevolent smile and carried on undaunted. 'They do this insurance stuff for the money,' she said confidingly to Charlotte. 'But Annie's trained. She was a Special Branch officer for years, you know, before she set up on her own.'

Charlotte looked impressed, but Annie said nothing. She'd never identified the moment Aunt Marian had turned her three months as a police probationer into her years in Special Branch. It had become too blatant a lie to contradict.

'But never mind all that,' Aunt Marian went on. 'Charlotte, tell Annie all about your friend who was murdered.'

'No, no. No one was murdered.' Charlotte jumped in with an alarmed glance at Aunt Marian and made a faltering start to the tale. 'It was a client of mine. I was counselling her. It's just that she had rather a nasty experience around here and I thought...'

So Charlotte was one of Margot's drugs counsellors. Annie, though not without sympathy for the woman, found some amusement in the way her aunt had turned her into a summer plaything, but the saga itself was not very interesting.

Charlotte told the story of a woman who, high on drugs, had taken off into the hills and, in trying to outrun the hallucinations of a bad trip, fell and lay unconscious in the undergrowth for several hours. She'd been lucky not to die. After the physical injury had healed, the psychological trauma reared up in nightmares and flashbacks. A rich family had plucked the woman out of NHS care and into the exclusive world of Margot's brand of complementary medicine. It jarred that Margot, for all her success, had only been able to provide this hesitant ditherer to counsel the victim. No name was mentioned, though Charlotte alluded more than once to the issue of 'client confidentiality' with worried looks towards Aunt Marian. Annie, thinking of the call she'd overheard, resisted the temptation to say, 'Oh, you must mean Lorraine.'

'Tell Annie about the murdered woman.'

'No, really, it wasn't. It's just that she hallucinated an old friend. Another drug addict. A friend of hers who must have died years ago. It was her subconscious bringing out all the guilt about her own drug taking. It was just with me coming up here. I thought it might be useful to me, as a practitioner I mean, to see the spot where ... where it happened. It was stupid of me. I didn't think. I've compromised client confidentiality, and I'm...' She gave Aunt Marian an agonized glance. 'I'm relying on your aunt not to give me away.'

'You can rely on me.' Aunt Marian sat back, looking smug.

Later that evening when her aunt, yawning, announced her intention to have an early night, Annie decided to wander down to the local pub for a more convivial atmosphere than the staid Mrs Watson's. On impulse, she asked Charlotte if she'd like to come along.

'Oh! Well ... I ... Um...'

Annie held her smile in place, but regretted the invitation as soon as it left her lips. As the stutterings turned into a yes, she knew she'd let herself in for an evening of forced conversation.

They walked down the hill together.

'Uh ... That's a nice jacket.'

'Thanks. It was my birthday present from Aunt Marian for my twenty-fifth.' Annie wondered what Charlotte would say if she knew she called it her Margot jacket. Her one piece of kit that made her old schoolfriend take a second look. 'How long have you worked for Margot?'

'Oh, not long. I was ... I'm only there as a temp. Covering for someone who's off ill.'

They found a seat at a table by the window away from the crowded bar. 'So, what brought you here on holiday? Have you been round here before?'

'Oh no. I've heard them talking about it at work. It sounded so nice. Then ... well, there was this business with this client. It kind of seemed like a good idea...' Charlotte's voice tailed off and she looked down, embarrassed.

'And ... um ... you're on your own?' God, what a stupid question. What did she expect Charlotte to say? *No, I'm here with my partner. He's in a trunk in the attic.* 'Sorry, I mean ... People usually come with friends. It's unusual for people to holiday alone around here.' For Chris'sakes, stop digging, thought Annie, taking refuge in her drink.

'Uh ... No. You see, I only moved to London quite recently. I haven't really made many friends yet. And there's no one special ... you know ... a man, I mean. I was married, but we split up. That's why I moved really.'

'Sorry. That's tough.'

'Oh, it was mutual. We were never well suited. Uh ... so how about you? Are you married?'

'Me? No. I don't really go for the relationship thing. I prefer to be on my own.'

Charlotte gave her a sly smile. 'There is, isn't there? Someone special, I mean. I can tell by the way you're all defensive about it.'

Annie laughed and wondered why the remark didn't annoy her. Maybe it was the slightly glazed look in Charlotte's eye. The alcohol was taking hold already. 'There's a guy I see quite a lot of, but it isn't serious. We like each other's company, that's all.' No way would she tell Charlotte that Mike had a key to her flat, that he'd call in to check it over while she was away. That would give the wrong impression altogether. For a moment, she let a picture run through her head. Her and Mike coming here. He'd enjoy the place and it would be fun showing him around. The problem would be Aunt Marian.

'I daren't bring anyone here,' she confided. 'If Aunt Marian disapproved, she'd make things impossible, and if she approved, she'd be talking wedding dresses before she finished shaking hands.'

Charlotte laughed. 'What does he do? Is he in the same line as you?'

'Nah, he's in a bank. Stocks, trading, all that stuff.'

A draught blew round them as the door opened and a crowd surged in. Annie recognized a few locals and exchanged nods of recognition.

'Of course, you'll know all these people, growing up round here.'

Annie smiled and shook her head. 'I know two or three of them. The rest are holidaymakers, like you. There isn't that much local trade.'

'Isn't there? Why not?'

'There's a religious sect, more or less a closed community. They have a lot of land round here. They don't drink, so it's killed the local pubs outside the season.'

'Oh yes, the Doll Makers. I've heard about them. I haven't seen any, though.'

'You never see them, except for the young girl. She delivers stuff to the post office up where my father lives.'

'Dolls?'

'Yeah, I suppose.'

'I was hoping I might be able to visit, but your aunt said they aren't like that.'

'A guided tour of the doll factory, you mean?' Annie laughed. 'No, they don't go in for that sort of thing. More likely to run you off if you were to turn up.'

'Is that how they make a living? Dolls?'

Annie gave Charlotte a sideways glance. The questions were jarringly avid. 'I shouldn't think so,' she replied. 'I doubt anyone but Mr Caine buys them. I'd swear it was the same row of dolls in his shop now as when I was little.'

'What about the young girl who delivers them? He must sell some if he takes regular deliveries.'

Annie shrugged. 'Yeah, I suppose he must. I hadn't really thought about it.'

'Did anyone buy you one when you were little?'

'No, I...' Annie paused at the ghost of a memory, the delicious squidge of a doll's middle between small fingers, as compulsive as popping bubble wrap. 'Not that I can remember.'

Charlotte relaxed visibly as her glass emptied, and was suddenly not at a loss for words at all. 'So what's this Caine man's involvement with them? Why don't they sell their stuff round here?'

Annie didn't want to get into involved explanations about the Doll Makers. There was nothing interesting about them any more. She and her friends had done the big curiosity bit when they were younger, sneaking on to forbidden land, even as far as the big wooden doors of the building they used for their services. She smiled, recalling the delicious terror of listening to Margot's tales of what went on inside. This was something to amuse Charlotte with. 'Margot used to terrorize the little kids with stories of what they did. Human sacrifice, black magic, you name it. There's this church thing where they hold services. You can't see in from outside but you always feel someone's watching you. We called it the building-with-eyes. Margot said there was a hand, a gnarled hand, that would reach out and grab you if it knew you'd been prying into their secrets. It could get you anywhere, even when you were at home in bed.' She laughed. 'None of the kids round here would sleep with the light out when Margot was in storytelling mood.'

'And is this Caine one of them?'

Again that eager tone. Annie took a sip of her drink before answering with a question of her own. 'Why are you so interested?'

'Uh ... I've heard people talking about them at work, that's all. I'm just curious.'

Annie knew that Margot and her up-market associates would not gossip about the rural eccentrics of her youth to the extent it impinged on the consciousness of her employees. Her aunt's new friend had an agenda of her own.

'No gnarled hand, though,' Charlotte added with a smile.

Annie chose her words with care. 'Caine had something to do with them at one stage,' she said. 'Ages ago. Before I can remember.' Aunt Marian would know, but she wouldn't tell Charlotte that. Their glasses were nearly empty. Annie drained hers and stood up. 'Same again?'

Charlotte giggled. 'I shouldn't really. I usually stick to Diet Coke or mineral water.'

'Oh, go on. Another one won't hurt. You're on holiday.'

She waited until Charlotte's glass was half empty, then asked, 'So who's this Lorraine person and why is it so important you follow her up?'

'Oh my God! How do you know about Lorraine?'

'Don't worry. I overheard you on the phone. That's all. So what's it all about?'

'Uh ... like I said. It's of interest to me as a practitioner.'

'It's a long way to come just for that.'

'It's not just for that. I ... uh ... I knew Lorraine.'

'You mean other than as a client?'

'She was never my client. I spoke to her briefly in hospital after her accident, but then...'

Annie waited for Charlotte to go on, but she twisted in the seat and looked out of the window as though expecting to meet the eye of a clandestine watcher.

'Then what...?'

'Uh ... nothing.'

Annie too glanced out of the window and made a bland comment about tomorrow's weather. Let Charlotte relax; let the guard go back down. She'd find out what she needed to before the visit was over. Not that she cared about the woman's hidden agendas. All she wanted was to be sure she was no threat to her aunt.

CHAPTER FIVE

At breakfast the next morning, Charlotte met Annie's eye and gave her a shy smile, a recognition of confidences shared the night before.

The day promised to be warm, but the rain lashed down in waves. Annie tried anyway to tempt her aunt into one of their usual trips, over the mountain to town, or across the loch for a change of scene, but was relieved to be given a firm refusal. Aunt Marian didn't know she'd sold the BMW, and was sure to ask questions about the ageing Nissan. It could be an opening to tell her aunt the truth about the business, but it wouldn't be fair to off-load it without her father here to soften the blow. *Soften it for whom? What exactly am I expecting him to do?* Questions she glanced at and set aside.

Annie didn't begrudge the time spent immobile in a tall armchair if this was what her aunt wanted, but the inactivity kept pictures flashing through her mind – straw dolls reached out, snatched away her childhood memories, stole all her security, then turned inward and ripped each other to shreds. She felt at the mobile in her pocket. Why had it remained silent? Why hadn't her senior partner, Pieternel, called from London to say she'd salvaged the business at the eleventh hour? For no good reason, she resisted the urge to ring. Mustn't tempt fate while there was still hope. Pieternel had talked about having irons in the fire and hers was the business mind. She'd get them through if anyone could. Except Annie knew her hopes were quicksand, or she would have heard something by now.

'Would you three like to join a Scrabble-bee?' Annie looked up into the benevolently smiling face of an old man as her aunt said sharply, 'My niece doesn't play. Charlotte and I might join you later.'

Charlotte looked from one to the other of them in surprise. 'Well ... I could soon teach you ... It isn't difficult.'

'Annie doesn't play.' Aunt Marian's voice set like concrete and was so unlike her usual anodyne tone that both Charlotte and the old man backed off. Aunt Marian rose from her chair. 'Come with me, Charlotte. We'll get some coffee for everyone.'

Annie kept a neutral expression as she watched them leave the room. Aunt Marian's voice, lowered but not enough, floated back to her. 'Never ask Annie to play Scrabble in company, dear. She fell in with a bad lot at school and you never know what she'll come out with.'

Annie ducked her head to hide her amusement from the other guests. She wondered what impression Charlotte had formed after a week with Aunt Marian, and whether having now met Annie, she thought it an accurate one. It didn't matter. From the depths of her own financial pit, Annie found herself nursing an avid curiosity about Margot. Just how successful was she now? Tonight in the pub she'd squeeze Charlotte dry of all she knew.

The pub was quiet and made a seamless end to a day of doing nothing. Annie hadn't expected to relax at all, with all that had happened, but her aunt's world still had the power to soothe her. She experienced the same feel of a few days' calm following 360 days at full throttle. She smiled. Her father wouldn't use the word calm in relation to Aunt Marian, but the tiny squalls over mealtimes, about the weather, or the timing of the newspaper delivery came so far under Annie's radar these days, they didn't puncture the smooth flow of the day.

She returned from the bar with two drinks, to find Charlotte kneeling up on the seat and peering out of the window. 'Anything interesting going on?'

'Uh ... no.' Charlotte twisted round to sit properly, though craned her neck round as though riveted by something outside.

Annie looked too, and saw nothing but early dusk enfolding the street outside. 'What is it?'

'No ... nothing. I thought I saw someone I recognized. But it couldn't have been. I'm sorry, I have to ask. What did you put?'

'What did I...? Oh, the Scrabble. It was nothing. I was only nine or ten. Someone had 'adult' across a triple word score and I put e-r-y after it. Aunt Marian was mortified. I didn't really know what it meant, I just knew it from the Ten Commandments.'

'What about this bad lot at school?'

'School? She doesn't know the half of it.'

Annie had no qualms talking about this time of her life to Charlotte. No worries about the woman blabbing to anyone. Aunt Marian wouldn't believe her, and Margot already knew the worst there was to know of Annie's past. She told Charlotte of the rush of both excitement and relief when she'd found the crowd that had the pills, who had contacts in town who'd smuggle in all sorts for a price. How she had plummeted to the depths before clawing her way out.

'It can't have been easy to get yourself out of it.'

'It wasn't.' Annie's mind tapped the horror of it. A black pit of memory she had barely to touch to ward off temptation. 'That's when I learnt to run. Really run. Long distances, the heavier the terrain the better. I could have done with someone like you to help me through it, but I suppose I ran the worst of it out of me.'

'Someone like me?'

'A counsellor, I mean. Didn't you say you'd counselled addicts?'

'Uh ... yeah...' Charlotte looked away. 'And you've stayed clean?'

Annie laughed and raised her glass. 'I overdo this stuff sometimes, but only when I'm led astray.'

'Oh gosh! I'm sorry. I didn't mean—'

'Joke. Don't worry. I've far worse than you to contend with.' She looked into the amber depths of her glass and thought of the workmate they'd had to sack. Casey Lane. A good worker and fun friend, but moderation wasn't in Casey's vocabulary. 'In fact, we've just sacked the world's worst bad influence.'

'For drugs?'

'Kind of.' Annie shrugged. It had been the official excuse. *We sacked her because one of our investors went bust at just the wrong moment and the business is going down the pan. If nothing turns up, we'll be history in a couple of months.*

'So it's just you and Pieternel? Does that mean you're on the look-out for work?'

Annie watched Charlotte key herself up to ask something – something a PI might have the answer to – and felt a stab of curiosity about the mystery Lorraine. She let a shrug be her only answer, and said, 'No, there's three of us. Dean's someone Pieternel knew from way back. He's an IT whizz. Cut Dean and he bleeds silicon.' She looked Charlotte in the eye, and held her voice steady, conversational. 'So you went to see Lorraine in hospital?'

Charlotte said nothing for a moment and then blurted out, 'Look, how well do you know Margot?'

'I never see her these days. I'm not going to talk to her about you, if that's what you're worried about.'

'I only went to see Lorraine because ... Well, because she knew someone I ... uh ... wanted to speak to. I didn't know anything about this accident she'd had. Or the hallucinations or anything. She told me a load of lies about why she was there. I didn't get to speak to her again. Her brother came and took her away. I only found out the detail when I looked out her records. Look, you won't tell Margot, will you?'

Annie shook her head. 'No, 'course not. And did you find the place where Lorraine fell?'

Charlotte blew out a sigh. 'I don't think so. The description was so sketchy. Your aunt helped me on where to start.'

'So you didn't find anything?'

'Oh ... well...' Charlotte's eyes slid away from Annie's and she busied herself with her drink.

Annie remembered the call she'd overheard. *I followed the path Lorraine took. There was something really odd...*

'There was something that didn't quite gel.' Charlotte's expression was troubled. 'I contacted Margot.'

So that's who she rang. Annie let her eyebrows shoot up. 'And what did she say?'

'It was out of office hours. Though it was odd … Anyway, I left a message. I expected her to get back to me, but she hasn't. I don't really like to ring again.'

'So what does my aunt think you want help with? From me, I mean, as a PI?'

Charlotte, with her glass at her lips, changed a sip to a gulp, and gave a laugh that was more to do with alcohol than mirth. 'It isn't to do with me really. People are always telling me not to interfere. It's a friend. A friend-of-a-friend, actually.'

'What's the matter with this friend-of-a-friend?'

'Her sister's disappeared and she wants to find her. Lorraine knew her.'

'Has this friend-of-a-friend reported her sister as a missing person?'

'No, she doesn't want to do that in case it was intentional. The sister's a bit of a headcase, and she might have got into trouble. She … look you mustn't say anything, but she had this plan to fake her own death. She said specifically not to make waves if anything happened … seemed to have happened…'

'And has anything *seemed* to have happened?'

'Uh … well, not really, but then suppose she faked an accident or something. It wouldn't necessarily get much publicity.'

'But wouldn't she have told her sister? What did she plan to do?'

'Oh, my friend didn't have any details. But she's worried that her sister's trying to blackmail someone. Someone dangerous.'

Annie noted that the friend-of-a-friend had now become a friend. 'And get away with it by faking her own death? Your friend needs to go to the police.'

'Yes, but … you won't say anything, will you? I know your father's … well, it's nothing to do with anything around here. I shouldn't really have talked to you at all.'

'No, I won't say anything. My father's got enough on his plate at the moment. He doesn't need to go looking for work.'

'How about you? Are you looking for work? I mean, just

suppose ... I'll advise her to go to the police, of course, but I know she'd want to try other avenues first. It's really difficult ... for my friend I mean. She got this note that said not to make a fuss if she heard her sister had died, but she hasn't heard anything.'

'What did the note say?'

'It said "I need them to think I'm dead". What would it cost to have someone like you do some digging?'

Annie felt through her pockets. 'I've a leaflet somewhere. Here you are. Retainer, hourly rates, expenses. It's all on the back.'

She saw Charlotte's eyes widen. 'Good heavens! I'd no idea it would be as much as that.'

'Like I said, tell her to go to the police. They're free.'

They sat in silence for a while. Annie listened to the low buzz of conversation and glanced out through the window behind Charlotte. It was dark now. 'When you said you rang Margot and left her a message, you said, 'though it was odd...' and you stopped. What did you mean?'

'Nothing really, just that the answer-phone clicked off.'

'How do you mean?'

'It was like someone had picked up the phone and put it down again. Like they'd listened for a while, then deliberately cut me off.'

Annie woke to a shaft of light that speared through the skylight and made her roll on to her side to avoid its glare. She let the momentum carry her over the edge of the bed. It was time to be up. Mrs Watson ran a tight ship and late risers missed breakfast.

Before going down, she threw her things into her rucksack. She'd stay with her aunt until after lunch, then head back to her father's via the smokehouse. They had made a stab at communication, and mustn't let it slip back, however unnerving it felt beside the polite-strangers comfort zone they'd developed over the years. She paused to peer through the sloping skylight. The loch was visible as a smooth sheet disturbed by an occasional ripple. She watched two birds land creating a rip in the water's surface that mended behind them. Her father thought the severed leg – legs – had been thrown in down there.

Would he expect her to stay on in Scotland once he knew about the business? She'd explain that she couldn't. She had to go back and fight side by side with Pieternel until there wasn't a glimmer of hope left.

As she reached the hallway, a door banged and footsteps click-clacked down the corridor. Annie turned to see Mrs Watson, face grim, brandishing an egg-slice.

'Annie. A quick word, please, before your aunt comes down.' The tone made Annie feel ten years old. 'I couldn't fail to notice, Annie, that ... Ah, Charlotte. This concerns you too.'

Footsteps pattered down the stairs and Annie was aware of Charlotte close beside her. The tactical naivety of cramming herself close to Annie, made them into errant schoolgirls and left Mrs Watson, with her egg-slice, in the dominant position facing them. Annie fought to suppress a smile at the picture they must pose, as they stood meekly to receive a lecture on coming in late and making a noise that might disturb the other guests. '...especially you, Annie. Your room's just above ours, as well you know. Both Mr Watson and I have to be up early. We're not on holiday.'

No, thought Annie, but I bet you charge Aunt Marian full whack for that box room I sleep in when I'm here. The lecture at an end, she turned to head for the breakfast room. But Mrs Watson hadn't quite finished. 'Someone called to see you, Charlotte. Late last night. I had to say you were out and I'd no idea where you were. No message.' With that, she spun on her heel and stalked back towards the kitchen.

Charlotte turned a horrified face to Annie. 'Oh Lord! Margot!'

'Margot? Why on earth would it be Margot?'

'That call I made. It must have been more important than I thought. Oh crumbs ... Mrs Watson?' Charlotte called out towards the retreating back. 'Mrs Watson, did she leave a name? What did she look like?'

For a moment, Annie thought Mrs Watson would express her displeasure by pretending not to hear, but as she reached the kitchen door, she half turned her head. 'It was a man.'

'Oh, thank heavens.' Charlotte almost sank at the knees.

Annie laughed. 'You've been spending too much time with my aunt. You're getting paranoid. Margot's not going to chase all the way up here after you.'

'No, I suppose not. But I wonder ... Oh well, never mind.'

They went to join the other guests at breakfast.

Annie wanted to spend her last morning on her own with her aunt. One morning of semi-normal holiday. Charlotte would understand. She probably didn't want to tag along all the time anyway. If the weather held, they'd amble round the shops or along the water's edge. Annie felt a chill at the thought of standing at the point where, if her father had it right, the leg had been thrown in the loch. She turned to locate Charlotte, to have a word before Aunt Marian appeared.

The breakfast room had the bleak early morning feel of a waiting room. A few of the guests sat reading newspapers as they crunched toast. Annie pushed herself to her feet and stretched. The view from the window showed the makings of a warm day, perfect for a morning's stroll down into the heart of the village, followed by lunch in one of the pubs. Aunt Marian would like that.

Charlotte was in the hall. Annie, about to speak, realized Charlotte was fiddling with her phone. She cast an anxious glance at the stairs, wanting to speak to Charlotte on her own. Her aunt would consider it the height of ill-manners to exclude their new friend. She kept half an ear on Charlotte's call, half an eye on the staircase.

'Hello ... uh ... You sent me a text ... asked me to ... Oh Lord! It's you... Yes, it's me, Charlotte.' Annie heard amazed recognition in Charlotte's voice, and saw her head duck down, as one foot twisted to rub the other ankle as though trying to polish her shoe on her trouser leg. No one special, eh? From the embarrassed pleasure in Charlotte's body language, Annie thought there soon may be.

'Yes, I know. I'm so sorry. The signal's really unreliable round here. I ... uh ... the landlady said someone had called. I never thought. And I could have sworn I saw you ... What? Oh, I ... uh ... I went out for a drink with one of the other guests ... Uh, no, a woman visiting her aunt ... Yes, that's right. How did you know? What? Oh, well, yes, I'd love to ... What? Now? I haven't had breakfast ... I'd half promised to join my friends here, but ... Yes, yes of course. I'll be there...'

Annie ducked back out of sight. Great timing. No need for a quiet word in Charlotte's ear. Charlotte shot back into the breakfast room, not noticing Annie behind the door, grabbed her bag and slipped back out. Annie heard the front door slam.

Their gentle amble round the village lasted all morning, and ended with lunch in a pub overlooking the water. Annie let her gaze move south to north along the shoreline. Where had he – or she – stood, bin-liner in hand? Had it been weighted down? Surely it must have been. And when? The early hours when no one would be out strolling along the front. Not a great place to choose. Hadn't her father said there'd been a report of someone dumping trash? She imagined a shadowy figure standing there, a quick glance round, then swinging the sack in a great arc and flinging it out to sea. Then what? Had the rock or whatever was used as ballast torn through the plastic? Had the killer watched aghast as the bag split open and one leg flew free into the water. That would be the leg that hadn't been found, or rather that *had* been found by the marine life. The other one, tangled in its protective plastic had swirled its way along the coast until the tide pulled it under the jetty and Freddie Pearson's rod snared it. If she'd been here a week earlier and looked out of the box room window in the middle of the night...

'I wonder where Charlotte got to.'

Annie shrugged.

'That business with that client of hers is really preying on her mind.'

'I wonder who it was who came to see her last night,' said Annie, curious to know who Charlotte had gone to meet.

'She asked around about the Doll Makers before I got to know her. Maybe it was someone to do with that.'

'I shouldn't think so.' Annie cast her gaze about. For all she knew, any of the people strolling around could be from the reclusive community on the hill. She wouldn't recognize any but the girl; didn't even know how many of them were left.

Aunt Marian nodded. 'No, you're right. It couldn't have been one of them. He looked quite disreputable. They're always neat.'

'How do you know what he looked like? You went to bed early. Mrs Watson said he called late.' Did her aunt miss anything!

'I was watching out over the water, from my room. You know that body young Freddie found in the loch, it probably went in around here, and not so long ago.'

Annie looked up in surprise. She hadn't said a word about her father's theories, and the local paper still speculated on the basis of a far older relic. 'Uh ... what makes you think that?'

'The tides are right.'

'Anyway, don't be morbid. And it wasn't a whole body. They aren't all neat, you know. The Doll Makers. That young girl looks quite a scruff.'

'I worry about her, Annie. No mother. Just that old woman to look after her. It isn't right. A young girl of her age should mix with youngsters. You should speak to her.'

'It's only once in a blue moon I see her.'

'Well, do try, dear. She needs someone to talk to.'

'OK, I'll keep a special look out.' Annie felt in no position to deny any favour Aunt Marian asked. 'But if you're really worried, you should get in touch with Social Services.'

'Now you know full well they wouldn't help. And I don't think she's neglected in that sense.'

Annie had only vague second-hand memories of the time three of the Doll Makers' children were taken into care. It had happened before she was born, but she'd heard the tale. The old man, father of the three, had made mincemeat of the authorities for their heavy-handedness in denying their right to an alternative lifestyle. For a recluse who shunned publicity, he'd waged such an effective campaign that he'd not only got his children back, but had blighted the career of a local politician. The old man died when Annie was young enough that he marked her awareness only as legend. What relation would he be to the girl who now scuttled wraith-like through the streets? Grandfather, maybe.

'What happened to the girl's mother?'

'I'm not sure, dear. She upped and left when Beth was just a bairn. It's a shame. She wasn't a bad lass, Ellie. Very intense, you know. Very religious. It looked as though she and her brothers might have grown up normal. They mixed in a bit after the old man died. Ellie took up with one of the tourists. He left her though, probably didn't even know she was having a baby. It's such a shame it didn't last: she was a beautiful girl, and having a normal family might have been just the thing for her.'

'Beth? Is that what she's called?' Annie was amazed, partly at her aunt's knowing the Doll Makers well enough to know their names, and partly that she hadn't found out till now. She'd grown up with the Doll Makers as background noise, never thought to wonder about them as people. Conversations years ago had been on a different tack altogether. Her aunt telling her that it was no sin to be different, that it *was* a sin to persecute people who chose a different way of life and that she must not join naughty girls like Margot who liked to go up there to make fun of them.

So the young girl she'd promised to look out for was called Beth, and her mother had been Ellie. Ellie and Beth. A combination of names from a different age, a different dimension.

The rain began to splatter down as they arrived back at Mrs Watson's. 'Just made it, dear. You'll have a nice cup of tea before you go?'

Charlotte joined them and coped well, Annie thought, with the interrogation from Aunt Marian about the disreputable young man, and who he was.

'I've no idea,' she said. 'I think it must have been a mistake.' Annie admired the ease with which the lie came to Charlotte's lips. If she hadn't overheard the call, she'd have been fooled herself, despite the uncharacteristic glow on Charlotte's cheeks and the cat-with-the-cream look that played in her eyes.

It was mid afternoon when Annie pushed herself up from her chair and announced that she must be on her way. The rain outside shimmered down in waves. She said her goodbyes, promised Aunt Marian she'd ring, wished Charlotte well and pulled her hood over her head.

As she strode from the guesthouse, her feet splashed down on the pavement and the rain soaked through the guaranteed shower-proofing of her jacket. She turned to give a vigorous wave towards Mrs Watson's, where her aunt and Charlotte watched from the big bay window, then turned to jog to the side-street where she'd hidden the Nissan. Somewhere nearby, a car engine sprang to life. She glanced at a big silver beast parked opposite, and experienced a pang at the smooth purr, barely perceptible over the drumming of the rain.

The sleek BMW Aunt Marian shelled out thousands for had been sold to keep the scavengers from Annie's throat a couple of months ago. It had been a toss-up between the car and the flat. She'd seriously considered keeping the car and living in the lock-up she rented. But the car would convert to ready cash, the lease on the flat wasn't so easy to cast off.

The door of the old Nissan opened with a metallic screech, and she slid in behind the wheel, relieved to be out of the downpour. It wasn't cold, just wet, but she began to shiver as the damp seeped through to her skin. Glistening sheets of water pounded down on the tarmac, and hammered on the roof of the car. That silver dream machine with the softly purring engine had moved along, and was now opposite the bottom of the side street. Or it might be a different vehicle. Maybe the if-only itch inside her head made her focus on symbols of what she'd lost.

It was good to know that Charlotte and her mini-mystery would keep Aunt Marian amused. Less fun for Charlotte of course, though the mystery caller might return and whisk her off. Why hadn't Pieternel rung?

Leaving the loch behind, she turned the car for the climb into the hills and headed for the smokehouse.

CHAPTER SIX

'How nice to see you, Annie. It must be a year since we saw you last. Nay, it's no trouble. It isn't late at all ... We wouldn't let your father down. We know how he likes his salmon.'

'Thanks. That's great. Only, it's a long drive and—'

'—and I want you to take this, Annie. It's a new line. He'll love it. Now, how about a nice cup of hot tea?'

'Well, I...'

'With a dash of something to warm you? You're shivering, Annie. You must stay long enough to dry out.'

'Uh ... well, OK, but I mustn't be too long. Thanks.'

The tea was welcome as was the sharp tang that warmed her beyond the heat of the liquid. As soon as she was seated with the cup in her hand, the interrogation began.

'Now, about this terrible business. A body in the loch. Tell us everything, Annie. You were there, weren't you? Is it true the rest of it was eaten? Some sort of animal...?'

'It was a leg ... part of a leg. I really don't know anything. I haven't heard about any animal.'

'Gives you the shivers, doesn't it?'

It was late when she left but the main road still had an air of summer-season bustle in the cars that thundered by. Another sleek, silver motor was parked down the lane from the smokehouse. The damned things haunted her. Maybe one day she'd climb back out of this pit, the way she'd climbed out of that other one all those years ago. Except now Aunt Marian was tangled up in it. If she went over the edge this time, there was nothing she could do that would be in time for her aunt.

She was tired. Too tired to go the long way round. She'd risk the pass, the road that cut a steep path over the high summit.

Not a route for tourists in bad weather, but Annie knew these hills, and she wanted to be home.

The road was flat for its first mile as it skirted fields, but even here it was barely wider than a farm track. As she turned into the first hairpin to begin the climb, Annie saw a flash of headlights across the plain behind her. Two vehicles attempting this pass on such a bad night amounted to heavy traffic. A glance in her mirror showed the flickering of lights through the trees as the other car traversed the flat stretch by the fields.

She was well into the climb when the temperature gauge swung into the red. She gave a grunt of exasperation. No choice but to stop and let it cool. There was space under the trees to squeeze the car off the road. Water dripped in heavy globules, splatting down as the leaves they'd gathered on could hold them no longer. It seemed drier than the constant downpour of the unsheltered road.

All this water. Surely she could capture some for herself. She pulled her showerproof over her head, struggled out and took an empty whisky bottle from the boot.

A tree root gave her a handhold as she tipped the bottle into the path of a trickle of water making its way down the slope. Small stones rattled down into the glass. Water and mud seeped through her trouser legs as she braced herself, watching the downpour become a meagre trickle when it found the neck of her bottle. Her mind wandered back to Aunt Marian's. Where would Charlotte be now? Down the pub? At the Scrabble board? Out with her scruffy suitor? Where was the Doll Makers' girl? Beth, as she must learn to think of her. It was odd to look face-on at the scene she'd taken for granted all her adult life. Beth must be twelve ... thirteen by now. Annie envisaged a primitive existence for her, but in all likelihood, she was far more comfortable at this moment than Annie, now mud-soaked as well as wet. The bottle filled and overflowed. Annie scrambled to her feet.

She heaved the bonnet up in a shower of rust and twisted the radiator cap. She held the bottle at arm's length in case the water should fountain out again as steam, trying to be quick without pouring gunge into the system, because all the time the bonnet was up, the rain swept in and threatened the electrics.

A thought struck. Where was the car she'd seen starting the climb behind her? She squinted through the worsening light. Had it driven past without her noticing? No, it couldn't have.

She slammed down the bonnet with a clang that reverberated round the small clearing. Maybe the other car had turned and gone back. A tourist taken a wrong turn. That was the most likely explanation. Nonetheless, she was puzzled its lights hadn't caught her eye as it travelled back across the flat plain.

If it hadn't gone back and hadn't gone past, it must have stopped at the first hairpin. A small shiver ran through her that had nothing to do with the weather. She peered through the trees. The lights of any car parked down there should show, but there was nothing.

The engine turned without trying to fire. She tried again. This time it coughed and rattled into action, but, as she pumped her foot on the accelerator pedal, the asthmatic engine laboured and died.

As the engine fell silent, she heard something that wasn't the downpour. A low hum, just audible through the drumming rain. An overactive imagination might interpret the sound as a vehicle creeping up the hill. She twisted round in her seat and stared hard. Nothing. Only a madman would drive up this road without lights. She tried to force herself to laugh.

The hill was steep. In reverse gear, she rolled the car backwards and slipped the clutch with too much force for the engine to resist. Stamping down on the pedal, she made it drag petrol through until the coughing settled to a steady rhythm, then she rammed it into first and it began to hiccup forwards once more.

'You've got water, blasted metal rust-bucket, what more do you want?'

Proper servicing, the engine spat back, but it dried itself of the rain that had crept in, stopped coughing and settled to a steady growl.

Annie let out a breath she didn't know she'd been holding. It was vital to nurse the engine to the summit, but she couldn't hold back a rising panic that made her floor the accelerator. The small car roared towards the next hairpin, its revs laboured, starting to protest.

Annie's hands clamped round the wheel. The protesting engine drowned out everything as she swung the car back and forth round the narrow turns. The climb steepened. It was hard enough seeing ahead through the rain and mist to take any notice of an occasional flash of light from the rear-view mirror. Every nerve strained towards one goal. The summit. If she could get across to the downward incline, she could coast it home.

The car screamed as though it would explode. Twenty metres more and she'd be off the killer slope. Ten ... Five...

She slewed the wheel, squinting through the fogged windscreen, knowing the road cut to the left, the outward curve wearing its only crash barrier.

A sudden glare of headlights blinded her.

Her gasp was involuntary. She scrabbled with the wheel, throwing a hand up instinctively to shield her eyes.

Her wrist hit painfully on the mirror. At once, the light vanished.

The road ahead was empty. Dark. It cut away from her round the rock face. She struggled to keep control. The sounds of an engine revving hard didn't match what her feet were doing. The car scraped and juddered as it grated against the barrier. She fought to hold it to the road.

A view flashed across her peripheral vision. The bold stripe of the barrier and then ... nothing ... a dense grey mist ... no sign of the patchwork landscape far below.

Her teeth clenched tight. She tasted blood as she accelerated out of the corner. The car rocked and steadied on to a short straight. Now she was off the killer climb. Just the gentle undulations across the top of the pass between her and the safety of the downward slope. But no more barriers.

The gale hit as she stamped the pedal down again, bouncing along the thin tarmac strip that snaked across the summit. Out of the trees' cover, the storm smacked the car hard as though the wind would pick it up and hurl it over the edge.

She threw it at the bends in the road, relying as much on memory as what she could see. Bright beams of light exploded in her wing mirrors and lit the interior of the car like bursts of flash photography. She knew this road. Concentration was total on the twists and turns.

Ahead, the road vanished, fell away into a void.

A tightening curve that dropped the road off the summit. No barrier here.

It rushed up too fast. With a gasp, she wrenched her foot across to hit the brake.

A blinding flash lit the interior of the car. She couldn't see. No time to think.

Her foot pushed hard on the accelerator. One hand wrenched the wheel, the other grasped the handbrake. The car skidded sideways round the outcropping of rock. Inches from the sliding wheels, a near-sheer drop to the bottom of the glen.

She slammed the handbrake back down, hearing herself whimper as though listening to a phantom passenger.

Something rational deep inside watched in horror as she hurled the small car at the oncoming brow and swung the wheel. The road dropped away in front of her. Now she could get maximum speed without forcing the car to its limits. The engine stopped screaming.

Safe now. Her panic faded. What in hell...? Adolescent Annie in her wildest days had never hand-braked that turn.

As the car flew back down into the cover of the trees, Annie straightened the mirror and looked up into it. All she could see was the short stretch back to the last hairpin, a grey and waterlogged view. She became aware of the pounding of her heart, and that she was panting as though she'd just done one of the killer staircases from the deep tube lines.

She was as high as the storm clouds. It was adrenalin ... couldn't be anything else.

Still geed-up, she raced through the village far too fast and jerked to a stop outside her father's house. The relief flooded through her. What in hell had got into her? And over that road of all places. Had she seen one single thing to justify pushing herself to the edge like that? OK, so a car had driven up behind and its lights had blinded her. She hadn't been concentrating. It had taken her unawares, that was all. She'd seen a few flashes of light. In the middle of a storm, for God's sake! She had her secrets, but nothing anyone would run her off the road for. This whole business was getting to her in ways she'd never dreamt of. And what really scared her was the sudden high she'd experienced, a chilling reminder of how good it could feel.

There was a rap at the window and she jumped round.

'You all right in there, Annie?'

'What?' She wound down the window and looked up into a lined and mournful face dripping with water, huddled in a scarf and narrow-brimmed hat.

'Uh ... yeah ...' She told her mouth to do its impersonation of a smile, as she opened the door. 'Thanks, Mr Caine. Yes, I'm fine.'

CHAPTER SEVEN

Early the next morning, Annie watched from an upstairs window as a small figure scuttled down the hill, head bowed, arms clasped round a fat basket. It was Beth heading towards Mr Caine's shop.

Mindful of her promise to Aunt Marian, she slipped out and followed. It was too early for anyone to be about, and a long walk for the girl just to bring a basketful of dolls. She was such an accepted part of the landscape that Annie had never questioned her presence before. There had to be more to it. She would ask her father later. She waited for the girl to return and head for the slope to the moorland track that would take her cross country back home.

'Hi Beth,' she said, trying for a tone of mild surprise at an unexpected meeting; no threat.

The young girl stopped and stared, her mouth falling open in surprise. After a moment when Annie thought she might just carry on without speaking, she said, 'Hello, Annie Raymond.'

All these years, this girl had known her name and yet she'd only just learnt to say Beth. Up close, there was no menace in Beth whose small but solid form was topped by the ragged edges of badly cut hair peeping from under a hat pulled down tight.

'How are you?' asked Annie.

Beth's face remained blank but her body language showed a desire to move away. She seemed in agonies in case they were seen. Annie struggled to remember what she knew of the Doll Makers from years ago. Was segregation a part of whatever rules they followed? What had Aunt Marian told her?

51

Beth looked up at her again with a sideways glance, as though sharing a secret. 'Annie Raymond. Special Branch,' she said. There was awareness behind the deep blue of Beth's eyes, and yet something was missing. Maybe Beth, with her strange way of living, hadn't seen enough of life, or maybe that hint of inadequacy hid something fundamentally wrong and explained why she'd been kept away from people. Whatever it was, Annie knew the girl echoed Aunt Marian's words without understanding them. Where had she heard them? What was she trying to say?

'If you want to talk ... you can talk to me. I won't tell anyone.'

Beth shook her head sadly, as though disappointed Annie hadn't understood her.

Annie felt her jaw muscles ache from holding her smile. What should she say now? This was like holding a conversation with someone who spoke a different language.

A crash in the undergrowth made Annie spin on her heel. A small deer broke cover and bounded up the hill. Annie watched until it blended with the scrub and disappeared. When she turned back, Beth was gone.

Back home, the smell of burning took her to the kitchen where her father fiddled with the toaster, trying to pry free a slice of toast that had cooked itself to the element.

'I'll make coffee,' she said. 'No Mrs L today?'

'She's having a day off. That salmon you brought is a real beauty, Annie. We'll have it for lunch.'

He gave her a smile that she returned. Today was ideal. No Mrs Latimer, just the two of them. She'd have breakfast, go and get washed and then sit him down and tell him everything. The panic was gone, her heart beat heavily in her chest, but she was ready to face him. There was sadness that a budding new relationship would be crushed underfoot. She stood here his equal, but by the end of the day, she'd be his little girl again. His bad little girl.

'Been out for a run?' He gave a nod to her tracksuit.

'Uh ... no. Just a walk. I saw Beth out there, Dad. It's a long way for her to come, all the way across the moor. Does she always come over this early? I've never really registered before.'

'Beth?'

'You know, the Doll Makers' girl. She takes stuff to Mr Caine. Dolls, I suppose.'

'Oh, right ... Yes, of course.' And Annie knew that his surprise was not that he hadn't known Beth, but that she did.

'Dad. If it's dolls she brings over, who buys them all?'

'He does pretty well out of the tourists every year.'

'Yeah, but not those crappy dolls. I wondered if he kept taking them because he was sorry for her or something like that.'

'Yes, more or less. He likes to do his bit.'

'But why her?'

'He's her uncle.'

'He's what! Her uncle? I never knew that.'

'No reason you should. He doesn't shout about it. I mean, would you? You wouldn't remember. You were only about six or seven when Caine's father died.'

Caine's father? That would be the old man whose children were taken briefly into care.

'Caine had a falling out with his brother and decided to leave the community,' her father went on. 'Actually, I suspect he wanted to leave long before that, but loyalty to the old man kept him there. He came to me for help when he wanted the post office. And I helped him.'

It twisted the knife to hear the shared confidences, him saying she was his equal now, but it wouldn't stop her. As his equal, she had to be honest. After breakfast, they would talk. 'Why did he come to you?'

'I'd got to know him a little a few years earlier. He and his brother and sister were taken into care briefly. You must have heard about it. I was taken round to meet him, a lad his own age, supposed to talk some sense into him, but I ending up taking his side. Not that I got to know him till years later, but he said he remembered me as an outsider he could trust.'

'What did you take his side about?'

'Oh, just hair washing and that sort of thing. You see he was fourteen. The little ones were only ... I don't know ... five or six. He felt he had to protect them. The people looking after them wanted to wash all their hair, but he wouldn't let them.'

'Why on earth not? Don't they wash hair? They always look clean enough.'

He laughed. 'Even you've held on to the old prejudices, haven't you, Annie? And it happened before you were born. No, he was quite right. They wanted to wash their hair, so they could say that all the children had had head lice but it had been treated.'

'But that's awful.'

'It was an eye-opener to me too. I've always been grateful to Caine for tarnishing a few of my ideals about authority figures. It's stood me in good stead over the years. Especially in this job.'

'What's his name?' Annie asked, suddenly curious. 'He's always just been Mr Caine to me.'

'It's Cain without the e. Cain was his first name. He took it on as his surname when he left the community. You won't make a big thing of it, will you Annie? It's not a secret, but it isn't something he likes to have broadcast.'

'Of course not.' She spooned coffee into the pot and waited for the kettle to boil. 'How's the case going? Any progress?'

'They're still racing round like headless chickens wanting to know how a van under close surveillance could give them the slip.'

'Yeah, right, they should have called you in sooner.' She'd meant the leg in the loch; had forgotten about the drugs thing. 'If they didn't know the roads round here it's no wonder really. And what about the leg in the loch? Any idea who it is ... was?'

He shook his head. 'There's so little to go on. We need to find the rest of the body.'

'You're certain there is a rest of the body? Dead, I mean.'

'Not a hundred per cent.' His tone told her he still worked at odds with his CID colleagues. 'But a body that was subject to that much heat is unlikely to have survived.'

Later on, after breakfast, she stood facing her reflection in the mirror in her bedroom. Any time today would do, but now she'd made her mind up to it, she kept putting it off minute by minute, knowing it would change everything. The house was warm and bright with the early sun. Breakfasty smells of toast and coffee still hung in the air. On some level her father had already responded to her need to talk to him. How else had this closeness sprung up between them?

'Annie. Annie!'

'I'm coming.' She called out her answer registering the distress in his tone. 'What is it?'

'Annie, I'm really sorry. I didn't know she'd do this.'

Annie looked uncomprehending at the paper he held out towards her. What was he saying? Do what? Who?

Then she took it from him and unfolded it. At the top, in Mrs Latimer's neat script, was the single word 'URGENT'. Mrs Latimer had taken messages while she'd been with Aunt Marian and, knowing she could use Annie's father's preoccupation as an excuse for it to slip her mind, had left the paper folded in a corner for Annie to find.

None of this mattered as she read the words Mrs Latimer had transcribed. The messages were from Pieternel. The first was an urgent summons to Annie to get her ass back to the office as fast as she could. Two days ago. It had come in two days ago. Oh Christ! The next two were more peremptory orders to Annie to get in touch, to get back at once. Mrs Latimer had let Pieternel believe she'd ignored them, and never said she was at her aunt's. This was salvation. It had to be. There could be no other reason for such a summons. She must leave now. Right now! Oh, why hadn't Pieternel tried her mobile? Maybe she had, and failed to get a signal; it wasn't great at Aunt Marian's.

'I'm so sorry, Annie,' her father said. 'I had no idea she'd do anything like this.'

It was the moment Annie had prayed for since she was eight years old. The moment Mrs Latimer overstepped the mark in a way that couldn't be hidden from her father. This was the moment she crushed the old enemy underfoot.

'It doesn't matter, Dad. So, she forgot. There's been a lot going on lately.'

'She didn't forget, Annie. Those notes were deliberately hidden.'

Foolish Mrs Latimer. Hidden somewhere she was sure I would find them, but I didn't. Not this time.

'Dad. It doesn't matter.' Annie heard her voice, firm, assertive. More like parent to child than the other way round. 'It's my fault for riling her. I know I said it was just sport these days, but maybe she doesn't see it like that. I should be more thoughtful. Please don't say anything. There's no point.'

'You're being very generous, Annie.' His expression was grim, doubtful.

'No, really. She's had a lot to put up with over the years. No harm done...' Annie sent up a silent prayer that was true. 'Just let it lie.'

She worked hard to suppress a smile. Partly, it was the image of herself defending Mrs Latimer, but mainly a sudden high, a rush of gratitude to whatever providence had kept her quiet until now. And anyway, her father would be lost fending for himself after all these years. The fact of being over-generous to the Latimer woman was an irrelevance.

'Dad, I have to ring the office.' She knew she couldn't hide the excitement in her voice, and saw that he heard it too and shared it, happy that something had buoyed her up. Her earlier reticence and worry must have shown through, but he hadn't pried then and didn't now. He gave her a grin and waved her to the phone in the hallway.

'You have reached the offices of...'

The answer-phone! She couldn't believe it. Why weren't they waiting ready to snatch up the receiver as soon as she rang? Maybe they had been two days ago.

She tried Pieternel's mobile, but it was switched off. That meant Pieternel was in a meeting. Oh please, please, let it be a really, really important meeting, one of the irons Pieternel juggled. Let it be catching fire so it lit the London sky. She was desperate enough to try Dean's mobile, knowing he never answered it. But he would check his voicemail and they'd know she was on her way. His terse recorded message hit her ear.

'Dean.' -Beep-

'Dean. I've only just got your messages … Pieternel's messages. I'm at my dad's. I'm setting off now. I'll be back as soon as I can. Before the end of the day.'

She raced up the stairs and threw her things into her rucksack. Pieternel's words, even filtered through Mrs Latimer, felt good. Not the message someone would leave if announcing immediate disaster.

Her father came out of the kitchen as she thundered back down the stairs.

'Dad … I'm really sorry. I've got to go. It's a big job. We weren't expecting it. I have to get back.'

'It won't be the first time your visit ends this way.' The grin lit his face again. 'At least I got my salmon this time. I'm just sorry you won't be able to share it.'

His expression, happy and relaxed, almost made her fall apart. She'd just found him again and here she was rushing off. And yet how much better like this than what she'd had planned for today. She might be back again in a week's time with all her bad news intact, no illusions, but suddenly there was hope. Impulsively, she flung her arms round him and gave him a real hug. 'Now promise me you won't have a go at Mrs L. She'll only burn your porridge if you do.'

He laughed. 'OK, Annie. Drive carefully.' The spark in his eye matched the prickle of a tear at the back of hers.

At the start of her drive, the rain was unrelenting, but by the time she reached the Midlands she found herself praying for it to return, to ease the heat of the southern sun and break the monotony of the motorway. The swell of traffic around the Birmingham junctions made her feel as she always felt, that she was nearly home. Why did she always fall for the deception that because the bulk of the journey was over, she was almost there? She boiled with irritation every last mile of the route.

Then at last, the weather and the aggravation was forgotten as she fought her way through the city traffic and slotted her car in behind Pieternel's. The fatigue and stiffness of the journey fell from her as she pounded up the staircase, too impatient to wait for the lift. She burst into the office panting as though she'd done the 400 miles on foot. Pieternel stood there, her slim form silhouetted against the glare of the sun through the windows, her dark hair scraped back and held untidily by an off-centre clip as she held a document out in front of her and raked her gaze over it. Dean crouched in a corner of the room, his small frame made smaller as he hunched over one of the machines, his mop of black hair looking as though it hadn't been brushed in days. He was the first to look up and see her. Then Pieternel's gaze snapped from the document to Annie, who knew her own eyes shone, and matched the fierce hope on their faces.

'What's happened? Tell me everything.' She flexed her fingers, resisting an urge to grab she wasn't quite sure whose lapels and shake the story out of them.

Pieternel's expression relaxed into a grin. Annie realized it was the first smile she'd seen on her senior partner's face in months. She grabbed for the words as Pieternel told them, barely letting the bones of the story emerge before she pitched in question after question. *When...? How...? Exactly how...? Who...?* Together, they savoured every re-telling, bounced possibilities back and forth.

'We're not rebooted yet, guys,' from Dean. 'But, hey...'

'Listen to me.' Pieternel's words were superfluous. Annie had no intention of doing anything else. 'I've met them twice now. They'll give us this one, but no promises. I've juggled a worse pack than this and come out unsinged, but we're right on the edge. Don't ever forget it.'

'Oh God, if I'd only got your message, or left you the number of the guesthouse. Of all the times for that to happen...'

'No damage as it goes. We couldn't get your side started till I got the file out of them, and I only got that today. But can't you get a transmitter put up near your aunt so your mobile works?

There must be a cash-strapped school nearby that could take a mast on its playing field.'

'Don't be daft. But Pieternel, this is brilliant! They're blue chip! If they'll sign us up ...?'

Pieternel's expression hardened. 'This landed on us because the outfit they usually go to went bust, and I played politics. We're on a knife edge here, Annie.'

Annie nodded, sobered. They only had hope because someone else had hit a bad patch worse than theirs, and now they descended like a wake of vultures before the bodies of their fallen rivals were cold.

'What we need out of this,' Pieternel went on, 'is a fast result and a good one. It's a routine claim, but sizeable. They're resigned to paying out, but they want it checked.'

'OK.' Annie flipped through inventories in her head. *Don't let us need anything we've sold off.* 'Where's the paperwork?'

'Here.' Pieternel passed across a bulky folder. 'I'm in the office while this one's flying. Dean'll take the day to day once he's got you set up, and you're in the field, Annie. Right then, it's a routine case and that's how we treat it.'

'Get outa town!' Dean had the words out before Annie. What was Pieternel talking about? Routine case?

Pieternel smiled back at them from one step ahead. 'One hint of desperation and they'll run like swimmers at a gate. It's got to look like it's all in a day's work. We go in fast and slick. You do the most professional job you ever did, Annie, and we might just reel them in. They need an outfit to take this stuff on regularly; let's make sure it's us.'

Annie wished Pieternel had used an image other than reeling them in, but shook thoughts of Freddie Pearson out of her head as she read through the papers. A straightforward surveillance. Was the woman as badly injured as she claimed to be? She paused, lost for a moment as a mental picture of the 66-year-old claimant described in the notes built up in her mind. She skimmed enough of the summary to get the picture. A thorough read-through would come later when she was on her own with no distractions. 'It looks routine,' she said, thinking of the extra impact she could make by pulling apart a complex scam. This was likely to be no more than a confirmation that the woman was on the level. 'To be honest, I'm surprised they're even checking it.'

'It's a multi-meg claim,' Dean pointed out. 'Those guys hate shelling out. It's how they got to be so hi-spec in the first place.'

'Annie, you're not thinking straight. If it'd been a more than routine, I couldn't have lobbied it into our laps. They'd have taken it to someone with a longer track record.'

True, thought Annie, but how was she to produce the triumph they needed out of a routine job?

She and Dean struggled with the bulky camera-housing. It was straight from the Ark, not the right equipment for a covert surveillance job, but the good stuff was long sold off. Annie thought back to her first ever real surveillance. She'd had good equipment then, someone else's, but no real idea what to do with it. Now she had the experience and the skills. Surely that outweighed the problems? Anyway she was set to follow a 60-odd year old who walked with crutches. How hard could it be?

'So it's all shoulders to the wheel again. Just like old times.'

'Yeah, kinda.' Dean's voice was heavy.

'We can do it, Dean. This is the break we need. And if we get out of the shit this time, we're really set up. We won't be relying on anyone but ourselves.'

'Yeah. If. It still means I've got to do all your shit while you swan about with this lot.'

Annie paused. It wasn't like Dean to be so negative.

'Pieternel,' she called over her shoulder. 'What did you mean you'd be in the office while this job's on?'

'They need to see us running smooth as an oil spill. Head of Ops full time behind her desk, not plugging gaps where there aren't any staff. They'll be over to check us out so I'm getting a temp in to sit behind a desk and look efficient.'

A temp. Annie's mind flashed momentarily back to Charlotte – the temp with the hidden agendas. But a temp couldn't do the specialist stuff. And that left Dean with all the case work on his shoulders. All the ongoing jobs. His own, hers and Pieternel's. All those not very lucrative loose ends and odds and sods of jobs they couldn't abandon without broadcasting to the world that they were finished.

'Dean can't manage on his own, Pieternel. We don't want to mess up any of the regulars we've got left. With any luck, we'll still need them.'

'I know. I'm buying in help till we're through this.'

'What with? Fresh air?' Annie was surprised Pieternel had found the funds for a decorative temp, but experienced help had to be out of the question.

'Casey Lane comes cheap. She's as unreliable as shit, but she can take over a full workload and hit the ground running.'

No puzzle now over Dean's mood. It wasn't so long ago that he'd got it together with Casey, and his desolation when she dumped him had left the place heavy with gloom. It had been a relief all round when Casey went. 'What if she won't come back? It's barely five minutes ago you sacked her.'

Pieternel ran her gaze across them in a way that reminded them why she was top dog. 'Turns out she just got the push again, so she's desperate. Word gets round, you know. She might be good, but she's high risk.'

Annie said nothing. She supposed Pieternel had dropped a word somewhere about Casey's drug habits. Her senior partner could be a real bastard when her back was to the wall.

Later in her flat, Annie spread the papers over the kitchen table, and outlined the key points in marker pen. She flitted from table to worktop, as she read and absorbed the detail, then returned to the camcorder to wrestle with its battery-housing. Dean had got it working, but she looked at it with misgiving.

She shuffled through the slices of a supermarket loaf, absently skimming the mouldy ones towards the bin. The last half dozen looked reasonable and she slipped a couple into the toaster, then leant across and pressed the button on the answer-phone that flashed one-message at her. It was three days old and the familiar voice brought a smile to her face.

Hi, Annie. It's Mike. Are you back yet? D'you fancy a night out? Give me a ring.

He'd expected her back early from her father's like she usually was. A night out with Mike was tempting. He had a knack of taking her outside her worries. He knew nothing about the desperate state of the business. It was just a casual thing between them so wasn't fair to offload her troubles on to him.

She picked up the phone. It was good to hear his voice.

'No, I can't take time out,' she told him. 'We've got a rush job on.'

'Oh, come on, Annie. You've always got a rush job on.'

'Hey, you know you said you'd like to come out on a surveillance with me? I've got one that might be just right.'

She spoke on impulse, half regretting the words, but why not? If it weren't for the context of the business going under, this would be the perfect job, routine, no fleet-footed quarry. And it would be an eye-opener to him to share the cramp and boredom of a routine stakeout.

'Yeah, great. Where and when? Now?'

'No, tomorrow. You'll have to take time off.'

'No problem. They owe me.'

Later that night, she gathered the papers back into their bulky folder. There was a single document that gave her pause. A copy of a fax from a hospital in Buenos Aires, slightly askew where the original hadn't been placed straight in the copier. She stared at it, asking it to give up any secrets it might have to give.

I'm nothing, it told her, just an off-centre copy.

The rational part of her knew it told the truth; knew she was desperate enough to clutch at anything that would turn this into a non-routine case that she could solve with a spectacular flourish.

CHAPTER EIGHT

Two days later, Annie manoeuvred her car into a gap at the end of the street, a discreet thirty metres from the target house. It was her second day trailing the woman she'd labelled Mrs Buenos Aires, who ranked with the easiest targets she'd ever had.

Despite his confidence, Mike hadn't been able to join her yesterday, but she expected him this morning and he would immediately learn a lesson about arriving earlier than this if he wanted a legitimate place to park.

The events in Scotland bugged her like a seed caught between her teeth. She'd checked the *Oban Times* website last night. The severed leg, literally and figuratively, was going stale. And she'd hear nothing from her father until he rang her. He wouldn't do email, except an occasional one-liner if she really pushed him.

'Email's for work, Annie. I prefer to talk.' Except of course he didn't. They hadn't talked properly in years.

As for her aunt, she might as well try to get her in a Formula One racing car as use email. She wouldn't even touch a mobile phone.

Mike's car pulled up beside her. Annie grinned and wound her window down. He clicked open his seat belt so he could crawl across the passenger seat to lean far enough out of the window to kiss her hello. The awkward angle made it a kiss on the level, as though they were in bed, instead of him bending down to bridge his almost-six-foot to her just-over-five. It felt good to have him close by. One day, when she shucked off some of her baggage, she might let him into her life properly. She knew it was what he wanted. Maybe it was what she wanted too, but if she ever let him close enough to see what sort of person she really was, he'd run a mile.

'There's nowhere to park,' he said.

'Just stay there. When she comes out, I'll move off. You park here and then come and join me.'

'Will we have time to do that? Won't she get away?'

Annie smiled at the tension in his voice. 'We'd have time for a complete change of clothes, not just cars. She's not too good on her feet.' She pointed across the road to the house. 'Just be ready to move when you see anyone come out. And keep an eye out for wardens, you might have to do the odd circuit. They're red hot around here.'

As the street began to wake, Annie outlined Mrs Buenos Aires' story for him. 'Her sister's lived in Argentina for a few years. They were visiting, her and the husband, and a motor bike hit her. She had a spell in hospital, then home by air ambulance with some pretty nasty injuries. It's a big claim.'

'Why does it need investigating?'

'They always look at anything this size. And you wouldn't believe the stunts people can pull. She could be exaggerating the injuries, be in cahoots with the biker, anything...'

'Is that likely?'

Annie shook her head. 'Nah, she's legit. I trailed her to the hospital yesterday. She wasn't putting it on.'

She almost mentioned the fax, but it was just an off-centre copy.

This case was a slow burner. It would bring a few more clients in its wake, a trickle, maybe enough to hold off disaster for a short while. Maybe long enough for Pieternel to reel in a real biggie, but more probably just long enough to keep them all hoping to the bitter end.

It was just after 9.30 when her phone rang. She picked it up without looking. 'Hello. Annie Raymond.'

'Hello, dear. Is that you?'

'Aunt Marian!' She shot bolt upright in surprise. Aunt Marian with her weird views on technology never rang a mobile phone unless she had to.

Mike's voice registered somewhere on the edge of what was important. She glanced across and saw a dustcart hassling him to move. She gave him a wave and twisted away to concentrate on the voice in her ear. The tone was excited. Annie imagined her aunt standing alone in the hallway at Mrs Watson's. She heard semi-audible muttering and heard paper rustling. 'Now where is it...? Ah yes...'

'What is it?' Annie tried to keep her voice even, but it came out a squeak. It must be bad news to make her aunt call like this, yet she sounded so calm.

'Your voice sounds odd, dear. I hope you didn't catch a chill in all that rain the other day. I expect it's your mobile phone. It must do all sorts to a voice, sending it through the air. Anyway, I'm on a proper phone so you can hear me clearly. That's the main thing. Now listen carefully, Annie. I've a job for you.'

'A job?'

'Yes, dear, a job. I was sadly mistaken in that lass and I feel responsible. If I hadn't taken her under my wing, Mrs Watson wouldn't have let her take advantage of the facilities like she did.'

'What girl? Charlotte?'

'Yes! There you are. Annie knew at once who I was talking about. I told you she'd know what to do.'

Annie readjusted her mental image of Aunt Marian, and set Mrs Watson in the hallway behind her. 'What's she done?'

'She's...' Aunt Marian cleared her throat and spoke self-consciously. 'She's ... done a runner.'

Annie smiled and relaxed. It wasn't a crisis after all. It was just her aunt grabbing an opportunity to brush shoulders with her niece's cloak and dagger world. Mrs Watson was probably every bit as impressed as she was intended to be. 'Done a runner, has she? What did she take?'

'Och no, dear. Nothing like that. She hasn't stolen anything out of the house, but she left owing a full week's half board. Now, you're to find her, Annie. Spare no expense. She mustn't get away with it. Heaven knows what sort we'd start getting if word got out. I must say though, I was sadly mistaken in her.'

Me too, thought Annie, I wouldn't have thought she had the gumption. Her opinion of Charlotte rose a notch. The thought came to her that maybe Charlotte simply couldn't stand another moment under Aunt Marian's wing and had cut and run.

'When can you be back here, dear? Later today?'

'I ... uh ... ' Annie scrabbled in her mind for a way to say no, without snubbing her aunt. 'I'll make enquiries at this end. She works in London, doesn't she?'

'Aye, of course. You can call on Margot. The old girl network. Anyway dear, I won't keep you. You call me when you've got Mrs Watson's money. A full week's half board.' There was a murmured exchange in the background. 'Yes, and two packed lunches.'

Annie clicked off the phone and blew out her cheeks. With any luck, her aunt's enthusiasm for the venture wouldn't last long.

She turned to look for Mike, but the dustcart now occupied his space, blocking her in. He'd be back round in a moment. Poor Charlotte, she must have been desperate to get away to run out without paying. The dustcart revved up and moved further on, clearing Annie's view of the road.

'Oh shit!' Mrs Buenos Aires' car was gone.

She leapt out to look up and down the road. No sign, but she couldn't have gone far. Her phone rang again.

It was Mike, his voice panicked. 'Annie, at last! She came out while you were on the phone. I followed her.'

Good old Mike, that would save her some time. 'Where are you?'

'On the main road. She's just turning into Tesco.'

Tesco? That was just round the corner. She'd be there before either of them found a parking space.

As Annie pulled into the car park, she saw Mike standing next to his car, jigging about, head snapping back and forth, a look of alarm on his face that relaxed into a slump of relief as he saw her.

'Over there. Over there.' She saw him mouth exaggeratedly, as he waved his arms and pointed over the tops of the cars.

People going past glanced at him and looked away. Annie gave him a grin and swung her car round to where he pointed, to where Mrs BA made heavy weather of backing her car into one of the disabled bays. Mike needed a beginners' lesson in covert surveillance, but that could wait.

It must be agony for her to drive, thought Annie, as she focused the lens. They hadn't had any money yet. Had they taken out a loan to adapt the car? Did she just struggle on when she had to? Why was she shopping on her own? Where was Mr BA?

She filmed the woman as she disappeared inside the store, then wandered over to the car and peered inside. No, as far as she could tell, it had all the standard controls. Just the blue badge in the windscreen to show there was anything wrong.

'That's her car.' Mike was at her side, his voice excited. 'She went in that way. Should we follow? She didn't look that bad on her pins.'

Annie looked down at the bulky camera, then up at Mike. 'Come on.' She pulled him back towards her car. 'For God's sake turn your collar back down and stop looking so guilty. See this?' She indicated the camera. 'How far d'you think we'd get carting it around a busy supermarket? We'll wait for her to come out.'

They sat in her car and chatted desultorily until Mrs BA re-emerged from the store.

Annie lifted the camera to her shoulder and watched through the lens. A woman in a Tesco tunic strolled at Mrs BA's side carrying a couple of bags. Yes, Mrs BA's bland face wore the mask of a smile. Aunt Marian would do just the same. Accept help if she had to, but not show the pain.

'You could use this, couldn't you?' Mike said. 'To make it look as though she isn't as bad as she says.'

Annie nodded, but said nothing as she watched Mrs BA, framed in the lens, climb into her car and reach for the seat belt. This was damning footage.

'It wouldn't negate the medical reports,' she told Mike, knowing as she spoke that it could do just that. There was something compelling about video footage; a magic that could counter reams of paperwork. Annie could weave a temporary spell over the case that would reduce the stratospheric claim to ashes. Mrs BA would have to go to court to fight maybe for years for her rightful dues. The medical evidence would restore the balance – eventually. And meanwhile, the business might stand up on its feet again on the back of some clever spin with a chance recording. And Mrs BA might die before she saw her payout. 'It's not the true picture,' she said. 'And I'd have to be an unscrupulous bastard to use it.'

A terrible fantasy played in her head, where this turned into the case of her dreams, the case where she pulled the impossible out of the hat, saved the client hundreds of thousands. A big case. Could make the papers.

But she'd seen the medical reports, seen Mrs BA and her elderly husband yesterday as they struggled to the hospital. They needed their settlement and needed it without delay. If the only thing on the other side of the scale were financial ruin, these thoughts wouldn't get off the ground. But there was Aunt Marian. If two elderly women are drowning in front of you, and you can only save one of them, which do you choose? The elderly aunt you've known all your life, who brought you up and gave you everything, or the stranger you've never even spoken to?

'Mike, I have to get back to the office. I have to take this lot back in.'

'What? Now?' He looked taken aback. 'Let's at least go and get some coffee.'

She forced a smile. If you only knew what I was really like, she thought, you'd keep your distance. He'd joined her at her request, taken time off work, she couldn't desert him like this. But neither could she sit and talk pretending everything was OK. She had to be on her own.

She glanced at her watch. It was early still. 'Give me an hour,' she said. 'Meet me back at my place. I'll make us something for lunch.'

'Ooh!' He waggled his fingers in mock excitement. 'Coffee and stale bread. Can't wait.'

'Oh Mike.' She ducked her head in some embarrassment at the accuracy of the picture, but he'd pulled a real smile from her. 'I'll call and get something, OK?'

Annie made straight for the flat and spread the case notes over the kitchen table. She needed space to think.

If Mrs BA had let herself wallow in self-pity, if she'd played the victim for all it was worth, she would never have struggled to the shops and jeopardized her claim. And if she'd been like that maybe Annie could have contemplated cheating her out of what was her due.

No, she couldn't even think about it. This woman was someone else's Aunt Marian. But what of her own aunt? One elderly woman was condemned to a future hell by Annie's actions. There was no middle ground. It was Aunt Marian or Mrs BA.

The click of the key in the door took her by surprise. Had she been sitting here so long? 'Mike.' She smiled up at him and tried to pull her thoughts back together. She was as muddled now as when they'd left each other an hour ago. What was it they'd arranged to do? 'Oh shit. I'm sorry, Mike. I forgot to get anything in for lunch. I'll go now.'

'Of course you forgot, Annie. The day I come round here and find a tidy kitchen and a meal ready I'll know something's really wrong.' He eased back a pile of dirty crockery and dumped down a carrier bag. 'Just sarnis from Pret. And I got some fruit.'

'Thanks.' She laughed back at him, and prayed that her thoughts didn't show. *Something really wrong.* This was the perfect time, by his reckoning, for her to be ready for him with a three-course meal in a candlelit room.

Annie intended to get into work early the next morning to start taking the load back off Dean, but eight o'clock found her at the kitchen table, riddled with indecision and still in her pyjamas.

She rifled through the case file and pulled out the fax. The supermarket trip meant nothing. The only thing that niggled at the back of her mind like grit in her shoe was that skewed fax copy. She stared at it until her eyes ached, but couldn't see anything, or even catch a glimmer of what might be there to see.

What she wanted was someone with whom to talk it through, like in the old days when she and Pieternel had sat for hours over the files, over Annie's notes.

The first time Annie had said, 'It's just a feeling ... I don't know...' Pieternel was scathing. 'We can't build a business on feelings, Annie. Get some evidence.' So Annie had dug out the evidence. Evidence that no one else had found, because they didn't look, didn't have *just a feeling* to guide them. After a while, when Annie said, 'It's just a feeling...' Pieternel pitched in to help, to dig through to find what had set Annie's senses to alarm pitch.

But this one was different. This wasn't her investigator's instinct scenting a trail, it was desperation trying to find a way out and she daren't tell Pieternel she might have found one.

She knew what to do and a weight lifted from her as she made the decision. Of course she couldn't doctor the Buenos Aires report. Aunt Marian wouldn't countenance it for a second. No matter what the consequences, she wouldn't have Annie overstep that mark.

The certainty she was right cushioned her through a morning spent closeted with Pieternel who interrogated her for every last detail.

'But Annie, are you sure? This footage...'

'She's on the level,' Annie told Pieternel again and again. 'They know it. They have to. They've seen the medical reports.'

'And the fax? You said you'd wondered about it.'

'Nah, I was clutching at straws. There's nothing missing off it anyway.'

It was stuffy in the small office. Pieternel's face was drawn, and Annie was sure it reflected her own expression. 'Let's get some coffee. I'm parched. What shall we do with it? D'you want me to write it up this afternoon? We can get it to them before the end of the day.'

'Hell, no! Let's get coffee, but get this straight first. I don't want to talk about things out there if Casey's about. The less she knows, the better. She can do her own caseload and as soon we can do without her, she's out.'

Annie fought back an instinct to tell Pieternel how unfair she was being. Let Casey fight her own battles. 'What do you mean, no? Don't you want me to write it?'

'I mean we don't rush round with it. We fitted them in, remember? As a favour. We rush round now, it's pretty clear we've put everything else on hold. I don't want them seeing a hint of desperation.'

'Fair enough. So what do you want me to do?'

'Leave it with me. I'll get it ready then you can take it round one evening. That makes us look busier. Where are we now? Thursday. I'll set up an appointment for next Tuesday. OK?'

They wandered out together to the main office, to hear a burst of laughter from the small annexe they used as overflow office, store and kitchen. Casey's voice, kept low, floated out to them. 'Time for a quick coffee? *Mein Fuhrer*'ll be closeted with Annie for hours yet.'

Annie tried not to smile as she met Pieternel's eye, and Casey's voice, this time in an unmistakable impersonation of Pieternel came to them again. 'For fuck's sake, Casey, use the damned spoon.'

Pieternel glanced at Annie with a look of distaste. 'Come on, we'll go across the road and get a proper coffee. There's something I want to run past you.'

As soon as they were settled in the coffee shop, Pieternel turned to Annie and said, 'You know what you were telling me about your aunt?'

Annie stiffened. Pieternel knew it was Aunt Marian's money tied up in the firm, but she'd never interfered in that side of things. 'What about her?'

'This job she wants you to do. Tracking down a guest who did a moonlight. I think we should take it on.'

'Pieternel, we're talking about one week's half board. The job'll cost them more than that in travel expenses.'

'You can warn your aunt in advance, can't you? She'll still want the woman tracking down.'

'That's not the point.' Annie was annoyed because she knew Aunt Marian would be with Pieternel on this one. *It's the principle, dear, not the money.*

'I'm clutching at straws here, Annie. I can't disguise that we're a tiny outfit, but I can make out we punch way above our weight. I could make a job like that look really good. I know it's not much on its own, but nothing's much good on its own. I'm desperate to pull in everything we can possibly use. Your aunt'll have to pay, of course, full whack plus expenses, unless you want to pay it yourself. We don't have any slack.'

Politics was Pieternel's side, fieldwork Annie's. They didn't interfere in each other's spheres. When Annie said 'It's just a feeling' Pieternel supported her. Now she asked Annie to trust her in return. She tried to get her head into the idea. The job itself was nothing. Tracking and search jobs had been her bread and butter at the PI agency

'Are you sure it's worth it, Pieternel? A bit of a fee and me tied up hundreds of miles away from the action.'

'If you must know, I've given the impression we're setting up new offices. So if they wanted to check up, I could send them to Scotland to see you.'

'No you couldn't. What do you want me to do, pretend we operate from my father's? And you know I can't do all that PR stuff talking to clients. It's not what I'm good at.'

'You underestimate yourself, Annie. Anyway, no one's going to go all that way. Maybe a phone call. I just want you to be based in Scotland for a few days. Trust me on this one. Please.'

Annie shrugged.

'I don't need you to go straight away, but we mustn't leave it too long and risk the woman turning up again. Stay and work with Dean for a couple of days so I can get Casey out of his hair. The last thing we need is him with his head all over the place again.'

That night Annie dreamt she had to carry cash from the supermarket to her car, but the cash was a viscous liquid and the trolley made of straw. Her hands struggled to weave the strands tighter. If the weave were thick enough and springy enough it would hold, and she would find her way out of the labyrinth. She felt the delicious squidge of fat, tightly bundled straw beneath her fingers, then the plumpness she'd created sagged again into empty dry strands.

It's my doll! It's mine. Mummy, it's mine!

She spun in triumph. Her mother stood behind her. Mummy. A hand reached out. A might-be smiling face. Then a roar of anger. *It's my doll!* The face changed just before it came into focus, a clawed hand ripped the doll from her arms. Alarms rang.

She found herself sitting up in bed, trying to interpret the sound. The phone. She fumbled for the handset, pulled it to her ear and mumbled, 'Hello?'

'Annie? It's her. I'm sure of it. No one else knows.' It was Aunt Marian's voice, full of tension. But before Annie could speak, the phone went dead.

Annie sat up, breathed deeply and blinked the sleep out of her eyes. It wasn't unusual for her aunt to ring with half a story and a promise to keep Annie up to date as events unfolded, though this one was more disconnected than most. Prior to ringing back to find out what it was about, she went through to the kitchen and flicked the switch on the kettle. If the day must start with an intense conversation with Aunt Marian, she would have coffee to sustain her.

'Hi, Mrs Watson, It's Annie. Can I speak to Aunt Marian?'

'You've just missed her, Annie. She's gone out.'

'Oh ... That's OK, it wasn't important. I'll ring later.'

Annie spent the morning working with Dean. Casey's name was never mentioned, but Annie didn't have to ask if the relationship were on again. His usually dour countenance wore a smile; he initiated conversations that weren't confined to the bits and bytes of the doctored system they unravelled. Pieternel was wrong. It would do no harm to anyone to have Dean happy, and if Casey could turn him round, then she was a better woman than either of them. Maybe Dean would repay the debt and help her to clean up her act.

In the afternoon she rang the guesthouse. The phone rang and rang and was eventually answered rather tentatively by one of the guests. No, he didn't know where Mrs Watson was and sorry, he wasn't sure he knew her Aunt Marian at all. Annie left a message for her aunt to ring back.

When she arrived home, she took in the flat's chaos. Cups heaped in the sink, the work surface invisible beneath the remnants of curling-at-the-edges sandwiches and Mars bar wrappers stuffed at random between stacks of clean and dirty crockery. Something didn't smell too fresh, maybe the battered carton of milk balancing on half a loaf of bread. She picked it up, wrinkling her nose at the clogged mess round the opening, and carried it to the bin where she tried to push it through the swing top. The bin was so full, the lid wasn't secure and tipped off, leaving Annie to recoil at the stench that rose from the packed contents.

She toyed with the idea of ringing someone to suggest a night out. Maybe Mike, maybe not. It wasn't wise, the way she'd come to rely on him. It would be great to have a wild night out with Casey, but she couldn't risk the aftermath. She skipped mentally through the list of friends who might be up for an impromptu fling, before realizing it would take more money than she could justify spending, given she was about to charge her aunt for a job she should offer for free.

With a feeling of giving in, she phoned Mike and left a message on his voicemail telling him to come round if he wanted to.

She jammed the bin lid down, balanced the milk carton back on the bread and looked in the fridge. It didn't smell too sweet either, but provided coffee. She'd need a good strong cup to face this lot, and wrestled the kettle into the gap between the tap and the stacked crockery, so she could fill it.

Invigorated by the thought of imminent caffeine, Annie hauled the rubbish down to the bins and started removing fur linings from inside the cups. When the phone rang just after nine, it reminded her that her aunt hadn't rung back. She dried her hands and picked up the handset.

'Annie?' said her father's voice.

Her father rang on Sunday mornings, and only then if he wasn't on duty, so she knew it meant trouble before she heard more.

'What is it, Dad? What's wrong?'

A pause. 'I'm sorry to call so late, Annie, but I'm a bit worried about your aunt. Has she been in touch?'

'Well … yes, this morning. What's happened? Is she all right?'

'Yes, yes, she's fine. Mrs Watson told me you'd rung. Apparently, there was a break-in at the guesthouse last night.'

'Oh my God! She never mentioned it.' Annie struggled to remember what her aunt had said. 'She wasn't hurt, was she?'

'No, no. Nothing like that. It was the girl who cleans who noticed someone had been through one of the bedrooms. No damage done that I know of. But Mrs Watson rang me when your aunt stayed out all day. She rang again now to say she'd just got back.'

'Just now!' Annie glanced at her watch. Her aunt had left just after she'd phoned in the morning. If she'd been out till now…?

'And she wouldn't say where she'd been, but Mrs Watson saw a ferry ticket.'

'A ferry ticket? Had she nipped over to Tarbert?' Even that short trip seemed impossibly adventurous for Aunt Marian these days, but if she were upset…

'No, not Tarbert.' Annie heard the echo of her own disbelief in her father's tones. 'She's been all the way to Glasgow.'

CHAPTER NINE

The next morning, Annie phoned the guesthouse as she and Mike zigzagged across each other's paths getting dressed and making coffee. 'Hi, Mrs Watson. Is Aunt Marian—?'

'Och, she's not up yet, Annie. She was exhausted after yesterday. I haven't woken her.'

'OK. Tell her I'm on my way. I'll be with you before the end of the day.'

'Will you want your usual room?'

'Uh ... no. I ...uh...' Annie had no intention of doing another stint in Mrs Watson's uncomfortable boxroom. 'No, I'll take Aunt Marian away for a few days. Up to my Dad's.' Fingers crossed that she could persuade her aunt and that her father wouldn't go off pop about it.

As she replaced the handset, Mike said, 'You don't seem to have been back home five minutes,' and gave her a smile that said he didn't want her to go.

Annie shrugged. 'I told Pieternel I'd go.'

'Does it make any sense, Annie? Travelling all the way from London for the sake of a week's half board?'

'Don't forget the two packed lunches.' She gave him a grin. 'No, of course it doesn't, but I'm glad of the excuse to go. Aunt Marian went across to Glasgow by herself. That's a hell of a journey. She hasn't done anything like that in years.'

'I suppose at her age, a break-in's quite an upset.' Mike stood up and headed for the hallway. He returned and tossed a pile of post on the table. 'I guess I should get going.'

Annie flicked through the letters. Bills, bills and more bills. None she could pay, and none she would open in front of Mike.

A fat brown paper package. Name and address handwritten. She froze for a moment as she took in the handwriting and then the Glasgow postmark. 'What the hell...?'

She tore off the paper and ripped the flimsy cardboard off the box inside. 'It's from Aunt Marian. What on earth has she sent me one of these for?' She held up the straw doll for Mike to see.

'What is it?'

'It's a doll. A post office doll.' The box and wrapping, upended and thoroughly shaken out revealed no explanatory note.

Mike looked at her, a crease appearing between his eyebrows. 'How worried are you, Annie, on a scale of one to ten?'

'I can't help thinking she might be getting to the stage where ... uh ... where she can't manage on her own.' She couldn't bring herself to say words like senile and dementia. Too close to madness, too wrapped up in lost memories.

'The break-in must really have upset her.'

She didn't want to discuss this with Mike. It wasn't his family, wasn't his problem. She pointed to the Margot jacket slung over a chair. 'Hang that back in the wardrobe for me, will you?'

She tried her father's number before she set off, but he'd left for work so she told the answer-phone she was using Mrs Watson's missing guest as an excuse for another visit. Her plan to bring her aunt up to stay with him was news she would break face to face.

Annie arrived outside Mrs Watson's late in the day, hot, tired and cross. She was here for her aunt, but knew she should be hundreds of miles away for just the same reason. If the business were to survive, it needed all experienced operatives on the front line fighting hard.

But Pieternel had been emphatic. Annie had rung again before she'd left. 'I'll get back as soon as I can, Pieternel.'

'No, Annie. I told you. I need you based up there for a few days. Just make sure you're back by Tuesday evening. OK?'

Mrs Watson's conspiratorial welcome irritated Annie as it became clear she and Aunt Marian had been winding each other to white heat over the break-in.

'We feel sure that Charlotte Grainger was a courier, Annie. She must have stashed drugs here and sneaked back for them. You'll get to the bottom of it, won't you? I don't want the good name of the guesthouse dragged through the mud.'

Annie's gritted teeth did service as a smile. She knew Mrs Watson would lose interest at once should anyone suggest that she foot the bill.

As soon as she was alone with her aunt, Annie pulled the doll from her pocket. 'Why did you go all the way to Glasgow to post this?'

'I'm sorry if I worried you, dear.' Annie watched as her aunt turned towards the window. 'It's a lovely peaceful view, isn't it? I've always liked it. But there was a killer down there just a couple of weeks ago. It's funny to think of it; it makes it all look different.' She let out a sigh, before turning back to Annie and the question she'd asked. 'I don't really know, dear. I was in a bit of a state about the break-in. I didn't want to trust the local post.'

Annie looked at her aunt perplexed. These weren't the actions of the sane and down-to-earth woman who'd brought her up. The age gap between her mother and aunt was almost twenty years, and her aunt was now an old woman, maybe one who could no longer manage even in the cosseted environment of Mrs Watson's. 'But why send it at all, Aunt Marian?'

'With Charlotte and everything. Her being so secretive, and stealing those tapes. Someone might have been after me and I wanted you to have it.'

'But why a doll?'

'Not just any doll, dear: it's your mother's.'

'My mother's! But why...? Where did she get it? Who gave it to her?'

'She came home with it, dear, just a few days before she was ... just a few days before. I kept it afterwards. I always wondered. Your father didn't think it was important, and I couldn't press him on it, not with what had happened, but I've never forgotten.'

Annie looked at the doll in her hand. Its plump lopsided form was a parody of the dolls that stalked her dreams. 'I never knew,' she said. Not that she'd ever known anything. Her mother was a 2-D image from photographs she couldn't remember, a face just out of sight in a dream. There was nothing left in her memory of the real person who must have been the centre of her world. 'Did she have a lot of dolls?'

'No, dear. Just that one. Why do you ask?'

'Sometimes I dream about her, only it's someone else when she turns round. And she has great armfuls of dolls, but I'm not allowed to touch them.' She stopped, as she heard her voice catch.

'You wouldn't remember, but your mother took quite an interest in the Doll Makers at one point. An unhealthy interest. It was the lad. He nearly led her astray. You'd have been about four and she'd had another miscarriage, so she wasn't herself, but I had to have some quite sharp words.'

'What lad?'

'He'll be a grown man now. I don't think he's there any more. I haven't seen him in years. He was one of the ones they took into care.'

'Not Mr Caine?'

'No, no. Cain's brother, Kovos.'

'Kovos? What sort of name's that?'

'Biblical, dear. I forget which bit though. He was younger than your mother by five or six years.'

A cold blade of suspicion sliced through Annie. Had her mother had an affair with one of the Doll Makers? The thought of it left her numb, not knowing how to react. It fitted with the sorts of things Mrs Latimer used to throw at her in anger. She put the doll on the sideboard and pushed it away. Her aunt's gaze tracked the doll's movement across the polished surface.

'I didn't think of it before, but I'd like you to have the doll when I die. I never thought to put it in my will, and it's something that would just get thrown away otherwise. But I'm glad you brought it back for me. I'd like to keep it for now, as a keepsake, but you be sure and have it when I go.'

Annie gave her aunt a smile to drive away these demons, and tried to turn the conversation. 'There can't be many people living up there now. You never see them these days.'

'I was glad when they stopped pushing themselves on the community,' said her aunt. 'It's not a normal life they lead, however clever the old man was. But I'm sorry for young Beth. I do wish you'd have a word.'

'I did. I spoke to her last time I was here.'

'That's good. How did she seem?'

'Uh ... fine. Aunt Marian, do you think you could get Mrs Watson to do some coffee? I could do with something to pick me up after that journey.'

'Yes, of course, dear. I'll nip down now.'

While her aunt was gone, Annie tried to call her father, but couldn't get a signal so was forced down to Mrs Watson's hallway to the house phone.

'Dad? I'm with Aunt Marian.'

'Will you be calling up here, Annie?'

'That's what I'm ringing about. Aunt Marian and Mrs Watson are spinning each other off planet with their spy theories. I need to get her out for a while. Can I ... well, what I thought was that I could take her across to town for a wander round and a bite to eat, then can I bring her back to you for the night? She needs a break from the Watson woman.'

His pause was so brief, Annie wouldn't have noticed if she hadn't been listening for it.

'Yes, of course. She'd better stay a couple of nights. I'll get Mrs Latimer to make something nice for supper tomorrow night. I might challenge her at the backgammon board if I'm not called out. Then I can run her back the next day. It's my day off.'

'Oh no, it's OK, Dad.' He'd got the wrong end of the stick altogether. 'I'll stay too. I won't land her on you.' *Except I will if Pieternel can't work her magic...*

'But aren't you needed in London, Annie? I don't mind entertaining Marian for a couple of days.'

Unexpectedly, she felt tears prick the back of her eye. She'd always known he'd come through for her; do his best. She knew just how much he hated his sister-in-law's fussing. 'It's OK, really. And like I told you when I rang, I'm half here on business. Mrs Watson wants me to make enquiries about a guest who did a moonlight.'

Annie took the long route to drive to town the other side of the peninsula. It would tempt fate to push the Nissan across the mountain pass too often. She decided to go straight to the heart of things and see if talking would help calm her aunt. 'Why didn't you tell me about the break-in when you rang?'

'I did tell you, dear. I told you I was sure it was Charlotte. You see Mrs Watson thinks it was drugs she came back for.'

'And what do you think?'

'I'm sure it was Charlotte, but it wasn't drugs. It was the tapes she was after.'

'The tapes she took from Margot's?' Annie remembered the call she'd overheard.

'Yes, she'd given them to me for safe-keeping. She insisted. I didn't want them.'

Annie kept her own opinion under wraps about who had insisted, because it was clear that however she'd felt at the time, her aunt didn't want the things now. 'Why should they have been safer with you?'

'Anyone could have found them in one of the ordinary guest rooms. I've my own furniture. I locked them in the tallboy.'

'And what were these tapes anyway?'

'I didn't listen to them, of course, but Charlotte told me they were the tapes of Lorraine, the drug addict, the one who had the fall in the hills and went to hospital. And Charlotte went to talk to her. I'm sure she told you. They were the tapes of Lorraine in counselling at Margot's.'

Annie wondered if Margot's clients knew that their sessions were taped. What a fertile field for blackmail. 'Dad said they'd taken Mrs Watson's booze.'

A crate of single malt, he'd said. Annie thought of the raw spirit Mrs Watson poured down her guests. She balked even at calling it whisky. It was the oldest insurance scam in the book, of course, taking advantage of a break-in, expanding the claim, but this one wasn't her problem.

'A decoy, dear. Just a decoy, so we didn't know what she was really after. And you will take the tapes back with you when you go, won't you? I'm getting too old for this sort of thing. I want to die in my bed. I'll keep the doll if I may, but now you know about it, you be sure it comes to you. I'll get it added to my will.' Aunt Marian's voice had lost all its bounce.

Once on the outskirts of town, Annie cast a look towards the ferry docks and put her own tiredness aside. She thought of the treats her aunt had arranged in the old days and how ungrateful she'd always been. The city today must be daunting to her aunt, but maybe she'd like to revisit some of the old haunts now they were together. 'We could nip across into Glasgow if you like; have a look round the lighthouse museum, or go out to the Rennie Mackintosh house. Then we could get a bite to eat in one of those little bistro places we used to go?'

Her aunt pulled a face. 'I'm not really in the mood for traipsing round museums. Couldn't we stay here and just go to the burger bar?'

'Yeah, fine.' Annie tried not to feel the rebuff. Not-in-the-mood was her line, when she, a pouting and sulky twelve-year-old, protested that she wanted chips and burger, not silly fancy food. Had her weekend jaunts with Aunt Marian been born from her aunt's determination to bring up her niece the way her dead sister would have wanted? Had they both been miserably bored with museums and fancy food? She turned the thought away, feeling suddenly empty. As though a part of her had just grown up and left a void behind. She headed the car for the main street and the burger bar.

As she slid on to the seat, Annie hoped she'd remember to get up slowly. Her skin would be welded to the plastic by the time they left. They ordered sausage, egg and chips. Aunt Marian sat back. 'Now, I phoned Margot, but she didn't seem to know what I was talking about, so you'll have to speak to her.'

'You've been in touch with Margot?' Annie's toes curled.

'Yes, to tell her about Charlotte. Good Heavens! I haven't told you yet, have I?'

Annie's thoughts were drawn irresistibly to a mental picture of Margot. Margot smiling that cold half-smile of hers as she listened to Annie's aunt's absurd theories.

'...you know the high pass, the short-cut back to your father's?'

'Sorry, Aunt Marian, what was that? Did you say Charlotte's been in a car crash?'

'Yes, dear. Pay attention. Last Wednesday. That's how I know where she is.'

The tables around them were empty, but cluttered as though they'd arrived just after a coach party left. The air was stale. Annie's hunger disappeared and she balked at the thought of greasy chips. 'Which hospital?'

'No, dear...' Aunt Marian stopped as a harassed and hot looking woman in an apron brought their food.

Annie caught the smell of freshly cooked chips, golden and crisp. Her hunger returned and she reached for the salt.

'No,' Aunt Marian repeated, watching the waitress walk away, 'not the hospital. The morgue.'

'Oh my God!' Annie looked up, shocked. 'Poor Charlotte. What happened?'

'She must have been going too fast and I suppose she skidded. She's not the first. The thing is, they don't know.'

'Don't know what? Who doesn't know?' She spoke automatically as the shock rippled across her skin. Only a week ago, she and Charlotte had shared drinks and confidences in a pub not so far away. Her aunt held the ketchup bottle out to her. On auto-pilot, she took it and watched herself inscribe her name in big loops with a thin line of tomato across the mound of chips. If she'd been twelve, there'd have been sharp words from her aunt. She stopped herself from dotting the i.

Poor Charlotte. That explained her sudden disappearance. She hadn't done a runner after all. Then it came to Annie with a jolt, a playback of the words she hadn't registered as Aunt Marian had spoken them. That road. It happened on that same road.

'They don't know it's her.' Aunt Marian speared a chip as she spoke. 'It was in the papers. They said they hadn't identified the driver, but, of course, I knew at once.'

'How do you know it's Charlotte? Was there a photo?'

'Oh no. I just knew.'

Annie felt a surge of relief. It was a complete stranger in the car, not someone she'd known, no connection with her own race across that mountain. What had Aunt Marian said, last Wednesday? That made one thing sure: Charlotte might either have died in the crash or been responsible for the break-in, but not both. Clearly her aunt hadn't done the maths. She'd let that dawn in its own time.

'It's sad to think of it,' Aunt Marian continued cheerfully, 'Charlotte lying there at the bottom of the glen.'

The plate in front of Annie came into focus as slabs of chip-shaped concrete over which someone had sneezed an ill-cooked egg and dribbled her name in congealed blood. A wave of nausea swept over her. She made a pretence at eating, while her aunt's voice, like a radio too loud to ignore, too soft to understand, played on in the background.

A torrential rainstorm. The car that vanished. A blinding flash of light from nowhere. And a terrifying race across a mountain ... Someone had tried to drive her off the road at that exact spot. Had they tried again with Charlotte and succeeded? No, it was just coincidence. It was all coincidence. She'd panicked in the thick of a storm. Charlotte was living it up miles away, having the rest of her holiday out of the reach of interfering old women.

A chill speared Annie. She desperately wanted her aunt to be wrong.

As they set off towards her father's, the first brushstrokes of dusk swept the sky.

Aunt Marian sat up and peered into the mountains. 'Let's go back the short way, shall we?' Her voice was interested, alert. 'We could stop at the top of the pass, and see where poor Charlotte went over.'

Annie was too tired to think of a good reason to say no, and it *was* the shortest route.

When they reached the windswept summit, Aunt Marian insisted Annie pull up so she could get out to peer over the crash barrier. 'I hope you're always careful when you come this way, Annie.'

Annie gave her aunt a smile but was glad of the failing light that hid what a poor attempt it was.

'Poor girl. She didn't have much of a life.'

Annie said nothing. She looked down at the road surface and imagined she could see tyre marks. It needed a conscious effort to stop her mind conjuring up the screech of rubber on tarmac; the picture of Charlotte terrified, stamping down on the brake, while her car was pushed closer and closer to the drop. She spun on her heel and ushered her aunt back to the car. There'd been no whisper of any other vehicle involved, and anyway there was nothing but her aunt's imagination to say it was Charlotte.

CHAPTER TEN

When they eventually pulled up outside her father's, Aunt Marian sighed and said, 'I'm absolutely whacked. I hope there's a bed made up. I need an early night.'

'I'm sure you can rely on Mrs Latimer to have the spare room ready.'

Annie's father came out to greet them and carry his sister-in-law's bag inside. 'What on earth's in here, Marian? It weighs a ton.' Annie heard a forced joviality in his tone. He'd seen the tiredness in her face.

'Just my overnight things.' She yawned. 'Dear me. I wish we hadn't stopped at the top of the pass now. That fresh air's really taken it out of me. We saw where that car went over.'

Once inside, Aunt Marian refused even a cup of tea, and headed for bed. Annie went straight to the phone to call Pieternel.

'Much the same, Annie. Still on the knife edge, but looking positive. Just you sit tight a few days. I'll let you know. How's your vanished guest going?'

Annie told her Aunt Marian's theory. 'It probably isn't Charlotte,' she finished. 'But if it is, it kind of wraps up the job.'

'Yeah, great. Put a claim on the woman's estate and they might get their money back.'

'You're a callous bastard, Pieternel. I quite liked Charlotte.'

After her call, Annie and her father sat cradling mugs of cocoa as she told him the bones of what had happened. She omitted any mention of the doll. For Annie, the trauma of her mother's murder was something she glimpsed in flashbacks of fractured memory or bits of dreams. For her father, it must have been a horrendous milestone that sliced his life in two.

He assumed his sister-in-law's trip to Glasgow had no concrete focus and Annie didn't enlighten him.

'What in heaven's name possessed you to go and gawp at the crash site?'

'It was Aunt Marian's idea. She's got it into her head she knew the victim. The guest who did a moonlight from Mrs Watson's. Charlotte Grainger.'

Her father shook his head. 'The woman in the car had ID on her. She wasn't Charlotte. She was Julia. Julia Lee. Though we can't find out where she's from. What was she like, this Charlotte person? Short? Tall?'

'Short. Shorter than me. Why?'

'Her body was thrown from the car before it hit the bottom so she was pretty badly smashed up but the fire that destroyed the car didn't touch her. I'm expecting to find she was a good bit taller than you once the PM results come back.'

'How come?'

'It was a hire car. The woman at the garage said Julia Lee was almost six foot. It'll be a disappointment to Marian. She always fancied herself as a bit of a detective.'

Annie rose early the next morning and went downstairs to find her father already at breakfast. He put the paper down as she came in. 'What have you in mind for today?'

'There's no point me going overboard after Charlotte. Minimal job, minimal fee. I'm here for Aunt Marian really. If she's up to it, we'll go round the village. I want to jolly her out of this mood she's in over the break-in.'

As they sat together, Annie told him about Charlotte, about her theory she'd been driven away by the fussing of the old women at the guesthouse. When she went on to tell him about Lorraine, the woman who'd fallen on the moor, he nodded. 'Yes, I heard about that. People do some stupid things. They don't realize how dangerous these hills can be.'

Annie was relieved. She wanted him to know about Charlotte's hidden agendas in case there was more beneath them than it seemed. Charlotte's face flitted across her mind's eye. Charlotte sitting next to Aunt Marian, desperate to stem the flow of her aunt's chatter; and in the pub; her avid questions about the Doll Makers; her unconvincing tale of a friend-of-a-friend. As she thought about her, Annie was struck by a sudden conviction that she would see Charlotte again soon. It was no more than a feeling, but reassuring. She saw herself apologizing for her aunt.

All morning, Annie trailed behind her aunt as she renewed a multitude of old acquaintances. Aunt Marian's stamina amazed her. In the post office, while her aunt swapped information on mutual friends with Mr Caine, Annie studied him. He'd been one of the Doll Makers and she expected some hitherto unnoticed glint in his eye, or secretiveness in his expression. But he was the slightly distasteful old man he'd always been, except now she knew he was only her father's age. She watched as he drank in the minutiae of the mini-scandals and squalls that upset village life, and leant eagerly towards her aunt to share from his own store of gossip. She turned away and looked into the faces and tiny eyes of the straw dolls as they hung from their rack, and understood their blank expressions. They had to listen to this stuff day after day.

It was as they left the shop, Aunt Marian grabbed her arm. 'Who's that? Over there. Who is it? I know that face.'

Annie looked. A group of children pushed and shoved each other towards the sea wall. 'Who?'

'No, he's gone. He went round the corner. Now where do I know him from?'

'I'll jog on and get a look at him if you like.'

'No, dear. No point. It isn't someone you'd know. He was a real blast from the past.'

Their morning stroll stretched itself to lunch in the pub and a further leisurely saunter round. It was late afternoon by the time they headed home. Annie had forgotten the incident outside the shop, until her arm was gripped again as they strolled back up towards the house. 'There, look! That's the man I told you about this morning. Don't look round! He'll see us.'

'How can I look and not look? Do you want me to see who it is or not?'

'Be careful. Pretend you're looking at something else. I've remembered who he is.'

Annie turned and saw a lanky individual leaning on the car park rail, looking out over the water. The sun was low in the sky and he squinted into its glare. His clothes had a slightly battered air. He looked nothing like her mental image of an old acquaintance of her aunt's. The reflection of the sun off the water made it hard to see his face, but she wouldn't have put him much beyond mid-thirties. He stood, looking at nothing in particular, but with a glimmer of a smile, a spark in his eye, as though waiting for life to toss him his next instalment of entertainment, and with every confidence that it would. She liked him immediately, but knew he was the sort her aunt would disapprove of on sight. The area attracted any number of people in the good weather, but he wasn't the type to be welcome at Mrs Watson's.

'So who is he?' They turned and continued their way up the hill.

'It's no wonder I couldn't remember. I had in mind I knew him from years ago, but of course I don't. He's the one Mrs Watson's nephew said he'd seen.'

Annie tried to head off a tangled explanation by having a guess at where this led. 'You think he was responsible for the break-in at Mrs Watson's?'

'No, no, that's the thing. Mrs Watson's nephew's in one of the front dormitories, and it couldn't have been long after he'd been on the ferry, what with his cases and things.'

Annie's head spun. 'What?'

'He saw him. Mrs Watson's nephew saw that man from his bedroom window the evening of the break-in. That's how we know it couldn't be him.'

Light dawned. Mrs Watson's nephew, along with his contemporaries, was a weekly boarder in town the other side of the peninsula, as Annie had been when she was his age. Crossing the high pass to and from school in town, even when the weather would allow it, made it too long a day for the children who lived this side of the mountain.

'He saw him before that too,' Aunt Marian went on. 'A week before they got that body out of the water. From his bedroom window again. Exactly a week. He remembered, with it being his friend's birthday.'

'It wasn't a body,' she murmured. 'Just a leg.'

'I know, dear. It makes it worse, doesn't it?'

Annie would have moved from local primary to weekly boarding in any case. It had been unfortunate timing that made it one more thing in an unrelenting series of changes after her mother died. Something else to resent her father for. First Mrs Latimer, then he'd packed her away to her aunt's. It must have been hell for him, she thought now. He'd had to pick up the pieces of his life and try to deal with open warfare between his daughter and housekeeper. It had felt to her then as though he'd chosen Mrs Latimer over her. And before she could make real sense of her new life with Aunt Marian, she'd been plucked off to big school. It must have been hell for Aunt Marian too. The unmarried elder sister, marvellous as an aunt, but clueless about how to be a parent. Annie knew it was the Monday to Friday of school that had given her an anchor, at least until she'd found and joined the bad crowd. Weekends with Aunt Marian were eccentric interludes, both weird and wonderful.

'But why on earth would Mrs Watson's nephew tell her about who he'd seen at school? She might be a world-class gossip, but surely she doesn't interrogate her nephews on what they see out of their bedroom windows?'

Aunt Marian laughed. 'Really Annie, what a thing to say about Mrs Watson. No, you see, she spotted him hanging about near the guesthouse and said what a shifty sort he was. And her nephew said he knew him. Of course he didn't. He just meant that he'd seen him, but we got all the details from him. And he'd seen him over in town, and of course if he'd been in town, he couldn't have been this side of the mountain at the guesthouse looking for Charlotte's tapes.'

'But why did Mrs Watson suspect him at all? Just because she doesn't like his looks?'

'No, no, of course not. He was Charlotte's young man.'

'He was what!'

'He was the one who called round for Charlotte. Not that I ever met him. He didn't come round again, but after you left, she took to slipping out without telling anyone. I saw them together in the distance, down by the shops. You saw yourself, he's a shifty sort.'

He certainly looked more the type to do a moonlight than Charlotte. Annie wondered if they were still together, and remembered her conviction that she would see Charlotte again. It would be ironic to bump into her here with Aunt Marian in tow.

She still hadn't told her aunt what she'd learnt about the crash victim, Julia Lee. It would save till after supper.

The cooking smells that greeted them made Aunt Marian sniff appreciatively and whisper to Annie, 'You can say what you like about Mrs Latimer, but she can cook.' It was clear that Aunt Marian's mind was at work as they settled themselves round the kitchen table. Annie's father carried the heavy dish from the oven and put it in front of his sister-in-law.

It occurred to Annie, that if Mrs Latimer were here, she would have commented on the unsuitability of game pie on as hot a day as today, at the same time that she drooled at the meaty aroma released as her aunt cut into the pastry. No wonder mealtimes had always been such tense affairs. Her sniping, Mrs Latimer flouncing. Her father in the middle with gritted teeth waiting for the next attack.

Aunt Marian made her first incision into the pastry before she spoke. 'Now, do you think we should tell Margot?'

'Annie's friend Margot?' her father said, surprised. 'Tell her what?'

'About the car crash.'

Annie explained the link between Charlotte and Margot, and added, 'But it wasn't Charlotte, Aunt Marian. Dad says they've ID'ed her. It's someone else.'

'I'm sure you're wrong. It must be Charlotte. If it isn't her, why did she come back and break into the house?'

Annie and her father exchanged a glance. 'A minor point, Marian, but wasn't the break-in after the crash?'

'Yes, it was the day that ... Oh, I see what you mean. She couldn't have been there as well as ... I see ... So it must have been her young man ... except for Mrs Watson's nephew of course...'

For a few moments, the only sounds were munching, the clinking of cutlery, and birdsong drifting in on the evening breeze. Aunt Marian's brow furrowed as she thought things through. 'So who was she, the woman in the car?'

Annie's father pondered the question, then said, 'Don't go spreading it all over the place, Marian, we haven't traced any relatives yet. Her name was Julia Lee.'

'Julia Lee!'

'Don't tell me you know her, Marian?'

Both Annie and her father looked up.

'No ... No, I suppose not. It's a common enough name, isn't it? The one I'm thinking of died years ago.'

'Not ours then. A pity. We could do with getting a handle on her.'

'Then it must have been the young man,' Aunt Marian said, knife and fork poised over her plate. 'The break-in, I mean. If it wasn't Charlotte, it must have been him.'

'Not unless he was in two places at once,' Annie pointed out. 'Mrs Watson's nephew, remember? And anyway, it could have been Charlotte, couldn't it, like you thought at first? If she wasn't in the car, she could have done the break-in?'

Annie's father shot her a don't-encourage-your-aunt look. Annie winked.

'I suppose so. But look, he's only a bairn, Mrs Watson's nephew. No one'll take much notice of him. And Charlotte was so nice.' She turned to Annie's father. 'I'm sure you can pin it on the young man. We can keep Mrs Watson's nephew out of it.'

Annie's gaze met her father's. Fleetingly, he raised his eyebrows and sought heaven with an upward glance. Without comment, he carried on with his meal.

After supper, Aunt Marian initiated a game of Scrabble, which she thought would be fun to play outdoors with some wine.

'Yes, why not?' Annie, allowed to participate in the privacy of home, surprised herself by thinking it might be fun too. 'I just need to check in with the office.'

Dean answered and gave her what sounded like an optimistic summary of new business queuing up. Annie smiled. It was clear from his upbeat tone that he and Casey were getting on fine. Pieternel came on and toned down his account of a suddenly booming business. 'It's Casey,' she said, deadpan. 'She overheats his chips.'

'Good news, dear?' Aunt Marian returned Annie's grin as she wandered out after the call.

Annie laughed. 'No, it was just something Pieternel said.' She decided to bury all ideas of replaying Dean's words to see what she could make of them, at least for this evening. This would be an old-fashioned family evening.

When the phone rang later, they were all sitting round the garden table, batting at insects, a few minutes into the game. Annie's father, who had leapt into the lead with 'analyse', went to answer it.

Aunt Marian watched him go, then scooped a tiny winged corpse out of her glass and said, 'At times like these I wish I still smoked.'

Annie had her turn, and Aunt Marian had hers. They turned to the house, to see if Annie's father was coming back out, and heard his footsteps down the hallway. The front door slammed and a moment later, a car engine revved. Just like old times, thought Annie. No sooner does some family activity get started than he's called away.

'I hope it's nothing serious.'

'It's an ill-wind, dear,' replied Aunt Marian, sweeping her father's letters back into the bag and putting a line through his score.

The letters' bag grew lighter, the shadows lengthened and Annie felt certain of victory now her father was out of the frame, until Aunt Marian instigated a new rule. 'If you insist on *that* word, dear, I shall deduct the points from your score.'

'There's nothing wrong with it. It's in the dictionary. It means—'

'Annie! I don't want to know. And it won't be in any dictionary of mine!'

'You look it up. I bet it is.'

'You won't catch me looking up words like that in anyone's dictionary.'

'Annie!'

Annie looked round. Her father stood in the doorway, beckoning her in. She hadn't heard him come back, but the still of the evening had given way to a breeze that rustled the bushes and promised a storm before the night was out.

She left her aunt to re-box the game, and rubbed at her arms as she went into the house. It was cooler than she realized. And darker. She had to squint at the Polaroid her father held out. 'I don't like to put this on you, Annie, but I've got to check. It seems bizarre ... There's no evidence to point to ... Anyway...' He held out the photo, and she peered at it, puzzled, not understanding what he was saying.

'That's Charlotte,' she said, and remembered her earlier conviction that she was about to see her again. 'Is it—?' She stopped abruptly, feeling the prickle on her skin as blood drained, and looked again, taking in the grey pallor of the face, the closed eyes, the unnatural lack of definition of the rest of the shot.

'The description didn't fit at all,' her father said. 'The Julia Lee who hired the car wasn't the same woman in it when it crashed. Far too short for one thing.'

Aunt Marian came in as Annie said, 'So it was Charlotte in that car.'

'I've been saying that all along. You never listen.' She turned to Annie's father. 'I have all the details for you; I knew you'd want them eventually. She's Mrs Charlotte Grainger, and I have her parents' address in my address book.'

He looked at her and for a moment Annie thought his mouth would open without words coming out, but he gave himself a small shake and blinked rapidly a couple of times. 'You have her *parents'* address, Marian?'

'Yes, I'll go and get it.'

As her aunt bustled off, Annie turned to her father and said, 'I hope to God she never meets Dean. She'd blow all his logic circuits.'

Aunt Marian came back in and handed across a piece of paper. 'Here you are. And don't lose it. I don't have a copy. Come with me, Annie. I've something for you too.'

Annie followed her aunt into the hallway. 'Here.' Her voice a whisper, her eyes alight with excitement, Aunt Marian pushed a scrap of paper into Annie's hand. 'That's Charlotte's flat. She'd only just moved in. Her parents are elderly; she hadn't even told them. I want you to go to her flat before the police find it. She might be an al Qaeda agent and if they find it first, we'll never get to know.'

'OK, leave it with me.' Annie shared a conspiratorial nod with her aunt, thinking that she'd pass this to her father at the first opportunity. Then she read the address and paused. Charlotte's flat, just off Tottenham Court Road, wasn't so far from Margot's offices. For no reason, she thought of that off-centre fax in the Buenos Aires file, then about the high pass; how easy it would be to push a car off the edge. It didn't sit comfortably with Charlotte's tale of a friend-of-a-friend; someone faking a death … She wondered about Lorraine. There must at least be a nub of truth in the story of her accident because her father knew about it.

She fingered the scrap of paper. Maybe she would pay a surreptitious visit to Charlotte's London flat before she passed the address on. What harm could it do?

CHAPTER ELEVEN

'I'll get Aunt Marian away down to Mrs Watson's as soon as she's had her breakfast,' Annie told her father the next morning. 'She seems quite happy now. And I'll come back up here for the night before I go back. How's your inquiry going?'

He gave her a look of exasperation. 'Customs still sniffing about, all looking to blame each other. They still don't know where the van disappeared to in the few hours between them losing it and when it was found burning. They came crawling back soon enough. Wanting chapter and verse on what's what. Only now it's mountain tracks they're interested in, not old smugglers' trails.'

'Oh well, I expect they'll track it down in the end. What about the leg in the loch?'

'Nothing new. They've done all manner of clever forensic stuff, DNA and what have you, but none of it's any use without something or someone to match it against. How about you? What will you do about the Watson woman's missing guest now you know it wasn't a moonlight?'

'I'll make a few discreet enquiries and see if Mrs Watson can put a claim on Charlotte's estate.'

'Would she want to?'

'Hell, yes. She's out of pocket. You know what she's like.'

After breakfast, Annie set off with Aunt Marian to take her back to Mrs Watson's. As they drove through the village, her aunt waved to Mr Caine. Annie shot her a curious glance. Charlotte's death seemed hardly to have made a dent yet she'd known Charlotte far better than Annie had. Annie had talked to Charlotte, laughed with her, just a short while ago. She couldn't mourn someone she'd known so superficially, but there was a nasty reminder of her own mortality in the loss of someone her own age. A reminder too that she was now older than her mother had been when she died.

Annie thought of the scrap of paper in her pocket: Charlotte's address.

The promised thunderstorm petered out and now it was going to be another scorcher. The air was oppressive, with a feel of building pressure. Hot-faced tourists wandered about looking strained, their children fractious. The exception was a group by the jetty. The shrieks and laughter floated into the car. Annie wondered at them racing about with such energy. Aunt Marian looked too, and laughed suddenly. 'Look at that little tyke with the football! He's pretending he's fished out a severed head.'

Annie didn't want to hear wild theories about Freddie Pearson's catch, so said at random, 'So who was the Julia Lee that you used to know?'

'I didn't,' her aunt replied. 'It was the woman on Charlotte's tape.'

'It was someone Charlotte knew?' Annie turned to her aunt in disbelief. Why couldn't she have said earlier? Her father needed to know this. 'But the woman on the tape was called Lorraine.'

'Yes, but Julia Lee was the one Lorraine said she'd seen. The old friend she hallucinated.'

Annie tried to remember the disjointed story Charlotte had told. 'Are you sure it was Julia Lee?'

'I think so, dear. You see, I never listened to the tapes. I'm going on what Charlotte told me.'

'And this Julia Lee was who exactly?'

'She was the drug addict Lorraine knew.'

'Who'd died years ago?'

'That's what Charlotte said.'

Annie mulled things over as they continued down the coast road. Dead women don't hire cars. At any rate, when they do, it should be looked into. She would listen to the tapes and unravel the story for herself before deciding if her father needed to know.

Aunt Marian dozed once they left civilization behind, leaving Annie with her thoughts. Why had Charlotte taken a hired car over that pass? Where was she going? Should she go to Charlotte's flat in London, or just leave well alone?

Annie parked outside the guesthouse and hoped the car wouldn't tarnish the image her aunt had painted of her successful city-businesswoman niece.

Mrs Watson hurried out as Annie carried her aunt's case up the steps. 'Ach, there you are.' Mrs Watson ignored Annie and rushed to Aunt Marian's side, her eyes bright with excitement. 'I've tea ready in the back kitchen. Come and tell me all about it. Have you found Charlotte?'

'Well, we have, but we haven't solved the mystery yet. Annie, would you take my things up to my room, dear?'

Aunt Marian was bursting with news, and Annie eased herself into the background as the two women gossiped their way down the corridor towards the back of the house.

Once upstairs in her aunt's room, and secure in the knowledge that no one would emerge from the back kitchen until long after the tea was cold in the pot, Annie went systematically through cupboards and drawers until she found two audio cassettes, labelled in an unfamiliar hand, lying next to the limp form of the old straw doll. She picked one up and clicked it into the radio/cassette.

It started mid-interview. Someone went over Lorraine's story with her. Lorraine herself did little more than say yes and no, as the interviewer outlined what had happened. Annie knew nothing about counselling, though she'd had an idea that it was the client who was supposed to do the talking. The story that unfolded was the same she'd heard from Charlotte.

'*You didn't go nearly as far as you first said, did you?*' The interviewer asked.

'*No,*' said Lorraine. '*I made that up.*'

It all sounded very pat, as though they followed a script. The issue of the woman who might or might not have been called Julia Lee remained a mystery, because the woman wasn't named, just referred to as a friend.

'*What made you think of this friend?*'

'*I'd taken some stuff. It made me think of her. I used to get stuff for her.*'

'*And why did you run? Was it because the memories of what had happened to her started to haunt you? You thought you were slipping down the same path she'd taken?*'

'*Yes, that's it. You can tell him it was just like that.*'

'*And that tale you made up, that was just to cover up how silly you'd been?*'

'*Yes, that's right. I felt foolish.*'

Lorraine's tone was mechanical. She wasn't at all fazed by the reprimand underlying the interviewer's words.

Annie found it hard to concentrate on the words as she tried to hear beyond the bad quality of the tape to listen to Lorraine's voice. This was no counselling session. Or was it? What did she know? Margot's acolytes would be sure to use unconventional techniques.

She checked the labels on the tapes. If the reference numbers made any sort of sense, she'd listened to the second one. She swapped it for the first. Maybe this would contain *that tale you made up*. Get as close to the source of the story as you can. One of the basic rules.

The interviewer on this tape sounded sympathetic, more as Annie would have expected. As for Lorraine, no hint of reading from a script this time. She was traumatized and sobbing.

'*Yes,*' the interviewer reassured Lorraine time and again, '*you take me through it, step by step. And any time you need to stop, we'll stop. Just try to relax. It's completely confidential.*'

Did Lorraine know it had been taped?

'*I set off up the path. The cinder track where people park at the bottom.*'

Annie knew just where Lorraine meant.

'*What made you decide to go up there?*'

The question, innocuous enough, startled Lorraine into convulsive sobs. It was a while before the interviewer coaxed her back to coherence, but then immediately knocked things back again by asking if she'd *'taken anything'.*

'No! No, I swear I hadn't. I know what you think, but...'

Once again the sympathetic voice nudged her back to the story. *'Nothing you say goes outside this room. Just take it step by step.'*

'Then I climbed up off the track. There's two stones, and a tree with a V.'

Two stones and a tree with a V. Hardly remarkable, but Annie identified the exact spot Lorraine had left the track. These hills were a part of her. She could climb that track with her eyes shut. She understood Charlotte's need to find a local interpreter, someone who could identify the *track where they park at the bottom* ... the *tree with a V.*

Lorraine described her scramble up through the undergrowth towards a higher track, when Annie heard voices in the hall. She clicked the machine off and took the tape out. Aunt Marian didn't need to listen to this woman sobbing her heart out.

'I fancy a walk up into the hills before I go back to Dad's,' she said, as her aunt entered the room. 'It's such a nice day. I haven't been walking round here in ages. D'you want to come?'

'No, Annie. It's too hot for me.'

'In that case I'll take Charlotte's tapes and have a listen.'

'Should you? I don't know that she'd want you to.'

'She's hardly going to object. You have an old Walkman, don't you?'

'Yes dear, your father gave me one when I went into hospital with my arm. I'll go and get it.'

Annie looked back down to the cinder track. The crowds thinned as she climbed higher. She followed Lorraine's path up through the undergrowth on to a higher, ill-defined track. Up ahead, she kept to the tree-line, her hand on the Walkman in her pocket.

'...and then I saw someone up ahead, coming towards me...'

Lorraine's voice slurred and Annie smothered a curse. It sounded as though the batteries were running down. She clicked the machine off. This would be the friend, the one Lorraine hallucinated. Julia Lee maybe. So far, no name was mentioned.

Aunt Marian's hospital stay had been almost a year ago. She might not have used the machine since. Annie kicked herself for not thinking to check the batteries, but with luck, she'd squeeze enough life out of them.

She stepped on to a wide swathe of green. The mass of trees stood to one side, in ranks ready for inspection, a thick cloak of greenery over the top. Under the cloak, a forest of bare poles, a crop of prison bars ready for harvest, grew from a spongy carpet of brittle twigs and leaf mould.

To the other side the land fell away, the slope gentle. Up higher, it steepened. Somewhere along here, Lorraine had taken off at a tangent to the tree-line and sprinted down the hill. Plenty of scope to fall wherever she did it. The later interview suggested she'd lied about how far up she'd travelled. Annie thought she might have chanced a sprint herself down the gentler slope, if she had a good reason to risk her neck. To try it further along where the land broke away would be suicide.

The green she walked on was a broad highway between the tree-line and the slope. It twisted away cutting down the forward view. This would be where Lorraine meant. She'd come round this curve and seen someone walking towards her. She clicked the tape back on.

'...a woman walking down the hill. It took me by surprise. I hadn't seen her in years. It seemed so strange to run into her in a place like that...' The voice began to slow and whine. Annie cursed, and stopped. The voice picked up. '...didn't say anything until...' but as she set off it slowed again. The machine couldn't cope with movement as she walked. She took it out of her pocket and sat at the edge of the trees. This was near enough to listen to the rest.

'"Julia Lee," I said, and she looked up, surprised.'

So Aunt Marian was right.

She listened to Lorraine describe a meeting between two friends who hadn't seen each other in years. The patchy sound from the tape made it hard to judge nuances of tone, but she felt a distrust of Lorraine's account. If the meeting had happened, it had not been by chance.

With the stop-start way she'd listened, she began to imagine she recognized Lorraine's voice. The scratchy sound quality made it sound old, as though it spoke from years ago.

She stopped the tape again and took herself through the version she'd had from Charlotte, that Lorraine eventually dragged herself to an isolated cottage and was taken to the local hospital where first Charlotte had found and talked to her and then her brother had come along and taken her away.

She wound the tape on with her finger to get beyond the latest bout of hysterics.

It came back on to the exaggerated breathing of Lorraine beginning to hyperventilate as she spoke. No holding back now. It all came out without prompting.

'We talked,' Lorraine's voice said. 'You know, just hello and how are you. Not for long. I could see she wanted to be off, and we said goodbye and that was it...'

Annie wasn't convinced. There'd been more to this meeting. Something in Lorraine's account was a lie. But not the fear. The fear was real.

Something made me turn ... I don't know what...

She'd gone. She wasn't there ... It wasn't possible ... There's nowhere to go. We'd only just walked on...

I don't know what made me turn. Maybe I heard something. I don't know.

I went back. I thought she must have fallen. I couldn't see her.

There was this stuff, branches and leaves and stuff, all tangled, at the edge of the trees. It was pushed apart.

I wouldn't have gone right into the trees. But she was there. Just there. Just two steps from the edge.

She was on her back, her arms flung out above her head. And red! This stain on the front of her jacket. Bright red ... on her back ... arms thrown out ... like she'd been pitched backwards into the

103

trees. *And this stain. I've never seen red so bright. It spread from the middle of her chest.*

I thought … she's been shot. Deer hunters. She's been shot from miles off. By mistake. It went through my mind in a second. I saw her lying there and I rushed back out of the trees. I was desperate to get help, to stop them shooting again. I froze. I didn't know what to do.

There was no one there. I was on my own. She was dying in the trees a stride away from me. I went back. I had to try to save her.

There was something different. It didn't register. I went forward, down to feel for a pulse at her neck. That awful red. Like I saw it again the first time. That spreading stain.

And a knife.

A knife in her chest. Right at the heart of that blood.

It hadn't registered, but as I bent over her, I knew I'd seen it. There'd been a knife in her chest. I saw my hand reach towards her neck. I saw the blood pulsing out of her. But the knife was gone!

I'd turned my back for a second … The knife was gone. Whoever'd done it was right there with me.

I don't know if I saw anyone. I just threw myself forward to the ground. I twisted over her, and I grabbed at the branches and the leaves. The dust was in my eyes, I couldn't see. I ripped the creepers out of the way, to get back into the open. I don't even know if I trod on her. And I ran. Straight. Right off the edge. There was no one to help. No one to shout for. If I could just keep my feet I could get away.

And I ran. I just ran and ran. It was so hard. I couldn't stop. I ran.

CHAPTER TWELVE

Lorraine's rising hysteria grated against the slowing tape. The sun was hot but Annie shivered as she clicked it off. She'd heard enough. But what had she heard? Fantasy, hallucination? Or a witness to murder? But her father knew about Lorraine. There couldn't have been a murder. She'd have heard about it. A body at the edge of the forest couldn't lie undiscovered for long.

Annie got up and brushed herself down. If anything had happened recently, there'd be traces. She remembered Charlotte's words. *There was something odd.* But Charlotte hadn't found the spot. Not much further on round this outcropping of trees and then she would be able to see ... But damn, there were people up ahead. She expected to have the hill to herself in the heat of the day, and didn't want to draw attention by poking about at the trees' edge. If there were anything there, the evidence mustn't be disturbed.

She decided to wait until they carried on up or came down past her, but they didn't seem to be going anywhere. Squinting against the glare, she saw the figures through a heat haze, one set swaying in a huddled group, others moving without apparent purpose, back and forth, round and round. Was it some sort of orienteering exercise she'd walked into?

It was too hot to wait about for hours, but Lorraine's story had her guts churning. She'd heard the original telling of it, and Lorraine's lying stood out like a beacon, but with an uncomfortable nugget of reality. Only one thing was sure: Lorraine had been scared half to death.

And what of Charlotte and the so-called friend-of-a-friend? Someone's sister planned to fake her own death? Julia Lee? But what use a never-reported fake murder?

Annie paced up and down, her thoughts a kaleidoscope of theories that tried to mesh into a coherent premise. Every theory had a jagged edge, a shard that didn't fit and ruined the rest. Maybe it was all a series of unrelated coincidences. She cast an occasional glance up to the stand of trees that hid the group of orienteers, but took care to keep out of sight. The heat haze lay over everything, a phantom shimmer that lent pseudo clarity to the landscape, but lay like a mirage where her thoughts should be. A headache threatened. Too much wine last night. Or maybe, not enough. She backed off under the trees where it was cooler.

How much would Margot know? She had to contact her sometime about Aunt Marian having been in touch, why not now? She retreated further into the shade of the forest, and sat against a scratchy tree trunk. The musty aroma of the forest floor rose, the dust making her cough. Her phone came to life with a beep, and after a second or two connected to a network. She hadn't been sure of a connection up here.

Margot's PA, Janice, answered with a smooth professionalism that brought to mind plush carpets and luxury offices bustling with people and the trappings of success. After a burst of classical music she couldn't identify, Margot's voice was in her ear. 'Annie! What a surprise. I hope you haven't rung to harangue me about your dear old aunt.' Annie's hackles rose at the mockery in Margot's tone.

'Of course not. It's Charlotte I'm ringing about. Charlotte Grainger.'

'Yes, the one your aunt rang about. Look Annie, I can't do anything about the sodding guesthouse. I'm not responsible for people on holiday. She was only a temp anyway.'

'It's not that. She won't be back. She's dead. She died in a car crash.'

'Oh, I'm sorry.' Margot sounded indifferent. 'Drop in sometime if you want to, Annie. If you need more on your mysterious Mrs Grainger. I'll look out her personnel file.'

After the call, Annie stood up and stretched her cramped limbs. What had Charlotte been up to? What had she said about Lorraine? *She hallucinated an old friend who died years ago.* Had Julia Lee died years ago? What of the so-called friend-of-a-friend; the sister who wanted to fake a death? And what went wrong that led to Charlotte's death, thrown from a car that exploded in flames as it hit the bottom of the glen? Her mind jumped back to a rain-lashed pass across the mountain; a sudden explosion of headlights; the screech of metal on the crash barrier.

Out on the green of the track, Annie hesitated. Time to return to Aunt Marian's to let Mrs Watson know her options for getting her money back. Then she must hotfoot it back up to her father's to tell him about Lorraine and about her own experience on the high pass.

She looked again at the tapes before slipping them back in her pocket, and fought an urge to hurl them deep into the forest. The idea of listening to Lorraine's voice again repelled her. She didn't want her father to hear it either.

As she turned towards the slope, a bright flash caught her eye and made her pull back. A momentary burst of light and scurry of movement from down on the lower track. She stared hard but there was nothing there now. Nothing she could make out from here anyway.

Lorraine's voice played in her mind. *Telescopic sights ... Shot from miles off...*

The path to Mrs Watson's crossed that track. Nothing in a random flash of light to force a change of plan, except the faint stirring of unease it spawned inside her. The instinct she'd learnt not to ignore. And there were a million ways out for those who knew these hills.

She turned and slipped back under the trees, wading her way through the debris of the forest floor. This was a longer route across forbidden territory from her childhood, the Doll Makers' patch.

The air was heavy. The scorching sun, visible only in bright shafts that pierced the canopy over the tracks and small clearings, crept into the forest as a heavy malaise with no warmth. In only a light T-shirt, Annie became uncomfortably cool as the woods became darker the further she descended.

She knew when she crossed the invisible boundary from forestry land to Torran Hill, the domain of what had once been a bustling, if eccentric community. The layered remains beneath her feet were deeper, spongier, the forest older, and shabby like a mansion now in the custody of people too old to care for it. The smell that rose up from her incursions into the thick carpet was at the edge of rancid. As children, they'd stepped over these boundaries for the thrill of facing hidden menace. Even now, her skin prickled, a ghost of the delicious taste of terror from years ago.

Threading her way through the trees, she had to steady herself on the roots and branches as she slithered down the steeper stretches. Her shoes felt gritty from the leaf mould and dust. Sweat dried on her clothes giving the gentle breeze a frozen edge.

The landmark bulk of a stone wall defined itself below her as she approached the road. This was the building-with-eyes, the source of the gnarled hand of Margot-generated legend that would reach out from the ancient stones and grab outsiders to drag them in. What surprised Annie was the shiver that surged through her as though to strip away rational thought and show the old legends to be true after all. She even felt a flutter of apprehension about what Aunt Marian would say if she found out.

She skirted the building, keeping to the slope instead of the easier track just below. The facing wall showed the same blank face as she remembered, with its tiny eyes too near the roof to serve any useful purpose as windows. And yet she felt them follow her through the trees, like the eyes of a portrait. For now, we're only watching, they seemed to say, but one day...

It was hard to reconcile the empty face of the edifice with the memory of a packed hall, people chanting, a choir singing. Was it faulty memory again? There was no image other than the blank wall to go with the remembered pageantry, but the feel of the pulsing noise came back to her as she scuttled past.

She slithered down the last stretch to the road proper and let out a sigh of relief. Childhood caught-on-their-land dread wasn't dented even now the right to roam was enshrined in statute. The panic ebbed only once her feet were on a public highway.

She left the building-with-eyes behind and strode down the narrow road, no thoughts other than to get to the main road and make her way back. But she paused again at a point where the road branched. One route was the straight one, down towards her aunt's. The other twisted back up the hill into the trees and led to the Doll Makers' house. She caught herself twisting her eyes sideways to sneak a glance. Then stopped to take a deep breath before she turned and faced the house. She wasn't a kid any more, and this wasn't private land.

It was as she remembered, a square plain-Jane of a house that sat some fifty yards up the track to one side. It should have nestled cosily under the trees, but didn't. Somehow the house and surrounding forest had weathered and aged on different scales and looked out of place side by side. An elderly couple with nothing in common, but too old to part company. The front door was open and Annie could see the small figure of Beth sitting at a table, a purple cloud round her neck, back to the door as she bent over some task.

Annie hesitated. Aunt Marian would want her to take the opportunity to talk to the girl who might be more forthcoming on her own territory.

She jogged up to the house, not realizing the breeze was strong enough to cover the sound of her footsteps until Beth, either too engrossed in her work, or made slightly deaf by the voluminous scarf at her neck, spun in shock to face her.

Annie saw a doll on the table, half-dismembered or half-made. The detritus of doll-making was spread out on the wooden surface amongst bits of straw and scraps of material. After her first shocked intake of breath, Beth whipped the doll out of sight behind her back, then crammed it into a basket, eyes wide with fear as she stared at Annie.

It was her nightmare! Just for a fraction of a second it was her mother. The dream. Trapped in a maze; the doll just out of reach. The face that changed from gracious to furious as it turned to look at her. She battled an irrational urge to fly at Beth, screaming, 'It's my doll! It's mine!'

She gripped her fists tight and felt the nails dig in. Her heart pounded. She bit down on the anger that tried to explode from her, but knew some bit of it leaked out as Beth, terrified, cowered back against the table.

'I ... I'm sorry...' She tried to keep her voice low, unthreatening, and heard it come out too high, breathless and dripping with anxiety. Another deep breath to steady the beat of her heart. 'I'm sorry, Beth. I really didn't mean to frighten you.'

'I shoulda kept the door shut,' Beth said, leaving Annie unsure if she meant a shut door would have prevented her being startled, or prevented Annie calling in at all. 'It's hot, see.'

Annie nodded, though it didn't seem very hot in the house, not with the trees towering around keeping it in constant shade. She glanced at a door the other side of the big room and wondered if Beth were alone.

'Uh ... my aunt gave me one of your dolls.' She hoped for pleasure or at least surprise, but Beth said nothing, as though the revelation wasn't worthy of comment. 'My mother bought it just before she died. I only just heard about it. No one knows why.'

'I don't know why,' Beth said, as though Annie had asked. 'I was minus seven years old when your mother went.'

Annie did a rapid calculation. Minus seven. If true, that made Beth thirteen, which seemed about right, but why would a 13-year-old have her mother's age off pat like that, for God's sake?

Annie couldn't read the expression in Beth's eyes, and couldn't frame the next question. What do you know about my mother? She knew she couldn't ask in any way that wouldn't sound hostile, because she didn't want to hear that Beth, minus seven, knew things she didn't know or couldn't remember herself.

They faced each other in silence, then Annie turned her attention to the room they were in and looked round. It felt cavernous, but was no bigger than the sitting-room at her father's. The similarities went no further than the dimensions. Where her father's room was bright, and crowded with the knick-knacks Mrs Latimer laboured over, this one was bare and faded as if the sun passed through a long time ago, leached out the colour and never came back. Rationally, Annie knew it was because the trees were too close and tall to let the light in, but she felt she'd stepped into another world.

The girl looked small and vulnerable in this empty cavern. Annie reached into her pocket for her wallet, and plucked out a business card. 'Here.' She held it out. Beth looked, but didn't reach for it, so Annie stepped closer and put it on the table. 'Call me if you ever need to. Any time.' She wasn't even confident Beth could use a phone.

Beth's gaze was suddenly riveted to something behind Annie's shoulder. She gasped and sprang forward, pushing Annie to one side. 'Someone comin'' she hissed. 'Go out the back.'

Annie needed no persuasion. Childhood fear of the Doll Makers had kept her senses tingling the whole time she stood there. As Beth threw herself at the front door and pulled it shut, Annie went the way Beth had pushed her, out through the other door. She found herself in the open air at the side of the house. A steep path wound down to the lower road, cutting off the corner she'd have had to go round the front way. A nifty shortcut they'd never discovered as young trespassers.

Before sliding down to the road and heading back, Annie crept to the edge of the house, used a thick creeper for cover and peered round. She was curious to see another of the elusive Doll Makers.

But it wasn't, and Annie was so surprised, she almost stepped out into view. It was the man Aunt Marian had pointed out. *Charlotte's young man.* He wandered up the road towards the house, looking around, up into the forest, as though not sure he was in the right place. Clearly, he too intended paying the Doll Makers a visit. Maybe visitors weren't such a rarity, but Annie had an idea that two in one day wasn't the norm.

He didn't look threatening and he probably knew things about Charlotte, but she wouldn't think of approaching him in such an isolated spot with only Beth for a witness. A pair of binoculars swung from a strap round his neck. Telescopic sights weren't the only things with reflective lenses. He looked hot and out of breath. It was possible he'd made it here by road while she stumbled her way down the hill. With his easy, unthreatening look, he'd have no problem hitching a ride.

She watched until he was almost at the front door, then turned and eased herself over the edge on to the twisty path that would take her away from Torran Hill and back to civilization.

CHAPTER THIRTEEN

A few moments back in her aunt's company were enough to show Annie a fully reinvigorated Aunt Marian, thriving on the stories she'd accumulated, stoking Mrs Watson with mix-and-match theories about Charlotte, the break-in and the world's security services.

Mrs Watson showed more finer feeling than Annie had credited her with and wrote off Charlotte's debt rather than pursuing her beneficiaries should there be any. Even so, a sense of unfinished business irritated Annie like a low-level itch. Her aunt and Mrs Watson would propound their theories to all and sundry. What if there was something genuinely nasty below the surface?

'Be careful what you say, and who you talk to about Charlotte,' she cautioned before she left. 'We don't know what she was mixed up in.'

'Don't worry, dear.' Aunt Marian whispered. 'I won't breathe a word about the tapes to anyone.'

Not without guilt, she allowed her aunt to write a cheque for the job, and watched as she settled back into Mrs Watson's with relief. To move her away permanently would be like taking a sick patient from a life-preserving drip. It racked up the urgency to get back to London to play her part in pulling the company round.

She called back to base before she left the guesthouse. 'I can come straight back now, Pieternel. Aunt Marian's OK.'

'No, Annie. Stay on like we planned. Trust me.'

It left Annie dissatisfied and trapped. Whatever Pieternel had cooked up, she didn't want to jeopardize it. Politics were Pieternel's game, not hers.

When she arrived back to her father's, he was out, and she wandered about the house with a feeling of being cut off from everything. No phone rang, no email beeped. The house sat in silence, no voices, no hum of equipment. She'd forgotten how to operate in a tranquil environment with no deadline clamouring. She needed to talk to someone. The problem was who, in the real world at this time of day, would have time for a call from someone with nothing to say. Of course, there was only one person she wanted to talk to who would also want to talk to her, who wouldn't struggle to hide the irritation when she said she'd just phoned for a chat. There was both comfort and disquiet in the realization of how at ease with each other she and Mike had become.

Her phone came to life with a battery-low warning beep, reminding her she hadn't charged it since the call to Margot. If her day were as packed as it usually was, she'd have had her phone on charge in the car. Somehow, because she had nothing to do, it had slipped her mind.

She made her way to the hall, but that phone thwarted her too. It hadn't been switched through. She'd have to use the one in the office; she went for the key.

The scene that met her eye made her stop and stare in amazement. Papers out on the desk, the chair pushed back. An office in use. A view of it she'd never seen. Her father must have been called out in a hurry to leave things like this. She approached the desk warily, like a trespasser. Could she justify using his office phone for such a non-urgent reason as wanting a chat with Mike? She told herself she would be scrupulous about looking away, about not touching anything she shouldn't.

Of course, it wasn't possible. If she looked away while she reached for the phone, she might accidentally touch the papers, disturb them. She must look, but that didn't mean she had to read what she saw. Even as the thought was in her mind, her eye caught the words. Habit stepped in; years of snatching at any opportunity to speed-read and retain from papers at odd angles, upside down, almost too far for the eye to focus. This was too easy. The words were in her head before her hand reached the handset. She pulled back, her original goal forgotten. These papers spoke of the leg in the loch case, and in one glance, she'd seen and absorbed a single fascinating fact. Her father's hypothesis had been confirmed. The leg – legs, maybe – had been thrown into the water not far from Mrs Watson's. They even had tide times and a precise date and a time 'to within half an hour'. That must be the reported dumping of trash.

Without touching anything, she looked at the partial story the documents revealed as she plucked the phone from its rest, her fingers tapping in the number before the handset was to her ear. 'Mike? Can you talk?'

'Hi Annie. Are you back?'

'Nah, tomorrow, but listen, Mike, I've found out some stuff about that body in the loch.'

'I thought it was just a leg.'

She grinned. Good old Mike. No time-wasting about why she'd rung, or where she'd found this stuff, or why it should be of the least interest to him. She told him about the times and the tides and how it had gone in near her aunt's.

'Both legs, did you say? How do they know? Have they found the other?'

'I don't know...' She looked at the papers on the desk, but couldn't bring herself to rummage through them. Her father would know they'd been disturbed. 'There may have been a witness when it was thrown in. Someone who thought they'd seen trash being dumped. Or...'

'Or what? What's up?'

'Just a sec. Let me think. It's the date.' The date Mrs Watson's nephew had seen Charlotte's guy from his bedroom window at school. What had Aunt Marian said?

He saw him before that too. A week before they got that body out of the water.

And the boy had fixed the date by a birthday, so it would be accurate. She looked again at the date on the page and did the calculation. Yes, exactly a week. So when the legs were dumped, he was on the other side of the mountain in sight of the dormitory windows at the school. When she explained to Mike, he said, 'So this guy's in the clear then. Was he a prime suspect?'

Annie laughed. 'No, he isn't in the frame at all. It's just that if I get the chance to talk to him, I'd like to know I'm not interrogating a murderer.'

'Why would you want to talk to him?'

'He knew Charlotte.'

And also, she would like to know why he'd been following her.

CHAPTER FOURTEEN

Recharged by her call to Mike, Annie savoured the knowledge that her father's deduction had been spot on. She wished she'd been a fly on the wall when he'd been vindicated in front of his CID colleagues.

Her lethargy dissipated. Aunt Marian was back to normal. Pieternel was working her magic. Her personal finances were still a concern, but everything would be OK. An unidentified leg and a drugs bust gone wrong weren't her worries. Her father was on the case. A dull ache labelled Charlotte still nagged at her. A life snuffed out. A person she could have grown to like, but also a person with her own agenda, who'd died in a dead woman's identity.

Her father already knew about Lorraine and her fall on the moors. Did he need Margot's tapes too? Annie pulled them out of her bag and looked with distaste, shrinking away from the thought of having Lorraine's voice in her ear again. Why should her father have to deal with it? He had enough on his plate.

Fed up with aimless wandering around an empty house, she went out and strolled down to the post office where she plucked a couple of local views from the postcard rack and asked for a book of first class stamps.

'You sending some cards to your friends down south, Annie?'

'That's right.'

'You write them now and leave them with me. I'll see they get on their way.' He handed her a pen.

She addressed one to Dean and one to Mike and wrote a few banalities on each. Weather good. Bit rainy. Very hot. See you soon. With their stamps on, she handed them to Mr Caine and while he busied himself reading them, looked at the row of dolls that hung limply from the rail inside the clutter of the window. They stared with forlorn tattiness, coated in dust, an absurd pretence at being saleable objects. It was only recently Beth had brought a fresh supply. Why couldn't he at least put new ones in the window? The dolls depressed her. Sometimes, when they appeared in her dreams, she knew that if she could just focus through the sad forms, she'd see her mother's face.

'You're back with your father then?' Mr Caine asked. 'Not down at your aunt's.'

'That's right. I'm going back down south tomorrow.'

'Did you want anything else?'

I'd like to know what makes you tick ... why you keep those stupid dolls... 'No, it was just the postcards and the stamps.' On impulse, she added. 'I saw that young girl the other day, the one who delivers the dolls.'

'What of it?'

'It's a long way for her to walk across the moor. I hope she doesn't have to do it in winter.'

'Long way from where?'

'Uh ... where she lives.'

'I'm sure no one makes anyone do anything they don't want.'

Clearly, his Doll Maker past was a sensitive area and her father wouldn't approve of her pushing him on it. She smiled a goodbye and turned to go.

The beginnings of a shower hung in the breeze. She let it caress her skin and smiled to see a family hurrying up from the shore. Father, mother, and two young children. The adults hustled the little ones towards the car park, rushing them to escape the rain.

Is this your first day, she wanted to ask, only this isn't real rain, the sort you've heard Scotland's famous for? That comes down in cascades, and washes the landscape to a brightness you won't see down south.

She sauntered on past them, to show how good it felt to be out in the gentle breeze and the mist that was scarcely rain. Father and mother bundled their offspring into the car, not giving Annie a glance. The small boy's gaze caught hers and he stared with curious eyes.

Then she saw a lanky form by the water's edge and the family was forgotten. The man her aunt had pointed out as Charlotte's young man, the man who'd followed her, stood by the rail staring out over the loch.

She began to move towards him, her gaze fastened on his face, half-turned from her. His hair was light brown and wavy. As she watched, his hand came up to push it back off his face. She saw the silver sheen of the mist where fine water droplets clung. He was older than she'd judged. Forty maybe, but something in his face made it hard to guess his age with any confidence. His hair looked soft, and as fine as the mist that coated it and now made him hunch into his jacket, as he looked up at the sky briefly.

It was clear he wouldn't rush to get undercover, yet his jacket was insubstantial and already showed signs of the damp creeping through.

She leant on the rail a couple of yards from him, knowing he was aware of her.

'Why have you been following me? What do you want?'

He gave her a glance, neither unfriendly nor surprised, and turned his back to the water. Leaning elbows on the rail, looking first up into the mountains, then turning his warm brown eyes on her, he asked, 'D'you know what happened to her?'

She hadn't expected this. Hadn't he heard about the crash, or was he asking why it had happened? Why did he think she would know?

'Um ... do you mean Charlotte?'

'Charlie, yeah. Where'd she go?'

The rather timid creature Annie thought she'd known took on yet another dimension, one that fitted the easy nickname, Charlie.

Seeing her hesitate, he spread his hands, gave her that half-smile again. 'I just want to know. She took my car.'

Her stomach knotted. He didn't know. She didn't want to be the one to tell him, but what could she say apart from the truth?

'She ... There was an accident. It was in the papers. The high pass.'

'I don't bother with papers. How is she?'

'I'm sorry, I'm afraid—'

'She copped it, did she?'

'I'm afraid so. Yes.' She looked up into his eyes, saw them cloud at her words. Then he put the smile on again, as though to reassure her. She smiled back. There was something insubstantial about him, not just his appearance, but his manner. It gave her an odd feeling. There was no solidity to him. If anyone were to lean on him the way she leant on Mike, there'd be nothing there. She wondered what Charlotte meant to him. He'd absorbed the news of her death as though accustomed to playing a difficult hand.

'Poor cow. How did it happen?'

'I don't know. Sorry.'

'Don't suppose you know what happened to the car?'

'I know it caught fire. I don't think there was anything of it left.'

'What about her?'

'She was thrown out. She didn't burn, but it's a hell of a drop. She didn't stand a chance.'

He leant back against the rail and tipped his head back, squinting his eyes as the rain washed across him. 'That's that, then.'

'What's what?'

'I thought she'd taken off with my car. It's been a hassle trying to find her.'

'How do you mean, your car? It was a hire car.'

'Yeah, I know. I've been following you,' he returned to her original question, 'because I wanted to know what happened to her. She just upped and vanished. I thought about knocking on that house where she stayed but the one time I went there, the old biddy looked set to run me off. So I came looking for you, but you kept getting out of reach, or you had an old biddy of your own in tow.'

Annie laughed, but didn't let on that her aunt had recognized him. 'Who hired the car? They know it wasn't Charlotte.'

He looked down and made a pretence of batting water off his jacket front, his expression sheepish. 'It was me.'

'Oh, come on...' Annie was annoyed at him trying to lie to her.

'Look...' He held his hands wide. 'She didn't want to get it in her own name and I've no papers that a place like that'd accept. She had this other woman's driving licence. I said she should use it, but she went on at me until I did, said it'd work, no trouble. I never thought it would, but she was right. They didn't look twice. Frock and a hat. Can't you see it?' He threw back his head and posed.

Yes, she could see it. She believed him. The tall, lanky Julia Lee described by the hire firm was none other than this guy in drag.

'Where did she get the driving licence? Was it someone she knew?'

'Search me. Look, I don't suppose...?'

When he stalled on the words, she prompted, 'You don't suppose what?'

'Don't suppose you could give me a lift back across to town? It's a pisser without a car, relying on your thumb.' He held out the digit and tipped it at the empty road.

She hesitated, but after all, why not? 'Wait here. I'll bring the car down.'

He gave her another flash of the brown eyes. 'Thanks, Annie. Charlie said you were a good 'un.'

It seemed inevitable that everyone round here should know her name. She looked the question at him. 'Jak,' he said, holding out his hand for her to shake. 'Jak without a c.'

Annie jogged back up to her father's, knowing how strongly he'd disapprove of her offering lifts to strangers.

Except for a moment's tension at the top of the pass, he was a relaxed passenger at her side as they drove away from the village and across the mountain. Deliberately, Annie kept the conversation light. She'd like to know more about his relationship with Charlotte, but didn't want to question him when she couldn't concentrate on the body language of his answers.

He guided her to a run-down area of town.

'Come in for coffee or something, Annie, please. You can't come all this way and go straight back again. You'll have me feeling bad about myself, and I don't do that sort of stuff.'

Again, why not? She might learn more about Charlotte, things her father needed to know.

He spread his hands in a gesture of excuse as he ushered her into the dank hallway and had to stand back to allow a morose and scruffy figure to shuffle past. Annie noted Jak's stare follow him out, his expression fixed, and felt some empathy. She'd had to forge allegiance on occasion with people she'd rather disown.

'I'm dossing with Dish while I'm here. It's not up to much, but he offered and I didn't think they'd be keen to have me where Charlie was staying.'

She laughed. It wasn't that he didn't look respectable enough for Mrs Watson's. It was the couldn't-care-less attitude that would have had the No Vacancies sign going up. 'So you're based in London? Same as Charlotte was?'

'Yeah, I had some work down there a while ago.'

'What work d'you do?'

'Whatever's going.'

'So how do you know Charlotte ... Charlie?'

'She came to me. Said she wanted to know something from me.'

'Why did she come to you?'

'She found out I knew people around here. She wanted to know about something.'

'What was that?'

'I dunno. She never got round to spitting it out.'

'I heard her talking to you on the phone, Jak. You sent her a text. I got the impression she wasn't expecting to hear from you.'

He looked up, surprised. 'That what she told you? She called me up a few days before, said she was up here, asked me to come. Said she had a job for me that she could pay for. I didn't say yes or no. Didn't know if I would. Then I texted her when I got here.'

It was plausible. Charlotte hadn't said anything about Jak. Annie had surmised all she knew from the overheard call. She looked again at the man in front of her. There was no feel of a hidden agenda as there'd been with Charlotte.

He smiled at her. 'You wanna drink while you're here?'

'Coffee?'

'I don't think Dish runs to coffee. He's got some nice booze in though. How about this?'

Jak slid a crate from behind a heap of boxes and pulled out a bottle Annie could see was a very respectable single malt. Her eyes widened in amazement.

'What's up?'

'Uh ... nothing ... well ... It's just that a crate of malt was reported taken from the guesthouse where Charlotte stayed.'

He let out a sigh. 'Look, I didn't ask where it came from. I think he bought it off a guy in a pub. Wasn't me, by the way. I don't do petty theft.'

'No, I didn't think it was.' She pointed to the bottle. 'Just a small one. I have to drive back.'

'I'll get something to put it in.'

She looked around the room. Boxes, heaped in towers against the walls, seeped their contents where the weight from above bulged the sides and split the corners. They seemed filled with ragged material and more boxes. The air was musty, stale. An unmade bed took much of what floor space remained and the only places to sit were a wooden chair, propped three-legged against the box mountain and a canvas foldaway seat with a rusty frame. She chose the canvas.

He returned with two chipped cups. 'Best I could do.'

He poured the amber liquid, and passed hers across. 'Absent friends.'

She raised hers to him, knowing she shouldn't do this. It was Mrs Watson's single malt, delivered via a guy in a pub, or maybe direct from the scruffy figure who'd shambled out as they arrived. There ought to be indignation on Mrs Watson's behalf but all Annie could muster was amazement that her aunt's landlady kept such quality malt.

'What does he do, Dish?'

'Nothing much. He's a lush. Never moves much beyond these two rooms. This is his world. Pretty crappy, ain't it?'

She said nothing. She'd had a glimpse of a glazed pair of eyes, near-death, looking out on a different universe. She remembered the deadly spiral she'd been caught up in at school, not so far from here – *there but for the grace of God* – and thought Dish's world felt fine to him as long as he had the money to keep it at arm's length. It was inconceivable that Dish himself had shambled his way over the mountain and raided Mrs Watson's.

'So what was Charlotte about? Why did she have someone else's papers?'

'How did you get to hear about it anyway? Oh right, your father.' He answered his own question. 'I suppose you get to know all the inside stuff.'

'Not at all. He's a stickler, lets nothing slip. What was this Julia person to Charlotte?'

'She didn't say.'

'Mrs Watson told us someone had called round for Charlotte on the Saturday evening. She had a face like she'd sucked on a lemon. I suppose it was you. When did Charlotte call you up?'

'The day before. Midday.'

So Charlotte had called Jak before she'd left the message for Margot. 'She told me she wasn't expecting anyone.'

He shrugged. 'I can't help what she said.'

'It was you who followed me up the hill, wasn't it? I saw you watching me through binoculars.'

'I only wanted to talk out of sight of the old biddies. What made you go all the way up there?'

'I always do. I like the hills.'

'Too bloody high for me in all that heat. I was waiting for you to come back down, only then you cut back.'

'I cut back because I saw you. I didn't know who you were. What made you go round to the Doll Makers?'

'The who? Oh, that creepy house in the wood. I wanted to catch you on the way down. You were there, weren't you? Watching me.' He laughed. 'I had a feeling you were.'

'But how did you know I'd come that way?'

'I can read a map. What other way would you come from that direction?'

Fair point. 'What did they say at the house?'

'Just some dozy kid. She hadn't seen anything. So what's your father said about this body they fished out of the water?'

'It was a leg.'

'Half a leg, I heard. Charlie wanted to know all about it.'

'Did she?' Annie didn't remember Charlotte showing any special interest.

'So what's the gen? I'd like to know, if it was important to Charlie.'

'But why? What on earth did it have to do with her?'

'I dunno. She was like that. All sorts of stuff she used to get wound up about. But I'd like to find out. It'd be like doing something for her, you know, now she's gone.'

Charlotte's death had shaken him more than he'd admit. She saw him as in alien territory trying to make amends. 'Yeah, I … I know what you mean, but I can't help you. My father doesn't talk to me about the cases he's working on.' Annie had no difficulty meeting his gaze as she spoke the lie. She would never betray her father's trust.

'Come on. He must do.'

'Nope. Never. He never has.'

She drained the cup, then stood up and wandered across towards the window. There was a curtain rail, but no curtains, just a stained sheet tacked across the gap. She lifted a corner and peered through filthy glass to the street outside. At once, anger mushroomed. 'The bastard's in my car!'

Jak was on his feet and out of the door before she could fight her way across the packed space. When she reached them, Jak had hauled Dish from the car and swung him round against the wall.

'Nah ... nothin' ... I got nothin' ... weren't nothin' there...'

'Leave him be, Jak,' Annie ordered, not wanting to be the cause of a deadbeat getting mashed to a pulp on the pavement, and feeling some alarm at the sudden rush of anger in Jak. 'He's right. There's nothing in there.' As she spoke she leant into the car, flicking open the glove-box, glancing in the door pockets. No, she kept nothing in the car that a lush like Dish could turn to ready cash.

Jak glared into Dish's face from an inch distant, gave him a final shake and pushed him away. 'Here...' He tossed Annie's keys over to her, and Annie realized Dish must have dipped her when he pushed past in the corridor. It said a lot about him that he'd retained such a light touch despite the state he was in: an expertise built in from childhood, and now instinctive. Annie looked round, and felt a little awkward. 'Thanks for the drink, Jak. I ought to get going.'

She saw Jak struggle to get his anger under control. 'You sure he's got nothing? Any secret compartments? He'll have ferreted them all out.'

'It's OK, really. There's nothing at all. I never keep anything in the car.'

He closed his eyes and took in a couple of deep breaths. 'Let me come back with you, Annie. If I stay another night in this dump I'll pan the little bastard.'

'Where will you stay?' she asked in some panic, in case he thought she could find him a bed.

'I'll find somewhere. Might head off up the coast. The weather's not so bad that a night in the open'll kill me.'

She didn't mind driving him back and felt only mild irritation that his motive was clearly less to do with distancing himself from Dish than in looking for further opportunities to interrogate her about anything her father might have found.

She didn't ask Jak where he wanted to be, but just pulled up on a deserted stretch of road close to her father's. She was surprised at a pang of regret that she was about to leave Jak to drift on through life, never sticking at anything, maybe meeting more

Charlottes along the way until age faded the charm that eased his path. 'Hope you find somewhere,' she said, wanting him to take the hint it was time to part company.

He made no move to get out of the car. 'In case I don't, a coffee would be nice.'

She almost laughed at his transparency. He was asking her to take him to her father's. Did he think she'd allow him to rifle through things in the office? No reason not to give him coffee though. She was twenty-eight years old and could bring friends home. He knew Charlotte. She knew Charlotte. More to the point, Mrs Latimer wouldn't be there and her father was unlikely to be back for ages. It was only coffee. 'Yeah, OK then.'

She felt relief that her father's car wasn't outside as they pulled up. He followed her into the house.

'Is this where he works?' Jak rattled the handle of her father's office as he walked past. 'He must have said something about that body.'

'Jak!' Annie spun round on him. No one threatened the sanctum. 'Coffee's all you're getting.'

'OK, OK.' He raised his hands in mock surrender.

She ushered him to the kitchen while she made coffee. 'Tell me some more about Charlotte.'

'What's to tell?'

'Whatever ... How did you get to know her originally?'

'Can't remember really.'

'She mentioned a friend. Someone who might have been in trouble. Did you know anything about it?'

'I don't think Charlie wanted your father knowing she was asking questions about that leg.'

Annie paused by the open fridge door. She didn't like the sound of that. It implied things like her father having to be involved in Charlotte's hidden agenda when he had enough on his plate, and somehow it felt like her doing, because she'd got to know Charlotte.

'You're not saying she had anything to do with it?' The severed legs had been thrown in just down the way from Mrs Watson's, but Charlotte hadn't been there then. She'd still have been in London working for Margot. At least, that's what she'd said.

Annie regretted bringing him here long before she finished her coffee. She'd learnt nothing of any real use about Charlotte. When they'd both drained their cups, she walked with him out of the front door. They stood awkwardly on the pavement for a moment.

'Annie, could you do something for me? Uh ... just a small favour. I wouldn't ask but...'

What now? Annie framed a refusal as she tipped her head in invitation to him to elaborate.

'You know the guy in the shop down there? He's kinda taken against me. Won't serve me. And I'm out of fags.'

He wanted a few minutes on his own here, knowing the house was empty, knowing she'd pulled the front door to without locking it. What sort of a fool did he think her?

'No, sorry.'

'Oh, right. You got a thing about smokes then?'

Suddenly she couldn't read him anymore. Was he on the level? Was she just being paranoid because of everything that had happened lately? An anger that she knew to be irrational rose up inside her. She had to clench her fists not to fly at him with the intention of doing real damage. It was like facing Beth across that room again. These were her own memories, her own worries, clouding her judgement.

'See you, Jak.' She turned on her heel and marched back to the house.

'Yeah, Annie. See you.'

She heard his footsteps retreat down the road and when she reached the door and looked back, he was gone, but her father's car was just pulling up so she had to paint on a pleasant smile and put a lid on the turmoil of emotion that threatened to flood out.

He smiled, too, and patted her arm as he came past her and headed for the office. She wondered if she could escape and have a run up into the hills, but his voice caught her before she could make a move.

'Have you been in the office, Annie?'

He always knew. She'd moved nothing, but he always knew. She wanted to be open with him and simply say 'Yes, I used the phone,' but knew that her voice would come out too high and he'd think she was hiding something. Damn Jak to hell and back. If he hadn't riled her, she'd deal with this.

'No, why, what's the matter?' She heard her voice, calm and measured, as she went to the door and looked in

'Nothing, I just ... I had to go off in a rush. I wouldn't normally leave everything out.'

The seed of doubt in his tone made her breathe an inward sigh of relief. Everything was exactly as he'd left it, she knew it was.

She left him rummaging through his papers and escaped to the kitchen. It was both irrational and unfair to feel anger towards Jak. She'd barely known him five minutes, yet felt he'd won her trust and then betrayed her.

As soon as she could, she would be out of the house, into the open to run her anger into the hills. But for now, she'd return to the office to act like a rational being and tell her father the things he needed to know.

'Dad, I found out something about the woman who died in the car, Charlotte Grainger. Well anyway, about a story she told Aunt Marian and me.'

He looked up from the desk, pen poised, clearly surprised she'd broken the taboo of no interruptions, but signalled her to go on.

She started on the story Charlotte had told about Lorraine, but he stopped her.

'It's OK, Annie. We know all about that.'

'It isn't just the accident on the moor, Dad. She knew someone called Julia Lee. Charlotte had her driving licence. And this Lorraine person claimed to have met—'

Again, his raised hand stopped her. 'We know about Julia Lee too. Now.' He gave her a smile and the ghost of a wink that made a brief intimate bridge between them, and at the same time asked her please to back off.

'Oh ... Right then ... And is it all connected? Is it important?'

This time, the look he gave her from beneath raised eyebrows was an unmistakable warning. 'Annie, you know better than that.'

'OK.' She retreated.

They were the wrong pair of shoes, and it was the wrong time of day, but she sprinted straight from her father's front gate to the nearest break in the houses that took her to the hills. It was a steep track, strewn with ankle breakers – holes, dips, loose rocks. Not a track at all, just a gully carved out by a small burn. None of it bothered her. As soon as she knew she was out of earshot, she let rip and cursed Jak to hell and back for making her feel so vulnerable.

She walked now, her legs on fire from the sprint up almost vertical terrain. What was it about him that had made her trust him as though she'd known him for years? What was it that he'd sparked inside her to bring out that reaction? She couldn't believe she'd acted so foolishly. Going off with a complete stranger after what had happened to Charlotte on the road where she'd been within a snip of going over herself. And yet ... what had Jak done? She'd had no business putting any trust in him, so why see him as under any obligation? He'd tried to find out what her father knew about the leg in the loch. He said he'd been doing it for Charlotte. Had he? His attempts had been ham-fisted enough that they were never in danger of succeeding and didn't dampen her first impression of him as friend rather than foe.

'Jak, you bastard,' she muttered as a way to push the blame away from herself as she strode through the trees. She knew she'd never see him again, not unless she sought him out and she had no reason to do that. Her task now was to forget him, forget all the things that had cluttered her mind up here. Tomorrow she had to be back at work. She had the Buenos Aires report to deliver in the evening.

She looked around. The light had begun to leach out of the woodland that surrounded her. It must be later than she realized. This was an unfamiliar stretch, the unattractive underbelly of the woods that the tourists didn't reach. Up ahead, she saw an irregular space between the trees and made towards it. The ground was cleared in a rough circle. She sat down in the middle of it, wrinkling her nose at the smell that rose from the disturbed earth.

Margot had said she would look up Charlotte in her personnel records if Annie wanted. There would be no harm in taking up the offer. Annie thought of the scrap of paper Aunt Marian had given her with the address of Charlotte's flat and felt a flush of guilt. There was no excuse to keep that to herself, but it could do no harm to have a quick look.

As she calmed down, Annie became aware of the feel of the ground beneath her. Soft ash, and quite deep. She'd pitched herself on to the site of a fire. Quickly she patted the ground. It was cold, but the sickly smell of burnt straw rose around her and made her nose wrinkle in disgust. She ran her hands through the ash and found it full of tiny globes, smooth, hard and round. As she rubbed at one and saw it glint back at her, she knew exactly what she'd found: tiny glass eyes and burnt straw.

Of course he didn't sell any. It was absurd to think he did. In this out-of-the-way and little visited area not so far from the post office, Caine disposed of his dolls.

A breeze whispered through the undergrowth making her skin prickle. She was sitting in a dolls' graveyard.

CHAPTER FIFTEEN

Annie twisted restlessly in and out of sleep that night. A parade of shabby straw dolls marched in the foreground distracting her from Jak as he rifled through files searching for the real Lorraine hidden inside a scratchy recording. Somewhere beyond them, way out of her reach, her mother laughed.

She'd planned to do the journey back without a break, but was already tired when she set off. When her phone rang just before the services at Leicester Forest and flashed Mike's number she was the glad of the excuse to pull in. She bought coffee before calling him back.

'Annie. Where are you? Why didn't you answer?'

'I didn't have the hands free connected. I had to stop. I'm on my way back. More than halfway.'

'Will you come straight round to my flat, Annie? Before you go home?'

'Why?'

'Uh ... I'll tell you when you get here. It's a bit tricky by phone.'

'I need to get back to my place, Mike. I have to go into work. I've that report to deliver tonight.'

'It's OK, I won't keep you. I mean I'll come back with you. But you will come here first, won't you?'

'What's the matter? Why the great mystery, for heaven's sake? OK, OK, I'll come round.'

When she arrived, he came out to meet her.

'You're running late.'

'The traffic was bad. Come on, what's this all about? I need to get back to the flat and get stuff for work.'

He climbed into the car. 'I'll tell you on the way.'

'OK, let's have it. What's happened?'

'I'm afraid you've had a break-in. Your flat's been trashed.'

'Hell, when? What did they take?'

He spread his hands in an I-don't-know gesture. 'I only found it this morning. There's papers and stuff all over.'

She fought an urge to tear at her hair. It was just one thing after another at the moment. 'Just mine, or did any of the others get hit?'

'Just yours, I think.'

'Oh well, my turn, I suppose. They missed me last time.'

First Mrs Watson's and now here. Annie's mind went at once to the tapes that were tucked into the glove compartment of the car; the tapes her aunt had been so sure had been the target of the thief. It was too ridiculous a thought to take out and look at now. Break-ins were a hazard around here where they were a rarity for her aunt's community. Back to the important issues – inventory, what was the worst they could have taken? Not much. There was stuff that would be awkward to lose, but nothing vital.

'Much damage?'

He gave her an I'm-afraid-so smile.

'Oh hell, clothes. Mike, they haven't trashed my clothes, have they? I've got to be all dressed up by this evening.'

'Everything's been thrown about, but nothing unbreakable's broken, if you know what I mean. Things have been thrown out of the cupboards. I guess they were looking for money.'

'Chance'd be a fine thing.'

She stood in the doorway and surveyed the wreckage. Pre-warned and prepared, she could take it calmly and felt grateful to Mike that he'd come to tell her.

Brute force had come through the doors, a jemmy forcing both door jamb and lock away from their housings. Annie took in the makeshift repairs. No subtlety here, she judged, just an opportunist taking advantage of an empty flat.

'The police said not to touch anything until you got back. So you could tell what had been taken.'

'Fair enough.' She waded through the debris. The kitchen was bad. Jars and pots overturned, smashed. Shards of razor-edged crockery and glass littered the floor. She left it and headed for the bedroom. Papers and clothes lay everywhere, strewn at random. Cupboards and drawers hung open. It wasn't nice, but it was OK. Given the amount of smashed crockery, she could feel lucky not to be finding her belongings drenched in the intruder's blood.

'I've had the locks changed.'

She blew out a sigh and reached up to put her arms round his neck. 'Thank you, Mike. It would have been awful just to walk into it, and still have to get to work ... Oh my God! The Margot jacket!'

She threw herself at the mounds on the bedroom floor and scrabbled through them, searching for a glimpse of real leather. They'd have taken it. The one thing she owned that had real value. It was to have been the cornerstone of her outfit for this evening. The touch of class with which to meet the prestigious client.

'You mean your good jacket?' said Mike, pointing across the room. 'Isn't that it?'

She dived for the glimpse of the familiar sheen and dragged it out, holding it up to him, twisting it back and forth, to try to see all sides at once. 'Is it OK? Have they damaged it? Is it torn?'

'Bit of something down near the hem,' Mike said.

She trampled across a heap of clothes to hang it over the wardrobe door and inspect it inch by inch. 'It's OK, it's brushing off. Thank God. Tonight of all nights I didn't need to be without this.'

At just after five, she entered the office, feeling finely balanced on several edges at once. None must distract her from what must be done. The flat could come later. She wasn't sure she had the means to dress herself in clean clothes tomorrow morning, but it didn't matter; none of it mattered. It could all come later. First and foremost, the Buenos Aires report.

She burst into an unexpected bustle of noise and activity. Dean's was the only familiar face. He sat on the floor, surrounded by computer printouts, intense concentration on his face. He grinned up at her.

'Uh ... Hi. How's tricks?' She aimed the question at Dean but stared in fascination at the bustle. There were four other people in the room who were all strangers to her.

Dean gave her a double thumbs-up.

The door swished open behind her and Casey marched in. As she hurried by, she slapped Annie on the back. 'Eh up. Double-oh-seven's back from the wilderness.'

Annie grinned. Something had happened while she was away. Something good.

'Ah, there you are, Annie.' Pieternel was at the far side of the room beckoning her into the small office.

Annie picked her way between the new makeshift desks. Pieternel closed the door behind them so they were alone.

'What's happened?' Annie breathed, not daring to believe the miracle until Pieternel spelled it out for her.

'A couple of lucky breaks came off the pack,' Pieternel summarized. 'We're not there yet. Not quite. But we're within that...' She clicked her fingers. 'Everything hangs on the next few days. I've a new investor. Don't you breathe a word out there, not even to Dean. He might spill the beans to Casey. We're flavour of the month right now. I've had to buy in experienced staff to cope.'

Annie swallowed, her mouth dry. Pieternel must be financing all this on fresh air. It was a last desperate throw of the dice. If her gamble with the new investor didn't come off... 'How ... how close are you to signing him ... uh ... her ... whoever?'

'Them. New money. Not used to playing the game. I need the name on the dotted line pretty damned quick, but I'll have them tied in tighter than a stallion's balls if I can just keep them dazzled for a few more days. I've been balancing them like prize salmon, Annie. It's been murder.'

'So why in hell did you send me away? I could have done everything from here and been on hand to help out.' *And missed some stuff I could have done without.*

'Believe me, Annie' – Pieternel ran her hand through her hair, making the dark tresses glint with gold as the sun caught them – 'it was important, but it's also complicated. I can't go into it all now. It's working, that's what matters. Just look around you.'

Annie knew Pieternel was hiding something, but if she could work the miracle, Annie was prepared to wait to get the full story.

Pieternel pushed the office diary across towards her, indicating a new entry for this evening. Annie felt her mouth curve to an even wider grin. One of their long-standing clients, a particular favourite of Annie's, was booked in.

'I thought we'd lost them. That's so good to see.'

'Yeah, great, isn't it? I want you to go round and see them.'

'But I can't. I've the Buenos Aires report to deliver.'

'Casey can take that.'

Annie felt her mouth fall open. Pieternel trusting Casey with the Buenos Aires report?

'Come on, Annie. It's a simple delivery.'

'I know, but...' She tried the idea for size. Certainly, their returning clients needed red-carpet treatment, someone who would flatter them, remember all the old cases. It would be all too easy for the wrong person sour the deal. But the Buenos Aires job was so important. 'Well, I suppose you're right. It's just a delivery and Casey won't have to talk to any of their bigwigs.'

'And if anyone wants to talk to her, she won't know a thing.'

'Is that a good idea?'

'Sure. Why wouldn't we send a trusted gofer, rather than an experienced operative? It's only a delivery.'

Annie let out a sigh. 'You don't want me to talk to them, do you? That's the real agenda here, isn't it? What's it about?'

'They've already been on to me, wanted to give you the third degree, talk through details of the case and so on. I had to say you were out of the country, out of touch.'

'Out of—? Did you tell them where?'

'I let them make their own assumptions.'

'But why? Why shouldn't they talk to me?'

'No reason at all, Annie. They can talk to you all they like in a day or two. Just not yet.'

Annie stared, perplexed. She was used to Pieternel playing a close game when things were rough, but this didn't make any sense and she said so.

'It'll all make perfect sense, Annie, I promise you. For now, I need you to trust me. Go out tonight and rebuild our client base and then I want you to duck out of sight for a couple of days. Then I'll tell you everything.'

'Tomorrow,' said Annie. 'You'll tell me everything tomorrow. I'll play along for tonight but that's all.'

'Not tomorrow, Annie. In a couple of days. Please. They mustn't speak to you before I've signed this deal.'

'But they're nothing to do with the deal. You said new money.'

'Please, Annie, it's complicated. Just a couple of days.'

Annie didn't know what to say. It was worth trying anything to save Aunt Marian, of course, and Pieternel hadn't let her down before. She ought to trust her, but why couldn't she know?

'So what do you want me to do for the next couple of days?'

'Great! I knew I could rely on you.' Pieternel leapt upon this query as full agreement and though Annie hadn't meant it that way, she said nothing, just let her gaze rise heavenwards. 'Go to the meeting tonight,' Pieternel went on. 'Then vanish. Mobile off. Don't answer your landline. No contact with anyone except friends and family until I get in touch and give you the all clear.'

'How will you get in touch if I'm not allowed to talk to anyone?' Annie asked, sourly.

Pieternel gave her an impish smile. 'Hey, don't I count as a friend after all this time?' Then she reached into the desk and showed Annie a tightly wrapped folder.

'Go and give this to Casey. She knows she's to deliver it on her way home, but I want you to have a word. Tell her how important it is. She listens to you.'

Annie opened the door to the outer office to see Casey laughing with Dean as she pulled her bag out of the cupboard. 'Oh, for fuck's sake,' she whispered urgently to Pieternel. 'Look at that abortion she's wearing. Has she got a coat? I know it's only a delivery but what sort of impression does that give?'

'Casey,' Pieternel called across, 'do you have a coat?'

'Nah, not in this weather. No need.'

'Right, well, you're to borrow Annie's for tonight.'

'Pieternel, it's my best,' hissed Annie.

'For Chris'sakes, Annie, she can't take mine. It'd swamp her.'

It was only a jacket. The wrong impression could cause all sorts of damage. It was no big deal. Annie tried to talk herself round but it was with great reluctance she handed over the Margot jacket and watched Casey fling it carelessly round her shoulders.

Later that evening, Annie left her meeting and strolled into the early evening crowds. It had gone well. They'd chatted like old friends and signed up a whole new contract.

The skies had opened while she'd been in there. They'd all joked about unsuitable clothing and how soaked they'd all be when they left, but the shower had been as short as it had been heavy and now only showed in the water trickling down the gutters and wet sheen of the pavement. As she stepped outside, Annie went automatically for her phone to turn it back on, then remembered Pieternel and left it off. Mike would be late back too tonight. There was nothing to hurry for. She let her thoughts skirt the edges of the city sounds. The roar of the traffic, too loud not to be intrusive, but background noise all the same. Something you got used to. She had no great incentive to get back to her flat and the mess that waited there, but couldn't muster much indignation over the way it had been trashed. It was nothing to the anger she felt about what the break-in at Mrs Watson's might have done to her aunt. On the surface, she was the same stolid Aunt Marian she'd always been, but she'd taken herself all the way to Glasgow on a fool's errand because someone had violated the safety of her environment.

Her thoughts turned to Jak and the squalid bedsit he'd stayed in. If it hadn't been Mrs Watson's single malt she'd shared with him, it was someone else's stolen property. She'd email her father about Dish and his sordid rooms in town. Those boxes must be stuffed with enough to make a serious dent in the local crime clear-up rate.

The high frequency wail of a siren made her flinch as it shot past. She watched it take a sudden dive to cut round the wrong side of a traffic island. No one expected her anywhere just now. No one could contact her.

Her feet already headed her in the direction of Tottenham Court Road. She fingered the scrap of paper in her pocket where Charlotte's address was written.

CHAPTER SIXTEEN

Charlotte's flat was in a converted house with a communal entrance and locked front door. Pseudo-carelessly, Annie pressed the side of her hand on to several of the bells, including Charlotte's in case of a hidden watcher.

A man in jeans and an unbuttoned shirt emerged and opened the door. He had a cordless phone in one hand and was obviously in the middle of a call.

'Sorry,' Annie apologized. 'I've come to see Mrs Grainger.'

'Uh huh.' He held the door open, and gave an indeterminate gesture that encompassed the rest of the house. 'Know your way?'

Annie smiled her thanks and strode in past him. He didn't look unduly interested, but idled in his own doorway a moment before he resumed his call. Annie's gaze ran a lightning inventory of the doors she could see and calculated that Charlotte's flat wasn't on the ground floor. She jogged up the stairs, hoping she exuded an air of someone who knew where she was going.

Assuming worst-case scenario, that the man downstairs was now phoning the police, she would give herself ten minutes. No more. If the official response to a potential intruder at Charlotte's flat came in under an hour, then she'd know for sure that the hidden agenda was momentous, but she wouldn't take chances.

She found Charlotte's door towards the back of the house. No one was about so she slipped out her credit card and bent over the lock to give it a try. It yielded at once. Annie stepped back in surprise. That was far too easy and spawned a gut-knotting moment where she was sure it would trigger an alarm.

When everything remained quiet, she slipped inside where she found a smallish room that mixed living, kitchen and bedroom space. She moved swiftly to the only other door and found a cramped shower and loo in what was little more than a cupboard. Back in the main room, her gaze raked the small space and she strode round the perimeter opening cupboards and drawers. The only places worth a second look were the chest of drawers and a wooden cabinet.

She took the cabinet first and raked through its contents; books, magazines and a small stash of papers in a folder, including a passport and marriage certificate. She flicked through everything, noting a few personal papers for a better look once she'd finished her initial sweep.

The chest of drawers was packed with clothes and books. It took only a few seconds to satisfy herself there was nothing of interest. She headed back to the cabinet.

She looked first at the marriage certificate, wondering for a moment if she would find that Charlotte's husband had been Jak. However, the name on the official document was Alan David Grainger. She retrieved the passport and looked through it with care. The Charlotte she'd known stared out from the photograph.

Next of kin ... Julia Lee.

Surprise caught her breath. She grabbed the marriage certificate again. She'd read over Charlotte's maiden name without registering, but sure enough, it was Lee.

Julia and Charlotte Lee. She remembered Charlotte's tale of two sisters and all that garbage about a fake death. Was it true? And if so, was it Julia or Charlotte? Had Julia faked her death on the moor with Lorraine as the witness no one believed? Had the car been intended to go over the edge empty and burn the evidence to dust at the bottom of the ravine? Poor Charlotte, if that had been the plan. There'd been nothing fake about that death.

Swiftly, she tucked the papers back into their folder and moved round the room putting everything back as she'd found it. One last glance to make sure she'd left no obvious trace and she slipped back out, pulling the door gently closed behind her.

It was impossible to work through the ramifications of what she'd found, but she knew she couldn't let this lie. She needed to know more about Charlotte. Margot had a personnel file on her, and Annie had a free day tomorrow because of Pieternel's agendas.

Mike was in the flat when Annie arrived home. He'd cleared enough space to sit in front of the TV and, in the kitchen, created a small oasis to stand the kettle and coffee jar surrounded by scattered food and shards of crockery.

'Ah, there you are. Did you know your mobile's switched off?'

'Uh ... yeah. Meeting.'

'Yes, of course, the report. How did it go?'

'Yup, all fine.' Please God that Casey had delivered it with no glitches. She hoped he wouldn't notice that she'd come back without the Margot jacket. She didn't want to attempt to explain Pieternel's reasoning before she understood it herself.

'Shall we go out to eat?' Mike said. 'I'll have to get back to my place tonight though. I'm in early tomorrow, and—'

'Sure.' He didn't need to explain. Any change of clothes he'd had here would need to be dug out and dry-cleaned if he had to turn into Mr Respectable for the merchant banking world tomorrow morning.

'Mike, thanks for sorting it.'

She swept some more of the mess aside and sat at the kitchen table, cradling her cup.

Mike ambled through and kissed the top of her head. 'Annie?'

'Hmm?'

'We need to talk.'

Immediately on guard at his tone, she looked up. What now?

Mike showed her the paperwork. The post that had lain behind the door had been ripped open in the search for anything convertible to cash. She glanced at the financial warnings, bills and threats that the intruders had raked through. What a disappointment they must have had. Even her identity wasn't worth taking.

'Why didn't you tell me?' Mike tried to keep the dismay out of his voice.

'You shouldn't have looked. It's not your problem.'

'But...?' He held up a page that Annie recognized as from the landlord.

'It'll take time to get me out. I've looked into it. I'll have something sorted by then.'

'But why haven't you given it priority? It's your home, Annie, for Chris'sakes.' He held out another statement. 'You've been paying off a piddling little unsecured loan.'

It was hard to explain to someone who'd never had to let go of the sides. Ending up on the street wasn't the issue. The important thing was to dive and dodge, to rob Peter to pay Paul to keep up a front as long as she could so that no one who didn't see the full picture could know how bad things really were. Her one and only priority was to cling to her financial integrity.

'Sit down, Mike. It isn't good.'

She told him everything. How the business was on a knife edge and would swallow her whole if it failed, about Aunt Marian; about Mrs Watson's; about all that her aunt had done for her. Everything she'd lined up to tell her father was suddenly easy to say.

At the start of the tale, she watched him roll a couple of how-bad-can-it-be phrases round his tongue but he swallowed them unsaid.

'Things are looking up for the business. I think Pieternel's going to pull off the miracle.'

'But your personal finances might still go belly-up?'

She nodded. 'If Pieternel pulls off this last trick, yes, the business'll turn the corner, with me or without me. If I go under, I won't take them with me, but I'll still take Aunt Marian.'

'And what's this trick Pieternel's after pulling off?'

Having gone this far, there was no reason not to tell him the rest. Mrs Buenos Aires, the case he'd joined her on. The routine job for a big prestigious client that Pieternel had turned into something big. 'I don't know what she's doing. Anyway, I don't want to know, not yet. I'll play along because it's working.'

'D'you want me to stay over? I can go early in the morning.'

'Thanks, but no. I'll be fine.'

'If you're sure ... Oh, and there was a message while you were out. Nothing important.'

Annie thought of Pieternel's injunction on her not to answer her phone. No contact with anyone except friends and family.

'Who was it?'

'She wouldn't give a name. She just said to say the girl at Torran Hill.'

'Torran Hill?' Annie felt her eyes widen in amazement. Beth had rung her. 'What did she say?'

'You weren't to ring back. She was adamant about that. I said I'd get you to ring, but she said no, her uncle wouldn't like it. So I asked if there was a message and she said, tell her the one she's after is keen.'

'Keen?'

'Yup. I got her to repeat it, said it back to her. The one you're after is keen. Who is she? Anything to do with a case?'

'No, not really. She lives near my aunt. She's a bit ... well, I don't know, not all there.'

'Talking to her, I thought learning difficulties.'

'That would cover it.'

Annie thought back to the last time she'd seen Beth in the dark house under the trees, urging her out the back way because she'd seen someone coming. The someone had turned out to be Jak and it was all too true that he'd been keen to find her. He was after tricking her into showing him her father's papers.

Beth must have gone to some trouble to phone to warn Annie. Aunt Marian was right. She was a good kid. She deserved better than to be shut away up there.

Morning brought the unwelcome news in the post that her road tax was due. That meant the need for an MOT test that she had no confidence the car would sail through.

She made a sudden decision. It was absurd for someone in her position to run a car in London. If she needed transport for work, then she could borrow a vehicle from Pieternel or Dean; meanwhile her car was going under wraps.

As Annie drove across town to her rented lock-up, her thoughts turned to Charlotte. The woman had gone to Scotland to try to find the spot Lorraine described, the spot she said she'd met Charlotte's sister, Julia. She hadn't found it, but something worried her enough that she'd called Margot. Annie had heard the call, but Margot never got the message. She remembered Charlotte's words. It was odd ... like they'd listened for a while, then deliberately cut me off.

A hot fight through heavy traffic made her decision seem all the more sensible. She turned the Nissan into the alley outside the row of lock-ups, a sea of crumbling concrete and rank detritus A couple of the garage doors showed deep cuts, bleeding new wood like injured flesh, but the damage was superficial, and hers had escaped attention.

Rank air rolled out to meet her as she heaved the door open. How had she accumulated all this stuff and why didn't she just dump it, could barely remember what was in here? The boxes piled high reminded her of Dish and his sordid bedsit. She had still to email her father about that. She piled things higher to make room for the car and drove it in. With the Nissan taking up what was left of the floor space, she had to squeeze herself out sideways, and patted the roof as she did so, an apology to the vehicle that had taken her so many miles, that she must leave it in this dark and cramped space. Chances were that the next time it came out it would be to be towed to a scrapyard.

An hour later, Annie walked down from Oxford Circus and stopped outside a coffee shop opposite the entrance to the building where Margot housed her empire. She wanted a moment to compose herself, fearing her imminent financial collapse would show in the sweat on her brow.

She pulled in a couple of deep breaths and walked across the road.

A long counter down the side of the entrance lobby policed access to the firms in the building, although it didn't physically block the way. A notice said 'Please switch your mobile off or on to silent mode, thank you'. Automatically, she lifted it from her pocket, but it was already off.

Although Annie had no reason to suppose Margot wouldn't tell her all she needed to know about Charlotte, she automatically put the security to the test and strolled towards the lifts ignoring the people at the desk. A young woman in a neat uniform scrutinized her as she went past and then turned away. High profile security, but lax. Lifts in easy reach, but no obvious route to the main stairwell. Annie glanced round and could see an access point behind the sweep of the long desk. However, there was a fire door, tucked away in a corner that must provide access from a minor staircase. Locked from this side, it would provide a way out to anyone needing to avoid the lifts. It won't come to that, she told herself, Margot'll tell me all I need to know.

The lift took her smoothly to the fourth floor where she stepped out into deep carpet and looked left and right, noting that the lift door itself wasn't visible from inside either of the big offices.

She found Margot's PA, Janice, at her desk.

'Good morning. Can I help you?' Janice gave her a smooth, professional welcome and then looked closely and did a minor double take. 'It's Annie, isn't it? How nice to see you. Is Margot expecting you?'

'Well, no, but she said to drop in. We spoke on the phone a few days ago about one of your ex-employees. I wondered if I might have a word.'

'Ah yes, Charlotte Grainger. I looked out her record. She was barely with us for a couple of weeks. Cover for someone who was ill. Do take a seat. I'll see if Margot's free.' Janice jabbed at an intercom and murmured into it.

A moment later, she stood up. 'This way, Annie. I'll take you down to Margot's office.'

Margot's private office was all Annie expected. Deep carpet, large expanse of gleaming desk top, huge windows overlooking the city, a larger floor space than the whole of the cramped operation she'd left behind. Towards one end was a low coffee table with comfortable chairs that Janice ushered her to. Margot stood up from behind her desk looking not so very different from the last time they'd met. Annie took in the slightly stockier figure, the neatly sculptured hair, the exclusive suit and felt that even the Margot jacket would have wilted under the brilliance of this assault.

'I don't want to keep you, if you're busy, Margot.'

'Always time for an old friend, Annie. Give me a minute to finish an email.' The words were friendly enough, but Annie didn't believe them. Margot would put herself out because Annie had something she wanted, presumably information on Charlotte.

Within minutes, a young woman entered bearing a tray. The smell of fresh coffee had Annie sniffing the air appreciatively as the tall pot, bone china cups and saucers and plate of luxury chocolate biscuits was set on the low table.

Margot strolled over from her desk and arranged herself in one of the armchairs.

'So Mrs Grainger won't be back with us. Did she mention that she wouldn't have been back anyway? She'd finished her stint. Resigned early, in fact.'

'No, she didn't. Janice told me she'd looked out her records. Was there anything of interest?'

Margot's eyebrows rose a notch, her voice diamond-edged. 'I'll say. Did you know how she came to be with us in the first place?'

'No, she didn't say.'

'One of our staff was mugged, had her arm broken. Our temp agency sent us your Mrs Grainger.'

'She's not mine,' Annie murmured. 'I take it there was a problem.'

'Not on the face of it. She had the exact experience we were looking for, which was unusual, it's a specialized post. She came; she was here just over a week and then didn't turn up one morning. She sent a message saying she couldn't come in any more, personal problems, so we got someone else. End of story until your aunt rang. I didn't know her, and she wasn't directly line-managed by Janice, but we looked out her records. And the woman she'd replaced, who's back now, went ballistic when she saw the photo on the file. Mrs Grainger was the mugger.'

'Charlotte? A mugger?' Annie was gobsmacked. 'You mean she did that just to get a job here?'

'We checked with the agency. Your Mrs Grainger turned up the day before the mugging and registered herself with a perfect-match CV. They'd had no time to do any checks when we called in and it wasn't the high-risk sort of post that needs positive clearance so they sent her along.'

'You said her work was OK. How did she manage that if it was a specialized post?'

'She blagged it for a week until she got at what she wanted, I presume.'

'Which was a set of audio tapes.'

'That's right. How do you come to know about them?'

Annie took the package out of her pocket and handed it over. 'She left them at the guesthouse.'

'So you've listened to them?'

'Not all through. I just wanted to see what they were so I knew what to do with them.'

Margot unwrapped the packet and turned the tapes to catch the light. 'Does your father know about them?'

'My father? No, why should he? What's it to do with him?'

'You know what a stickler he is. I want to deal with this myself, not have some country cop putting in a report and making all sorts of waves. And don't look at me like that. It's nothing I can't sort.'

'You're not going to reassure me without telling me more than that. There's some weird stuff on that tape and it turns out Charlotte was asking questions about that body that was found up near my Dad's.'

'I don't give a damn what's on the tape. It'll be something someone can blackmail someone else with. That's the nub of it. OK, listen, this is strictly in confidence. It's one of our franchises. I've had some doubts for a while, but they make us a lot of money...'

'So you didn't want to look too closely.'

'More coffee?'

Annie pushed forward her cup. Margot's blackmail theory wasn't a comfortable fit. The story on the tape was the murder – or fake death – of the blackmailer, depending on how the pieces of Charlotte's story fitted together. Or it was all drug-induced hallucination, if Lorraine's later account was to be believed.

'So what are you going to do?'

'I'll play it carefully. That's why I need you to keep quiet. I want to ditch that outfit, but it isn't something I can just do at the drop of a hat. For one thing, I don't want it causing any ripples with our security firm.'

'Why would it?'

Margot pulled a face. 'They were the ones who recommended them. And they're good. Very good for the money. They do a lot for us. I don't want to lose them.'

Annie thought about the security she'd seen. High profile, fancy bells and whistles, but she could drive a coach through it if she had to, but if they did what Margot wanted and saved her money at the same time, she wouldn't touch them.

'How about I make a few enquiries with the agency that hired Charlotte? Which was it?'

'I'm sorry, Annie. I can't have you ferreting about there. We have a good relationship with them, recent events notwithstanding. I can't let you go in with your size nines.'

'I'd be very discreet.'

'I'm sure you would, but I've no intention of employing you to go snooping.'

'If it's some other outfit, why do you have their tapes?'

'We have legal ties, responsibilities. More hassle, but more money. And they use our consulting rooms. Everything's recorded. It's all kept under lock and key, of course. It's sensitive stuff, but we have to keep it. Can't risk being sued, and people will pounce on anything these days.'

'Can't you get sued for keeping confidential data like that?'

'People sign forms,' Margot said, vaguely. 'And anyway we don't keep it long. Those tapes would have been destroyed if that woman hadn't taken them. They'll be ashes in the basement furnace before you've left the building.'

'Margot, you can't do that. They're evidence.'

'Of what? That a dead woman got away with confidential data? I don't want to headline that, Annie. I'll get to the bottom of it and sort it, but I need you to keep quiet.'

'I'll keep quiet for now, but if this turns out to have any bearing on anything big, it's got to come out.'

'Who else listened to them?'

'No one but me. Oh, and Charlotte I suppose.'

'Not dear old Aunt Marian?'

'No, she hasn't a clue about them.' Annie had to speak the lie because she must keep her aunt out of the frame. Whether or not Charlotte's paranoia or Lorraine's hysteria had substance behind them, no one must ever think Aunt Marian knew more than she should. She wondered suddenly how many people knew that her aunt had travelled to Glasgow and sent a parcel to her niece. Had the raid on her flat been someone frustrated with not having found the tapes at the guesthouse? Yet, the obvious conclusion should have been that the tapes were in the car with Charlotte.

'D'you keep the client records too?' she asked Margot. 'Names and addresses, that sort of thing?'

'Of course we do. Why?'

'Could you check up on a couple of people? No details, I'd just like to know if they really were your clients, or if Charlotte made them up.'

Margot hesitated, but then went to her desk and looked at her PC. 'What names?'

'Julia Lee for starters.'

After a minute, Margot said, 'I've got half a dozen J. Lees, but I don't think ... No, none of them's a Julia or even a Julie.'

'How about Lorraine then? The woman on the tape.'

'What's her surname?'

'I've no idea.'

Margot gave her a look. 'I can't search just on Lorraine.'

'There's a reference number on the tapes. Can you use that?'

Margot turned the tape in her hand, glanced from it to the screen and shook her head. 'Doesn't look like it.'

Annie swallowed a comment about geriatric computer systems and asked instead, 'Who does your IT stuff? Do you buy it off the shelf?'

'It's purpose built for us. It's a subsid of the security firm. That's another reason I don't want to piss them off.'

So the security firm that gave Margot such a good deal had access to her IT systems. Annie thought of Charlotte and the call that had been cut off. Who might be in the office out of hours? Security guards could prowl these offices with impunity when everyone else was gone. She toyed with voicing her suspicions, but knew Margot wouldn't want to listen, probably wouldn't care what anyone else got up to as long as it didn't interrupt the flow of money into her coffers.

Belatedly, a hint of impatience in Margot's tone filtered through to Annie. Margot had what she wanted now and Annie was in the way. 'Am I stopping you working, Margot? It all seemed really busy out there.'

'Don't worry, I've plenty of dogs to do the barking for me these days. But we've talked enough about me. How are you getting on? How's business?'

'Actually, it's pretty busy at the moment. Maybe I should get going...'

As Annie headed back towards her flat, she reflected on how much time it could take to do very little. The day was all but gone. She pushed open the door and heard voices from the kitchen. Mike's voice was instantly recognizable, but the other was more so, and so way out of context that it rushed the blood from her skin.

It couldn't be.

It was.

Something was wrong. Terribly wrong. That other voice was her father.

As the door slammed shut behind her, both voices cut off. In the fraction of a second it took her to get from the hallway to the kitchen, the silence rushed to fill every corner. The hammering of blood in her head deafened her.

'Dad ... Dad, what is it? What are you doing here? It's Aunt Marian, isn't it? Tell me. What is it?'

Her father's face, white with shock, was a momentary image, then she was crushed in a grip that pressed her to a shirt front that smelt of Mike.

'Annie ... Annie...' His voice was in her ear, the words struggling to escape.

'What is it? What is it?' Her words muffled, she tried to pull away to speak clearly, to make sense of the impossible picture of her father in her kitchen, sitting now as though his legs had given way. Mike buried his face in her neck. She could feel him shaking. And across him, she looked into her father's eyes, and saw how they glistened. She held out a hand that he clasped convulsively. While she felt panic rise inside her, there was a need to comfort them both.

For what seemed like whole minutes, she made no attempt to break up the tableau where one arm clasped Mike to her, the other hand grasped her father's.

It had to be Aunt Marian. Nothing else would bring her father this far south, but she must suppress her panic or she wouldn't be able to ask, and they wouldn't be able to tell her.

'What is it? Tell me, please.'

'You wouldn't answer your phone.' Mike's voice was still muffled in her shoulder.

'Oh Annie.' Her father spoke for the first time. 'Annie.'

'But what is it?'

Mike answered her, the words spilling out in a rush. 'They found a body in a fire at the other side of the city. We thought it was you. You wouldn't answer your phone.'

She pushed away from him so she could stare into his face. A body? 'I've been to see Margot.' She sat heavily in one of the chairs. 'For God's sake, tell me what happened? Please just tell me.'

Her father stared at her as though frightened she'd disappear if he blinked. He took in a deep breath and began to speak. Fire-fighters going in to damp down after a fire in what they thought was an empty warehouse, had found a body badly

153

burnt. Nearby was one of Annie's business cards. That led to Pieternel, and via her to Mike, and then her father. And no one could trace her. They had all panicked. Her father came down on the first flight from Glasgow.

'My God! Aunt Marian! She doesn't—?'

'She knows nothing. It's been going round inside me all day. How was I to break it to her?'

Thank God for that. She must ring her aunt without delay in case rumour should get there first. She pulled the phone from her pocket.

'But Pieternel knew my mobile would be switched off.'

'I guess she panicked too.'

'But just a business card? Didn't anyone see the body?'

'They're doing DNA tests on what's left of it. I must get on to them to tell them you're safe.' He looked incapable of movement, so she reached out and patted his arm, pushing her phone across to him.

'Use that. I'll ring Aunt Marian in a minute. And Pieternel. It must have been one hell of a fire.'

He nodded. 'Small, but intense. Very little was left. The card must have fallen out of a pocket.'

'I saw a photo, Annie.' Mike's voice was unsteady. 'It was your jacket, your good one.'

Her jacket? Her cards? 'Oh my God! It's Casey. It's Casey Lane.'

CHAPTER SEVENTEEN

While her father spoke into the phone, Annie sat with her head in her hands and tried desperately to pull the pieces together, to work out what could have happened, what she needed to do about it. Mike's arms came round her from behind. He said nothing, just held his face to hers and rocked them both gently. He didn't let go until they heard her father's call end.

'Dad, where are you staying? I can make up a bed on the couch and...' She ran her hands through her hair, suddenly aware of the chaos; the fallout from the break-in that between them she and Mike had cleared just enough to look like terminal bad-housekeeping. It wasn't a million miles from her bedroom at home in the old days. She bit her tongue on a confession that she'd been burgled which would only make her father's worry-load heavier.

'No need, Annie. They've put me in a hotel while I'm here. I should get off, now I know you're safe. They've asked me to call in. I'll see you tomorrow. Will you be at work?'

Who're they? Call in where? 'Uh ... yes. Yes, I'll be back at work tomorrow. Listen, I must ring Pieternel.'

'You make your call now. She'll be worried. I'll get on my way, but I'll see you tomorrow.'

Annie berated Pieternel soundly for not telling everyone that her mobile would be off, then broke it to her that the dead woman was almost certainly Casey.

'My God, I hope she delivered the report first.'

'Pieternel!'

She clicked the phone off and turned her anger on Mike. 'What did he say? What did he think about it? What did you tell him?'

155

'Who? What?'

'All this!' she screeched, a wide sweep of her arm taking in the mess. 'What on earth did he think?'

'I don't think he noticed.'

'Didn't notice! Of course he noticed. Just look at it all! You should have said something. No, you shouldn't. Oh, I don't know.' Her father had never lived in a big city; didn't know how much a part of life casual break-ins could become.

'Annie, I'm sure. I'm sure he didn't notice. Not properly. If we have it tidied before he calls in again, he'll never know. He was living a nightmare when he got here. He thought you were—'

The abrupt stop, the catch in his voice, jolted her. What was she doing, carping on about a few broken pots? Mike had lived a nightmare too. While she'd poured expensive coffee down her throat and stuffed herself on Margot's thick chocolate, someone had told him she was dead. What a heartless cow. He didn't deserve this. She flew to him and reached up to pull his head down to hers.

'I'm sorry,' she murmured into his hair. 'It doesn't matter. Of course it doesn't matter.'

'Annie, we could have a go at it tomorrow. Take the day off. You're not really going into work, are you?'

She held him tighter. 'Mike, I have to. I've been away too long. And if Casey ... well ... I'd rather stay with you, you know I would. But I can't.'

The next morning, Pieternel greeted her with haunted eyes and drawn features. 'Christ, Annie! What a mess. How in hell did this happen? C'mon.' She signalled her to the privacy of the small office. 'It turned me over when they said it was you. Then no one could reach you.'

'But you knew Casey had my coat. Why didn't you say? And you could have told them I'd have my mobile off.'

'I forgot about the phone and what's your coat to do with it? No one mentioned a coat to me. Oh, I don't know what I thought.'

'How's Dean taken it?'

'He was knocked sideways when we thought it was you, but he's OK now.'

Annie felt her jaw drop. 'I meant how has he taken it, knowing it's Casey?'

'Oh ... well, OK I think. I mean, we don't know for certain, do we? We won't know till later. Hey, where are you going? I haven't finished.'

Annie marched out into the big office, her gaze raking the space for Dean. She found him in a quiet corner surrounded by boxes and files. His face was blank, but drained of colour, a pulse beat at the side of his head.

'Dean?' She spoke softly, not knowing how to reach him. Only Casey had known that. 'You don't have to be here. We'd all understand.'

'All?' He turned eyes full of bitterness towards her.

'Pieternel isn't really a heartless cow. She just doesn't think.'

'She never liked Casey.'

'Well, maybe not ... but she knew how good she was.'

The flounce of his shoulders signalled his disagreement, or maybe just that it made no odds.

'Look, Dean, why don't you get off home? No one expects you in work after this.'

'No, Annie. I'd go mad. I'd sit thinking about it.'

'What are you doing now?'

The files that surrounded him were Casey's notes, all the cases she'd ever worked for them by the look of it. His gaze followed hers.

'I'll go through them, Annie. I'll pitch any that aren't anything and I'll go through the rest and see what I can find. Then it's up to you. You're the one who can do this stuff. It's up to us. We've got to find out who did this.'

'Dean, did Casey say anything to you? What makes you think it's to do with one of her cases?'

'It has to be, Annie. What else could it be?'

Annie blocked the thought that came to her mind, the voice that said she knew the answer only too well. She couldn't think this out just yet. There was too much else in her head. Dean knew the sordid world Casey sank into now and again. She might have pissed off her dealer ... tried to scam the wrong person ... taken contaminated stuff and fallen unconscious in the wrong place ... fallen victim to a mugging gone wrong. A connection with one of her cases was way down the list. But this was the only thing left that he could do for her, so she'd play along for his sake and to buy time for herself before she had to admit to him that she knew he was right.

What must it have done to her father that Casey's body ended up in a fire?

'OK, Dean. We'll do this. And hold on to the memories. Remember her face. Remember the good times.'

'I'll never forget her face, Annie.'

Annie expected Pieternel to kick off about Dean's extra-curricular activities, but she didn't.

'I suppose he must be fairly cut up, poor kid. This'll get it out of his system. Bit of a bummer for us, though. We'll be two experienced bodies down for a while. It's going to be a struggle.'

'We'll cope.'

'Yup. Uh ... You'd better sit down, Annie. Something I need to tell you about the Buenos Aires report.' There was something shamefaced in Pieternel's expression. 'I was hoping you wouldn't need to know about this yet. I leaked a few key bits of the report early. That's why they wanted to talk to you, why I pushed you into going to Scotland.'

'You leaked...? What key bits?'

'Where d'you think the work piled in from? We became the miracle workers, the ones to do business with.'

'You used that footage, didn't you? You spun it to make her look a fraud?'

Pieternel nodded.

'Now what? They've seen the full report and know you weren't straight with them, I suppose. How much damage is this going to do us?'

'No. No. It's kinda worse than that ... uh ... better than that. Depends how you look at it.'

'What do you mean?'

'Well, of course, the report matched the bits I leaked early. I'm not fool enough to feed them outright lies. I was just careful the way I spun it.'

'And?'

'The claimant's lawyers have got wind of it; they're kicking up a stink.'

'Well, of course they are. What did you expect? Did you think they'd roll over and just take it?'

'No, I assumed they'd fight it out. I expected the client to take our report to one of the big boys to get the extra proof they need that we're right.'

'And what when the big boys couldn't find their extra proof?'

'It'd show that they were no better than we are.'

'Bloody hell, Pieternel. You know full well there's no extra proof to find. The woman's on the level. Poor cow. What's happened?'

'They didn't go to one of the big boys like I expected. They came back to us. They want us to dig out the proof.'

'Yeah, right. What's the damage if we come clean?'

'Annie, don't be stupid! We're not throwing in the towel like that.'

'If the claim's legit, we've no option.'

'You're back on the case, Annie. I want you to find some real proof the woman's a fraud.'

CHAPTER EIGHTEEN

Out in the big office, Annie cleared herself a space as best she could on a stained and pitted desktop, thinking of the empty acres of polished wood in Margot's office. Once again, she spread the papers from the Buenos Aires file in front of her.

There was no sense of anticipation this time; no sense of secrets to ferret out. And one big difference between now and the first time: Casey had been alive then. There seemed little point even looking at the papers again. She knew every corner, could recite them practically word for word. But it gave her something to do that she could turn all her concentration on, blocking out all other thoughts.

She put the fax at the top of the pile. It said nothing to her any more. It was just a piece of paper, a slightly skewed copy. No instinct sang. She hadn't expected it to.

All she could do was go back to basics, first principles. Find the source. Look at the originals. The name of a clinic was on the fax. It was the source she must investigate. Nothing in the file gave any useful contact data. She reached a keyboard towards her. If the net wouldn't cough up a contact, she'd try the official healthcare channels.

Before long she had a phone number that might or might not connect her to someone who could trace the original communication. She clicked again at the keyboard to figure out the time zones. No point antagonizing anyone with a 2.00 a.m. call. Her fingers flew across the keys. She wanted this to be over.

Through the clamour of the office, beyond faces of new people she'd yet to get to know, she saw Dean in his corner, rifling through a mountain of paper. Pieternel, at the far end, was hunched over a phone, putting up barriers, Annie hoped, for when this new pile of shit hit the fan.

Her mobile rang.

'Annie, can you spare any time today,' her father's voice said. 'They'd like a statement from you about Casey Lane.'

'Yes, of course. I can come now. Dad, why are you involved in this?'

'Uh ... we can talk later, Annie. How long will you be?'

She checked her watch. 'Twenty minutes.'

As she headed for the Tube, she thought of the grey post-mortem photograph of Charlotte her father had shown her the night they'd played Scrabble in the garden. Her mind superimposed Casey's face on the memory. Only from what she'd heard, there hadn't been enough of Casey left for her face to be recognizable.

A young detective constable from the local station took her statement. There was little she could say, other than to describe the circumstances of her last meeting with Casey. He already had a statement from the client Casey visited before she was killed.

When everything was signed, he gave her a mock-stern smile. 'I understand you might have made some work for us.'

'What do you mean?'

'With that report of yours. Uncovered a fraud by all accounts.'

'Oh, I don't know.' She felt herself colour up, and cursed Pieternel. 'It's early days. It might come to nothing.'

He stood up. 'If you wouldn't mind, Ms Raymond, we'd like you to look at some CCTV footage from outside the building Ms Lane visited. We'd like it confirmed as her by someone who knew her well. You know we've found no family?'

'Yes, I know. She never mentioned family to any of us.' Not even Dean.

Her father joined them to watch the tape.

The resolution was good and the film in colour, so that even though Casey had chosen to obscure her face under a large hat, it was unmistakably her who strolled down the steps and out on to the pavement, looked right and left then jogged across the road and off the edge of the frame.

Annie felt a chill to see Casey alive and carefree. 'I'd forgotten how it rained that evening,' she said.

'Would you look once more, just to be sure?'

She nodded and paid attention again to the flickering frame. 'Yes, it's her. I'm quite sure. Uh ... How soon after...? When did it happen?'

'Probably soon after she left. We don't think she was killed where she was found. Chances are she was bundled in a vehicle and driven to where they burned the body.'

She felt he was telling her things he wouldn't have divulged had her father not been there. She also thought she felt her father's disapproval sweep over them both, but when she looked at him, his face was ashen. He caught her eye and tried to smile. 'I'm so pleased I didn't see that yesterday. It looked just like you coming out of that building, Annie.'

Annie couldn't meet his eye. She heard her voice rattle out questions. Who found her? When? Did they have any idea who did it? Could it have been an accident? A mugging gone wrong? If she heard the answers, they disappeared from her head immediately.

Before she left, she arranged to meet her father for a meal that evening.

Back in the office, Annie looked with distaste at the Buenos Aires file and the phone number she should ring later. Nothing must interrupt her evening with her father.

She took Dean aside to tell him about the CCTV image of Casey.

'Why didn't they ask me?'

'They might.'

'How's it going?' She nodded towards the heap of paperwork he was working through.

'Nothing yet, Annie, but it'll be there somewhere.'

Leaving him to carry on, she went to update Pieternel.

'I'll call the clinic later tonight. I want to catch them at about the same time of day the fax was sent, maybe catch the same shift, you know.'

'It's a routine query. Leave it with one of the new guys if you want. Have a relaxing evening with your dad.'

Relaxing? Hardly. 'Thanks, I'll do that. I wouldn't usually leave something like this with ... well, anyway.'

'Give me the gen and I'll pass it on.'

Annie went to retrieve the fax. 'This is what I'm after. Another copy faxed from source.' She showed Pieternel the numbers she'd dug out, reminded her of the time difference. 'It might take some fast talking to get the info out of them, of course.'

Mike was already there when Annie arrived home. He sat at the kitchen table drumming his fingers on the surface and saying 'Um,' to her queries on whether he'd had a good day or her mention of the CCTV images of Casey that she'd seen.

'For heaven's sake, Mike,' she snapped, 'can't you find anything better to do? I'd like to get this place cleared up a bit before Dad gets here.'

'He can't come tonight. He rang. Something came up. He asked if it would be OK to come round about midday tomorrow before he goes back to Scotland.'

What was it with her father? This summer was the first time in her life she wanted to talk seriously to him and he was never there. 'Yes, of course it will. I can come home at lunchtime, work late if I have to. What did you tell him?'

'I told him yes.'

'Good. Then we can have a real go at this mess tonight.'

He made a face. 'Let me get in one of those firms that'll come in and blitz it. I could do it tomorrow morning while you're at work.'

'Don't they cost a fortune?'

'Well, yeah, but—'

'And anyway, you couldn't get anyone at this notice.'

'I could. I checked in case you said yes. But...'

'But what? Come on, Mike, spit it out. You've been on edge since I got back.'

'Come and sit down, Annie.'

'For crying out loud, I'm fed up with people telling me to sit down. What is it?'

'I've done something you won't like, but I don't want you going off on one.'

'What? What have you done?'

'I paid the electricity bill.'

She stared, nonplussed. 'Oh, OK. Thanks. I hope you don't need the money back in a hurry.'

'I don't want it back at all. I spend enough time here. But that's not all. I've paid the rent too. The rent on the flat's back up to date.'

'Bloody hell, Mike. What are you playing at? I said I'd sort all that. I'd rather owe them than you.'

'I thought about it when I was here with your father. When we thought that you ... I didn't want him thinking you'd died on the point of becoming homeless.'

'Oh Mike, you idiot.' She tried and failed to hold on to her annoyance at his interference. He was a sentimental fool at times but somehow he suited her.

'I will pay you back when I can, but don't do anything like this again, will you? I'll get back out of this myself. I always have before.'

'I don't want paying back, Annie, but I can't afford to pay your bills as well as mine. Couldn't we compromise?'

'What do you mean?'

'Why don't I move in? Then we can share the bills, well, I can pay them till you're back on your feet.'

Annie stopped. The idea was preposterous. How could she let anyone into her life so irrevocably? Yet, how different would it be? He spent most of his time here as it was. And the idea of having someone to share at least part of the financial burden felt like a weight lifted already.

'That could work. You know, I racked my brains a while ago wondering if I could cram in a flatmate but there just isn't room. But if you were to move in...'

'It's a yes then?'

'It is. I don't know what's in it for you, but it's perfect financial sense for me. Of course it's a yes.'

'Or you could say that I'm the person you want to share your life with and you want me to move in whatever the financial implications.'

'You don't want me spouting that guff.'

'I wouldn't mind once in a while. So, do we shake on it or, since your father's not coming round, maybe we could seal the deal some other way?'

Annie laughed. Mike was right. It would be good to have him here all the time.

'Why's your father here, Annie? I know why he came to London, but why did he stay? Why is he acting like he's part of the inquiry? He didn't know Casey.'

Annie didn't meet his eye as she shrugged, hoping he would interpret the gesture as a don't know.

CHAPTER NINETEEN

Annie arrived at work before six the next morning, but found the office already manned. Dean was by his paper mountain, still sifting through, still looking bewildered. She would offer to help him in a while. The case file he sought wasn't in his heap.

She made them both coffee, then went to flick through the diary and papers on Pieternel's desk. Paradoxically, although they were busier than they'd been for months, there was little for Annie to do. The workload had been divvied up without her whilst Pieternel had wanted her out of the way. All she had to work on was this second bite at the Buenos Aires case and once she'd sucked that dry, the credibility-sapping result would likely be another sudden diminution of their client base, this time fatal. None the less, she flicked through Pieternel's notes deciding where to muscle in to get herself back into the thick of it.

She strolled back to her desk as the door opened and Pieternel came in. They murmured hellos. Annie sat cradling her coffee as the office filled up around her.

The new guy Pieternel had spoken to the night before marched over and handed her a sealed brown envelope.

'It's that fax you wanted, Ms Raymond.'

Annie smiled her thanks, the formal 'Ms Raymond' underlining the isolation she'd felt these last few weeks.

She slit the envelope and took out a page of notes, neatly written, and another copy of the fax she remembered from the file. So he'd done the job. Well done, him. He'd be a useful member of the team, supposing there was still a team left when the dust settled.

The Buenos Aires file came out again and she rifled through the sheets until she found the original copy. With the two sheets side by side, the only obvious difference was in the auto-lettering at the edge giving the date and time of faxing. The new copy gave yesterday's date; on the old one the information was lost in the angle of the off-centre copy.

Left to right. From top to bottom. Letter by letter and word by word, alignment and spacing. Every detail. She went through with a finger on each sheet following the printed captions and handwritten data.

She found it in the box captioned Date of Appointment. A pause, breath held in, heart thudding in her chest.

On the new copy, the figure eleven sat at the left of the box, its European-style arrowheads making it imitate seventy-seven to the English-reading eye.

On the old copy, the second digit had a line through it making it a seven.

Annie breathed out slowly, her fingers tight on the figures. Her hands moved once again from letter to letter, box to box. She reached the end. Everything else was the same.

She pulled the file in front of her and went over the chronology. The date of appointment had been altered from the eleventh to the seventeenth.

This wasn't the time to rush and she stepped through the story bit by bit, event by event. Eventually, when there could be no shadow of a doubt, she stood up and stretched. 'Sorry, Mrs BA.' she murmured.

In Pieternel's office she went through what she'd found.

'I have to unravel all the detail, but it won't take much now we know what to look for. Maybe they pulled the biker into it to stage some sort of crash with Mrs BA, maybe it happened for real. Whatever the original accident was, it didn't happen to her. She wasn't in the country on the eleventh.'

'But the injuries are real enough. They can't have faked that.'

'Yeah, sure. One of them's badly injured and my bet is that it's the sister and there was no insurance to cover what happened.'

'You'd better see how last minute the booking was. The whole holiday thing might have been so they could swap and make a packet on the holiday insurance.'

'They'll be devastated, you know.'

'Sod that. It's their own fault. Let's tell Dean. It'll cheer him up.'

'No, wait. Let me tell him quietly. This is not going to make it better for Dean.'

Annie told Dean later in the morning, kept her voice low, dropped it into the conversation as though it were nothing. He received the news as routine.

'Sure, I knew you'd crack it, Annie.'

At lunchtime, she hurried home to be there before her father. The sight that greeted her as she opened the door stopped her in her tracks. It was so different it might have been the wrong flat. Mike and his wonder-workers had done their magic, but it was too much. The place was absurdly tidy, surfaces gleamed, uncomfortably like Mrs Latimer's work.

Not a dishcloth was out of place in the kitchen, not even a teaspoon by the sink. A bunch of flowers stood in a vase on the table. An antiseptic smell hung over everything.

Her father would think she'd gone mad. She grabbed the vase and rushed it through to the bedroom. The wardrobe doors not only shone, they shut. She thumped the vase down on the bedside table, and raced back to the kitchen to search the cupboards for coffee and cups. On impulse, she flung open a couple of cupboards and plucked random tins and jars out to stand on the work surface. Then she stopped herself. Hadn't she enough to worry about without manufacturing extras?

Annie saw her father's amazed double-take as he stepped inside, but unless he said anything about it, she would keep quiet and let him think what he liked.

They sat over coffee and the sandwiches she'd bought on her way home. 'They've confirmed it as Casey Lane,' he told her.

'That's quick.'

'Did you know she had a criminal record?'

She nodded. 'Why are you here, Dad? I mean, I know why you came, but why have you stayed? Why are you involved in the inquiry?'

He looked at her, surprised. 'I thought you'd worked it out, Annie. The way she died...'

It came at her in a rush. *There was nothing left of the body to ID.* 'What did they find of her after the fire? Exactly what?'

His gaze wouldn't meet hers. 'Just her lower legs.'

The picture in her mind showed a sunny day by the loch-side. 'But, Dad,' she pleaded, 'they can't be linked.'

'It's so hard to tell with fire. It destroys so much. But you see ... The accelerant was an unusual mixture.'

'But was the other body burnt? The one in the loch? Have you found the rest of it?'

He nodded, but said nothing.

A memory came to her. The suffocating smell of the aftermath of fire; the acrid odour that seeped through all attempts to disguise it. A killer had tried to burn her mother. The fire had barely touched her, but the sickly-bitter tang filled her nostrils from two decades ago. She saw her own thin child's arms, almost doll-like, reach out towards the lifesize but lifeless form in the coffin. Strong hands clasped themselves round hers, dragged her back. *No, no. Let me. I need ... I need ...* The memory snapped, fractured. She was back at her kitchen table watching her father who sat, eyes lowered, waiting for his wayward daughter to demand the detail of what he'd found.

She mustn't force these twenty-year-old echoes of violence and estrangement on him; didn't want to face them herself.

'I suppose I shouldn't ask you for any detail.'

He looked relieved, but surprised as though he expected her to demand information from him. She didn't need to. If they'd found the rest of the body, her aunt would have all the detail she needed.

'Dad, you know about Casey and Dean. It's been hard for him, especially that we know so little. Is there anything I can tell him? How she died, for instance? Anything's better than not knowing and ... well, it's awful to think that she might have burnt to death.'

'I'm sorry, I can't help you. I only wish we knew. With just the lower legs to go on, it's all speculation.'

After she saw him off, Annie sat back down to take a moment to herself before she went back to the office. It was time to look face on at the fact that Dean had been right all along. He knew the connection went from Casey alive, through the work of the firm, to Casey murdered. He just hadn't worked out what, but Annie had. Had her father worked it out too? On some level he must have, but maybe he couldn't bear to face it.

Her skin tingled as invisible mites crawled over her body.

Casey hurrying off to Annie's meeting, in Annie's coat, under a hat that hid her face. It was no random killing. The killer knew just who he was after, but in the rain and the dark, he'd hit the wrong target.

CHAPTER TWENTY

Annie made her way back to the office. Casey's photo had been in the paper today. If the killer hadn't realized his mistake the moment he'd attacked and killed her, he would know now. Her gaze darted left and right, a wary eye on every face in the crowd.

Dad, I've got bad news.

She arrived at the office knowing she couldn't share this. Not yet. How could she tell Dean that it was her fault Casey died? She could only make amends if she could find answers for him, and to do that she needed his skills.

Whatever the strand that led from the loch-side to a deserted warehouse near the Thames, it was a tenuous one. There was only one place she knew where the trail might be picked up. The overwhelming temptation was to hand it all on to her father and let him mobilize official channels, but she couldn't give him enough to stop the real evidence being spirited away, whatever and wherever it was. She needed more, something solid, to put in front of officialdom.

Dean gave her a sideways glance. She returned it with a quick look, unsmiling, a jerk of her head, as she strode towards the bank of filing cabinets. He leapt to his feet and scurried after her. 'You've found something, Annie?'

A curt nod. 'I've found the case, but I've no hard evidence. That's what we're going after and the minute we find it ... the second ... we take it to the official inquiry. OK?'

'OK. What are we after?'

'I want a proper look at some electronic files that I don't think I'll get legitimate access to. I need your help.'

The smile he gave her was the first she'd seen on his face since Casey died. This was back inside his comfort zone where logic held sway and targets bled silicon.

Dean looked at the paperwork she lifted from the drawer. 'That wasn't one of Casey's.'

'No, I know, but it's the one that'll give us the answers, trust me.'

She set the file on her desk where Dean picked it up and flicked through, his mouth slightly open as he puzzled over the notes in the case folder labelled Charlotte Grainger.

As soon as she reached home that evening, Annie rang the guesthouse. Her aunt's grapevine might not give her the contents of the forensic reports, but she'd get close to a full story.

The clack-clack of Mrs Watson's footsteps receded as she stalked off to get Aunt Marian. Annie heard them return together, voices an indistinct buzz that cleared to individual words as they neared the phone. She heard her aunt say, 'Annie's father told me how busy she was, but I knew she'd find time to call.'

At once, a rubber-stamp slammed down on her forehead, *Ungrateful Niece of the Year* blazoned for all to see.

She'd planned it as a quick call; even run through the excuse of a mock appointment to bring it to an end. Now she sat and batted the conversational ball back up to her aunt, and dredged her memory for things to say to show what an interest she took in the minutiae of life at Mrs Watson's. 'And how's that nephew of hers? Does he still call in at weekends?'

'Fancy you knowing Mrs Watson's nephew. When did you meet him?'

'You told me about him seeing ... uh ... the guy Charlotte hung about with. Remember? It gave him an alibi for the break-in.' And the murder.

'Oh yes. I do remember. Do you know, Annie, they wouldn't pay her for that whisky she lost. Isn't it a disgrace?'

As she murmured sympathy, Annie shook her head to clear an image of herself and Jak as they lolled in that awful room and toasted each other in what must have been Mrs Watson's good single malt. She *must* email her father about Dish.

'Any news on the leg in the loch?'

'Och yes, dear. It's terribly exciting. It definitely went in from just down the way. The police haven't said anything. You know how they are, but we all know. It fits the tides and the times. We've worked it out.'

'Yes, you told me before.'

'Just fancy, if we'd looked out of the window in the box room, we might have seen the killer.'

'Do you think he threw in the whole body?'

'That's rather' – Aunt Marian cleared her throat and spoke self-consciously – 'rather sexist, isn't it, dear? The killer might have been a woman.'

'Aunt Marian!'

'It's all right, dear. I've found out what it means.'

'I could have told you what it meant! I had that X on a triple-letter score. Anyway...' How did her aunt immerse everything in trivia and draw her in so easily? 'Yes, you're right, I suppose. So ... uh ... have you worked out if the rest of it will wash up?'

'Oh no. They've found the remains of a body in the forest. Burnt to ash. They haven't said, but one of Mrs Watson's nephew's friends who was staying over at...'

Annie covered the mouthpiece and took some deep breaths ... in and out. She wanted to dive in with questions, but her aunt would get to the point eventually, and it would be a fuller account for letting her get there in her own time. '...They haven't said, of course. You know what they're like, but we all know it was the body.'

'Where did they find it?'

'Up in the hills. It was all cordoned off. It was just the other week. The day you dropped me off here. Remember? You borrowed my tape recorder. The little one with earplugs.'

A chill rippled through Annie. She was back on that exposed hillside with the sun blazing down. She'd retreated under the trees for shade. And to wait. She remembered the aimless milling about of that group of people who prevented her going just where she wanted to go. They hadn't seemed to move one way or another. Orienteers, she'd thought. But no. They'd been securing a crime scene. Her father had been called out in such a rush he'd left papers out on his desk. If she'd waited, she'd have seen him arrive to join them.

She thought back to her odd encounter with Beth; later that day, her meeting with Jak, the way he'd blundered in with his unsubtle questions about Charlotte and the leg in the loch. Where had he tried next? He was the link, the one who'd made her a target. Anger was pointless. His body probably lay rotting in a basement somewhere and might never be found. Who'd notice when a drifter like Jak disappeared?

'Aunt Marian, was it the room Charlotte had been in that was ransacked in the break-in?'

'Yes, dear, of course it was. They were after those tapes.'

Her aunt had been right all along; the tapes had been the target of the thieves who struck here too.

Lorraine had witnessed a real murder. The body had been burnt to ash. And the leg that had been fished out of the loch had belonged to Charlotte's sister, Julia Lee.

Saturday morning, Annie arranged to meet Dean. She needed something solid, something her father could use. She couldn't rely on Margot handing over the tapes intact. What she needed was a look at Margot's client database.

She sketched out for Dean what she knew of Margot's operation.

'I'd need some unsupervised time with one of her networked machines,' Dean said, 'and I'd soon get everything off for you. I could probably plant a Trojan that'd email new data to you.'

'It's an open plan office with CCTV all over the place and it's busy, but let's give it a shot. If you can't get anything, see if you can figure out how I can do it if I get myself in there one night after hours.'

'How will you do that?'

'That's the other side of what we're after today. They run evening courses. Not Margot's outfit, but it means the building stays open and the ground floor's heaving with punters so there's some cover.'

'So you want timings, distances, camera blackspots, all that?'

She nodded. 'Everything we can get.'

Janice was surprised to see them, and put no warmth into her professional smile of welcome.

'Margot's not in today, Annie. I don't believe she was expecting you.'

'No, she wasn't. We were passing. I had a business proposition to put to her. Maybe there's someone else I could have a word with?'

'Take a seat; I'll see who's available.'

Annie slipped a gold-coloured hooped ear-ring from her pocket as she and Dean stepped towards the reception's seating area. As Janice turned away from them to speak into her phone, Dean sidled out into the corridor. Annie saw him head towards the open plan office. She sat briefly, just long enough to slip the ear-ring down the side of the chair, then stood again and moved over to the window where she was in Janice's peripheral vision, and feigned interest in the view over the city.

'Annie?' Janice looked up at her. 'Can you give me a rough idea what this is about?'

'Margot and I were talking about a security problem you'd had. Off-site, I mean, not here. It occurred to me that we might be able to help out with that sort of stuff. I know it doesn't happen often, but it's as well to be prepared.'

Janice spoke into the phone again, voice low.

Annie craned her neck as though to see some distant feature of the cityscape and wandered close to the back of the reception area. Through an open archway was a back entrance to the big office area next door. As she glanced in, she saw Dean deep in conversation with a woman sitting at one of the PCs. She couldn't hope for him to get at any data in that crowd, but he was clearly pulling out the stops.

'Annie.' Janice's voice grabbed her attention again. 'Do take a seat. Someone'll be along to have a word in a moment.'

'Thanks.'

'Where's your colleague?'

'Oh, he just nipped to the loo.' She saw suspicion flare in Janice's eye and gave her a smile.

Footsteps in the corridor. Annie turned to the entranceway

to see a mountain of a man stride in, tall, broad and solid muscle. He wore a uniform with discreet silver braid edging the lapels.

'Ms Raymond?' He held out his hand to engulf Annie's and give it a bone-crunching shake. 'I'm head of security here. I understand you have a security problem.'

'Not exactly.' She outlined her wafer-thin story, mentioned Charlotte and the conversation she'd had with Margot. 'We're experts in insurance fraud, and it struck me that with the work you do here, you need to be absolutely sure of your data integrity.'

The words meant nothing and he gave her a condescending smile.

'Annie?' Janice's voice cut across them. 'Your colleague's not back.'

'No worries. He's probably got talking to someone.'

Janice stalked out of the room and was back within a minute with Dean at her side. 'I'm sorry,' Annie heard her say, 'but we're very busy. If there's anything you want to know, you must make an appointment and we'll do our best to help you.'

That was that really. The uniformed man-mountain escorted them back to the lift, going as far as to reach in and press the ground floor button before giving them a curt 'Good day.'

Back downstairs, Annie collected brochures about the evening courses. She waited until they were across the road in the coffee shop before turning to Dean.

'Well? Any luck?'

'Too many people about to get at anything, but it's a piece of piss, Annie. Their whole system's geriatric. They've no security at all.'

'So if I can get in there on my own, you can give me the tools to do the job?'

'No sweat. It'll be a bit of a bull-in-china-shop job because they use bespoke software. I'll write you something that'll just trawl everything up, then we can sort it out when you get it back.'

'Does bull-in-china-shop mean it'll take longer?'

'Yeah, probably minutes rather than seconds. But if you can give me anything to narrow it, I can cut that down.'

'I want Charlotte Grainger's personnel records and the client files of someone called Lorraine.'

'OK, depends if the data's encrypted or not. If not ... quick sweep of the system ... copy ... thirty seconds tops.'

Thirty seconds? It seemed disproportionate to expend all the effort that would be needed just for thirty seconds.

'No way we could grab thirty seconds while the office is open? Some sort of diversion?'

'Not that I could see. Too many eyes in the place, not to mention cameras. Did you know they deal with the money from all the smaller outlets? Be great for money-laundering.'

'Or blackmail.'

'When are you going in? You'll need to practise to get these timings right.'

'Sooner the better. I shoved an old ear-ring down the side of one of their chairs. I want to use it as a reason to go back.'

'When?'

'Monday.'

Dean took a piece of paper from his pocket and began to sketch on it. Annie saw a plan of the office materialize with desks, camera sweeps and timing, shaded blindspots. With mixed feelings, she watched the blueprint emerge of her breaking and entry to Margot's offices.

On Monday morning, Annie sat with Mike in the kitchen. Her day was mapped out in intensive practice runs. The length of the flat from the front door to the back of the bedroom just gave her the requisite distance, and by tonight she must be stopwatch perfect and sure of sprinting it in a few seconds.

'Did I say I'd be late tonight?' she said, as Mike stood up and reached for his briefcase. 'Not sure what time.'

'D'you want a lift in?'

'No, I'm not going in till later.' She looked at the piece of toast in her hand and thought about Casey Lane, burnt to ash, and the body on the hill the same. 'Mike? What do you know about crematoria?'

'Not a lot, other than it's where they burn people.'

'Ah, but did you know that even a crematorium oven doesn't burn people to ash? They have machines to crush up what comes out of the furnace.'

'No, I didn't know that. How do you know?'

'I worked a case once where someone accused someone ... this woman ... well, the details don't matter. It was all to do with the guy being cremated with a ring on his finger. But the point is I'm sure you could get forensics off what comes out of a crematorium oven. I'll check it out.'

'Yeah right. What's this to do with anything?'

'Casey. You don't burn someone to ash in an ordinary fire. Nowhere near.'

And, she added to herself, you don't burn two people to ash in two ordinary fires at opposite ends of the country.

CHAPTER TWENTY ONE

'Annie? Hello. What can I do for you today?' Annie heard the hint of exasperation under the smooth professionalism of Janice's voice at the end of the phone.

'It's my ear-ring, Janice. I must have dropped it the other day when I was in your office. I've looked everywhere else and I know I was wearing it.'

'I'll ask the cleaners and if they've found it I'll let you know.'

'Uh ... could you have a quick look now? I was in that end seat talking to your security guy. I'm sure it must have slipped off then. Could you just have a quick look down the side of the seat?'

Annie heard Janice draw in a breath as she put the handset on the desk. After a moment, her voice was back in Annie's ear sounding surprised.

'Yes, it's there. A gold loop thing. I'll put it in the post for you.'

'No, I'll call round. I need it tonight.'

'I'm about to leave, Annie.'

'I'll be ten minutes, Janice. Less. I'm on my way.'

With that, she clicked off the phone and sat back with her coffee in the coffee shop just across the road from Margot's building and waited. She would give it another five minutes, wanting as many as possible of Margot's crew to have left without Janice giving up on her and shutting up shop. Crammed in one of her pockets was a long, flimsy shirt that would cover her from neck to knee and hide the clothes Janice would see her wearing. In the other was a balaclava with bank-robber style slits for eyes, nose and mouth. If she'd been sure of access, she'd have slipped in after they'd all left, but it would be too much to hope that lax security went as far as leaving the fourth floor open to anyone who wandered up there.

The ground floor lobby was a press of people waiting for the evening courses to start. Annie threaded her way through to the lifts, but a uniformed woman stopped her.

'No access to the higher floors.'

'I'm here to see Janice Craig. She's expecting me.'

The woman spoke into a walkie-talkie giving Annie an anxious moment that Janice might choose to come down. If she had, it would have been the end of the evening's task because the lifts had been switched to key access. She didn't like the feel of this heightened security.

Margot's floor was in semi-darkness but Annie could hear the muted conversations of the few people still around. Please God they were all packing up to leave. Surely Margot didn't run to a night shift.

She stood in the full glare of the camera in the corridor as it swung to face her and looked one way then the other as though not sure where to go as she counted its sweep. She must be aware of its exact position from now on whether she could see it or not.

She marched round the corner to see Janice sitting at her PC typing furiously.

'Ah, Annie. It's here.' Janice lifted an envelope from her desk, her tone undisguised irritation.

'Thanks, great.' Annie grabbed it and turned to go, but there were voices outside. People heading for the lift. She needed to be alone out there. She stopped and turned back.

'Uh ... Janice? Did that guy have a word with Margot about my idea?'

'I don't think so, Annie. He didn't see any mileage in it, I'm afraid.'

Sounds of the lift door clanking open.

'Oh well, never mind. Maybe I should have another word with Margot sometime.'

'Hmm, maybe.' Janice didn't look up from her screen but was now clearly closing things down.

The whine of the lift headed back down the building.

'OK, well, thanks. See you. Bye.'

Annie raced back out into the corridor and jabbed the lift call button. The camera was full on her now. Hurry up, lift, before anyone else comes along.

The lift arrived. She stepped inside, jammed her foot to the door to hold it open and counted the camera round. Three seconds to its next blind spot, then she hit the ground floor button and leapt back out.

Quick glance either way and she dodged round the side of the lift housing to cram herself into a tiny space between a tall pot plant and the wall.

The camera wouldn't see her here, but a late leaver might if they happened to glance the right way. In the six seconds the camera was trained on the other end of the corridor, Annie pulled out the flimsy shirt and slipped it on. Seventh second and she stood tight against the wall. Footsteps down the corridor. The lift whined. The last of the main lights were extinguished.

She stayed still, knowing she must wait long enough to be sure. But not too long. The count inside her head would slip out of phase with the camera.

At last, there was just the quiet hum of the building at night and the muted sound of traffic from far below.

Time to move. From here, on the forward sweep of the lens, she could outrun the camera and give herself from one to three seconds leeway once inside the big office space.

She pulled the dark balaclava down over her head and neck. If the camera caught a glimpse, it would show a masked intruder who looked nothing like the Annie Raymond it had filmed earlier.

Deep breath, a push off from the wall and she sprinted down the short stretch to the big office. Round the corner of the wall, she threw herself to the ground and slid under the nearest of the desks.

A moment now to get her breath and peer out to check how well the count in her head had kept pace with the camera in the room.

Not great. She ducked straight back down. Damn. Not sure now if the corridor camera had caught her or not. Keeping low, she moved between the desks to the back corner of the office where the cover was better.

She headed for the computer nearest the archway that led into Janice's office, a back way out should she need it.

Once in position, she reached up and pressed the on switch, making the PC above her hum into life. She kept her head low, all the time keeping up a mental count and checking the angle of the camera every now and then. The memory stick Dean had given her slotted smoothly into the USB port and she watched it fire up as a rapidly flashing pinpoint of blue light.

The office remained quiet but for the low hum of the building's life support – air conditioning, water systems, echoes through the wiring ducts. On the next camera cycle, she risked clicking on the monitor. It showed a standard login screen dead centre, and down in the corner Dean's rogue program played out below the software's security radar and showed her its progress.

It was at 53 seconds of an estimated total of 3 minutes and 20 seconds. Longer than Dean had predicted, but just two and a bit minutes to go. She clicked the monitor off again and crouched down to wait. Two counts in her head now, the camera sweep and the program countdown to zero.

The second count had decreased by less than half a minute when something jarred her to full alert.

A noise that didn't fit in with the mechanical breeze of the building at night. She strained to listen.

Pad ... pad ... pad...

Soft footsteps coming down the corridor outside the office.

She sank into herself, till her head was down beneath the desk, her cheek on the cool surface of the floor.

A mass of desk and chair legs spread out in front of her. A pseudo forest, not so neat as forestry planted pine. She could see the length of the room, right to the main entranceway at the far end.

Pad... pad... pad...

Routine patrol by the security guard. It had to be. He'd walk down the corridor and go on his way.

A sudden burst of static. A crackly voice over a two-way radio. '... not clear ... access violation ... less than a minute ... tagged record...'

The replies were murmured, the voice too low to hear at all. Pad ... pad ... pad...

Her insides turned to ice. They had electronic alarms on the files. Dean had underestimated them. She had to get out, but that soft padding of footsteps was in the main corridor barring her way.

She kept low, watching the short stretch of corridor visible through the entrance. If whoever-was-there went past, she'd creep out behind him and get away. If he stopped at the doorway, she would slide backwards towards the other entrance and slip through into Janice's office.

A pair of feet stepped into view and paused in the entranceway. She felt her eyes widen with the shock; the breath catch in her throat, as her stare glued itself to the muted red and black leather of the newcomer's shoes. They were familiar. She'd seen them before. But where? Who? They stayed still for a few seconds then advanced a couple of paces into the room.

She saw one leg step in front of the other. The bent knee came into view.

For a moment, she froze, mesmerized; lost the counts in her head. No idea where the cameras were or how close to finished Dean's program was.

Whoever was there was kneeling down to check the office the quickest way possible, along the floor under the forest of desk legs.

There was no way not to be seen. She snatched the memory stick from the machine and hurled herself towards the rear entrance.

She heard a gasp behind her, the scrambling of someone fighting to get to their feet and then pounding footsteps, crashing the desks out of the way, coming after her.

The hammering of feet obliterated everything from her consciousness as she swung round the corner to Janice's office. He was close. Too close. She fought through treacle; he flew behind her on speed.

A sudden vision flooded her mind. Car headlights, full beam, coming at her ... a crash barrier ... a handbrake turn. It was the same chase. The same pursuer.

The adrenalin of terror propelled her on. In a suicidal leap, she hurdled Janice's desk in an explosion of papers and wire trays. She was aware only of gaining the fraction of a second that was enough to evade the arm that reached out to grab her.

She skidded round into the corridor and dived for the staircase she'd never seen, could only sprint to where fire regulations said it had to be.

A red sign with an arrow. Fire exit. She threw every effort into reaching the top step. Seeing no further. Every sense felt her pursuer within a breath behind her.

With a heart-lurching brush of something at her shoulder, she leapt, five steps, six. Grabbing at the rail. Swinging herself into the corner. She hurled herself down the next flight almost taking the dozen or so steps in one desperate leap. Everything focused now on the task. Land softly, crumple legs and ankles, spring forward from the first limb that felt solid surface beneath it, relying on hands and arms to grab the rail, to take the strain when there was nothing solid beneath her feet.

The distance between them increased, but that was only because her pursuer thought her trapped in a dead end, and had slowed, not wanting to risk a broken bone.

And he'd thought he had her on the downward bend, the treacherous hairpin off the summit. She focused only on speed and balance.

Now she was at street level and there should be a corridor.

There was. She let her feet and ankles take back the load and sprinted. The footsteps behind her skidded round the corner. She heard panting breath coming closer now they were back on the flat.

Her eyes fought to make sense of the darkness up ahead. It couldn't be a dead-end. The fire-door had to be here.

The gleam of a bar. It was there. She threw herself at it wrenching the metal, feeling a tremendous rush flood through her as it gave way. She burst out into a mass of people, a bright glare. Balaclava ripped off, head ducked to avoid the inevitable camera. A vicious slam backwards to close the door.

'Sorry ... sorry ... beg your pardon ... excuse me...' In the first couple of seconds of her zigzag scuttle through the mass of bodies, the shirt was shrugged off her shoulders and back in her pocket.

In the density of the crowd, as she shoved through, head down, on a fast track to the exit, she took one quick glance backwards at the far wall. The top of the fire door remained shut. No one on the desk took any notice of her as she strolled past and out into the night.

Her heart thumped in her throat but her mouth curved to a smile of triumph. The memory stick was in her pocket. She'd made it.

Why hadn't her pursuer come through the fire-door or radioed the front desk to stop her? If it had been just a security guard doing his job, what stopped him at the edge of the crowd?

CHAPTER TWENTY TWO

Annie pushed open the door to her flat and marched inside with a feeling of relief, of refuge found.

Mike looked up surprised. 'I thought you were going to be late,' and Annie realized that robbing an old schoolfriend might have been a huge deal in her head, but hadn't made a blip on anyone else's radar.

'It didn't take as long as I'd thought.'

She emptied her pockets on to the table. The bundled old shirt went straight into the bin to be safely in a landfill site before there was the remotest chance of Margot seeing it in any context that connected it to Annie. With a smile, she clasped the memory stick in her hand and rubbed its casing as though for luck.

'What's that?' Mike asked.

'Just something I got for Dean.'

A part of her wanted to rush back out now to find Dean and pass it on. Let him get started, find out as soon as possible whether she had what she needed or if she'd ripped it free of the machine too soon. This would get him back into the swing of things, or so she hoped, because the business needed him at full throttle. It needed both of them back online full time. It was early days but Pieternel had got them round a corner. The business finances might yet stay afloat.

She looked across the table at Mike. If she allowed him to bail her out for just a few months, she could face her debts head on, go and talk to people, offer them deals the way you were supposed to when you found yourself in too deep. Maybe she should consult one of these debt counsellor outfits. Maybe she could pull herself and Aunt Marian back from the edge.

Had she let Mike into her life solely for his ability to drag her personal finances out of the shit? Would she have let him in anyway? She knew she wouldn't cut her aunt's lifeline by shoving him back out, but she wished she could be clearer about her motives.

The next morning, when she handed the memory stick to Dean, she told him she'd had to remove it before it had finished, and added, 'Whatever you find on it, I'm not touching it till the weekend so don't neglect anything to do it.'

'No worries. It won't take a minute to decode anyway.'

'How's the Buenos Aires case going?' she asked Pieternel, who gave her a wide grin.

'Unravelling beautifully. The sister, like you said. They're twins, and crossing continents made the swap all the easier. It looks like the biker was down to get a cut. We're coming up really smelling of roses on this one.'

'Poor Mrs BA.'

Annie threw herself into helping clear up the routine paperwork as penance for her recent neglect of the office. Dean too, she was pleased to see, took up the reins again, although several times during the day, she saw him frowning over his PC with an intensity that could only mean he was working on Margot's records. In a quiet moment she caught up with him.

'It's a hell of a mess, Annie. A kid in primary school could have hacked together a better database than they're using.'

'But can you get the information off it?'

'Probably. Thing is, it'll be riddled with errors. Theirs, not ours. Whoever put this together couldn't normalize a database to save their lives. I'll bet this software costs more to maintain than their whole hardware budget.'

'I doubt Margot cares. As long as the outfit looks good and keeps the money flowing, she's more interested in up-to-date carpets than backroom machines.'

'I'll have whatever's there to find by the end of the week, Annie.'

'That's great, thanks.'

Annie struggled to take on Casey's workload. Mike living in the flat didn't seem so much of a change. Their only bumpy patch was on Thursday morning when a crash from outside rushed them both to the kitchen window to see a heavy pickup truck sitting across Mike's car in an embrace that looked terminal for both vehicles. Annie had to leave him remonstrating with the other driver as she hurried in to work.

Mid-morning the same day provided her own heart-stopping moment when she picked up the phone and heard Janice's voice. 'Janice ... Hello. Uh ... what can I do for you?'

'Sorry to bother you, Annie. I just wanted to check something.'

Annie worked her tongue round her mouth to ease the dryness.

'When you were here on Monday did you see anyone in the office?'

'Uh ... no. Well, only you. I was only there for a minute. Why?'

'I don't want this going any further, Annie, but we had an intruder on Monday night.'

'Oh ... uh ... did you lose much?'

'No, luckily security were on to them before they had time to do much. Margot's desk was broken into. Otherwise, just a bit of damage, things thrown about.'

Margot's desk? But she'd been nowhere near Margot's office.

'Margot said to tell you they took the tapes you gave her.'

Annie's head spun. Had the guy who'd chased her gone back for the tapes? Was that why he hadn't come after her when she made it to a public space, or was Margot using the break-in as an excuse to be rid of them?

'Annie, did you leave the building straight away?'

She pulled in a breath. 'Uh ... more or less. I tried to find the loo downstairs before I went but it was so crowded I nipped across the road into a coffee shop instead.'

'And you didn't see anyone hanging about?'

'It was packed, Janice.'

'I meant upstairs.'

'No, I didn't see anyone except you.'

As she put the phone down, Annie let out a huge sigh of relief and scuttled across to find Dean and drag him to a quiet corner to go over every second of her excursion to Margot's. What might have been caught on camera? How closely would they check her out? Her theory that her pursuer had gone back for the tapes.

'Maybe that's why he didn't follow you out. He wanted time to go back and get at those tapes.'

'It's all fits together, Dean, but I haven't got enough yet. It isn't clear. That night in the car, the break-in at my place...'

'What night in the car?'

'Sorry, nothing. It doesn't matter for now. I need to get at whatever's in those files and then get all this lot back to my father. Will Margot connect it to me because of the tapes?'

'Why are you worried, Annie? You've done this stuff before.'

'Not to an old schoolfriend.'

Saturday dawned bright. Too bright. Annie wanted to see the days contracting. It hadn't been a summer to hang on to. Mike took advantage of the weekend and slept in.

She took the transcripts Dean had given her and spread them over the table. His program had found nothing on Charlotte Grainger, employee. He didn't think it was because she'd snatched the drive before it had finished its trawl, he guessed there were no electronic staff records on the networked system. There were several Charlottes from Margot's client list, but Annie discounted them. It was Lorraine she was after.

She read through the fragmented data.

'Look at all the crap, Annie,' he'd said. 'Typos, mistakes, and all just sitting there. It'll look OK on their screens, all banged out in neat boxes to make it look something like. Seeing it raw like this shows up the crap.'

The name Lorraine cropped up dozens of times in four different spellings.

'Three different surnames and three addresses, but if I've decoded the date of birth right, then there are four of them.'

'And the rest?'

'Spurious duplicates, typos, data entry errors.'

Annie sat now with the transcripts in front of her and redid Dean's calculations. It was tedious, but important she got it right.

By the afternoon she had distilled the data to two possible records. At thirty-five and forty they were both older than she'd estimated from the scratchy voice on the tape.

She signalled Mike to be quiet as she picked up the phone and put on her call-centre telesales pitch for the thirty-five year old Lorraine.

The voice she spoke to had no resonance with the tones she remembered. Mike gave her a quizzical look as she chirruped, 'Thank you for your time. Have a nice day,' and put the phone down.

He busied himself rinsing cups at the sink and she told him briefly what she was doing. 'I'm not sure what she'll be able to tell me but I know she's the link back to why Casey died. But I don't know anything for certain, Mike. I'm trying to figure it out.'

'Shouldn't you go straight to your father with all this?'

'Believe me, I intend to, just as soon as I have something concrete to give him.'

'How will you tell if it's her?'

'The tapes weren't great quality, but I think I'll know her voice.'

'What will you do when you find her?'

'Get her to agree to talk to someone.'

Mike sat at the table and watched as she punched out the number.

'Hello...' The voice that answered was low, rich... A shiver speared Annie from head to toe.

'Uh ... Hello...' She struggled with her script. 'I'm calling on behalf of—'

'Why, Annie...' The voice was smooth as chocolate silk. 'I wondered when you'd call. They told me you might. Why the phone, why not a visit?'

'Uh ... I ... uh...' Annie fought for control. This woman couldn't know anything. She'd known Annie's voice – never mind how – and was fishing for how much Annie knew. That was all. Maybe Margot had guessed more about Monday night than she realized. Whatever, she'd blagged her way through that and she'd do it now.

'I don't have an address,' she said. 'Just have a piece of paper with a name and a number.'

'And what does the name say?' the voice purred, trying to caress her as though seeing inside her soul.

'Just Lorraine.' She kept her voice clipped and clinical.

No doubts that this was the voice on the tape, but without the fear. This was Lorraine in control. 'Let's meet, Annie. I'd like to see you again.'

Again?

'Yes, I'd like to. Where can we meet?'

Lorraine's laugh was light and velvet. 'We'll meet, Annie. Somewhere nicely public where we'll both feel safe and secure.' She named a coffee bar near Kings Cross Station. 'Shall we say an hour?'

'Can we say two hours? I can't get to King's Cross in an hour...' Automatically, Annie played for time.

'Then you'll miss me, won't you?' The voice flowed seamlessly into the click of the receiver going down, and the buzz of the dialling tone.

CHAPTER TWENTY THREE

Annie leapt to her feet and grabbed Mike's arm. 'Come on, hurry. We've got to get to her before she runs.'

'Who? Where?'

'Lorraine. She might believe I don't know where she lives. We've got to try. Brackenbury village. We can make it if we hurry. Come on. Get your shoes on.'

'But you said King's Cross.'

'She'll have been on to someone to get a reception party organized, but it won't be Lorraine waiting for us there.' She took in a deep breath. It wasn't Mike she needed. This was no routine surveillance. She needed experience. Dean or Pieternel. A pain stabbed her as she thought of Casey. It was Casey she needed for a job like this. But they must be on Lorraine's doorstep in minutes, had to catch her before she ran. No matter how in control she'd sounded, she wouldn't wait around for Annie to find her.

She leapt down the stairs. Every second was vital now. Mike could drop her at the end of Lorraine's street and— 'Hellfire!'

'What is it?' he panted from behind her.

'No car. We haven't got a damned car between us. Come on. We can still do it.'

Annie tried to talk Mike through what might happen as they ran towards the Tube station, but it was difficult to say anything useful. It would be play the hand as it was dealt and rely on experience to get it right. But Mike didn't have the experience. Her instinct told her Lorraine had been alone. She could only hope they could get there before anyone else, because her instinct told her two more things. Lorraine was the key to something far more than Casey's death and if she didn't confront her now, she would never find her again.

It was a quiet, tree-lined suburban street. Big houses stood back from the road in well-tended plots that said money in a clear, but understated way.

'If she knows my voice,' Annie told Mike. 'She might know my face.'

'But how does she know you?'

'I've no idea, but we can't risk walking past. If I can see a way in, you're to wait out here. Try not to be conspicuous. Look as though you're just waiting for someone.'

'Leave you to go on your own?'

'Yes.' She shot him a look that dared him to try to overrule her.

He shrugged. 'You weren't thinking of breaking in, were you?'

'Round here? No way. They're all alarmed to the hilt. Right, it's that one up ahead with the tall hedge. Slow down a bit. I can't see any way to get to the door without being seen. But look at the house next door.' She tipped her head towards the professional lettering on the discreet board at its gate. 'Corporate, not residential. With luck, that means empty at weekends. I'm going to chance it through their garden. Wait here, but don't stand where you can be seen from the house. And don't stare after me.'

Annie sensed reluctance in every move as Mike turned away and made play of checking his watch, but he did as she asked. She marched up the gravelled driveway. A high wall hid the houses from each other. The building itself would be impregnable, she was sure, but that was fine. All she needed was access to its garden.

The breeze rustled the leaves high above her as she approached the house. Alarms bristled from the tall stone frontage, but there were no cameras. The closed blinds at the windows were reassuring. Once the curve in the drive shielded her from the road, she veered off and made her way down a narrow, overgrown pathway beside the house.

The rear aspect of the house was as inattentive to her presence as the front. Her feet crunched softly in a carpet of twigs. A row of spindly trees stood subservient to the cityscape around them. She strode through the undergrowth, keeping to the shadow, heading for a thick creeper that smothered the wall between this garden and Lorraine's.

The stones wore a thick ivy coat. This creeper would suck the life from the wall if it wasn't cut back. She hoped it wasn't too close to collapse as she pulled on her gloves and took a good grip on the thicker stalks high up the wall.

This had to be done in one quick move. She might be visible from the top of the wall so had to trust to luck to give her a soft landing. The creeper stayed firm as she hoisted herself up and then flattened herself into a sideways roll over the top. She experienced a moment's panic as she clawed at ivy that wasn't there the other side, then landed hard on her back.

She pressed herself close to a sagging remains of a wooden trellis and spat out the mouthful of dust the creeper had given her. Keeping low, she peered round into the garden. It was the weirdest she'd ever seen. The ground was wooden decking and manufactured stone slabs. Cast-iron trellises and tall gazebos grew from it. Plant life was restricted to a couple of exotic shrubs that drooped from fancy pots like sad prisoners in an alien world.

Tall trees from the neighbouring gardens flew branches out over the sterile iron and woodwork. Annie saw that the dancing shadows were allies. They would shield her movement as she skipped lightly round the edge of the space. A quick recce of the windows showed no one in sight.

She ran, dodging the obstacles, dancing in time to the shadows, until she could press herself to the side of the house and edge along to take a proper look through the French windows.

The room was large, but dark. It held no conventional furniture, just statues and tall sculptures of snakelike animals.

She tried the handle and felt it give under her hand. Heart thumping, she eased the door open and slipped inside.

Footsteps padded from within the house, heading her way. Annie sped across the floor and crammed herself behind a gargoyle figure.

The door opened. A woman stalked in.

Annie saw the mass of red hair, a tiny form where she'd expected a tall one.

'Hello, Lorraine.'

The woman spun round, fury and fear blazing in her eyes. The fear came at Annie too. It came fast, stabbed her before she could put up a defence. She couldn't pretend, knew that the raw emotion sat naked on her face. All her planned words deserted her. She could only stare, and whisper, 'Who are you? Who are you?' as the intense blue eyes glared at her from within the frame of deep red curls.

'You are in so much trouble, Annie Raymond.'

'Lorraine?'

Lorraine tipped her head in a couldn't-care-less gesture, then turned on her heel and stalked out of the room.

Annie leapt after her, keeping close behind. Her gaze flew everywhere, noting the doors, the stairs, searching for hidden watchers.

The room where Lorraine led her was more conventionally furnished, with high-backed chairs and settees. The floor was polished wood. No carpet. No rugs.

Lorraine sat at one end of a long settee. After a moment's hesitation, Annie perched at the other end. Lorraine settled back, pushed her hair off her face and said, 'Well?'

'I want you to come with me. To make a statement.'

'A statement?'

'I heard the tapes, Lorraine.'

'The tapes are gone now, aren't they?'

'Yes, probably.'

'Burnt up in Charlotte's car.'

Annie tried not to look shocked at Lorraine's matter-of-factness.

'Anyway, it was all a dream.' Lorraine's tone was disinterested, and didn't even try to convince.

'No, Lorraine. It wasn't. They found a body. Just where you said.'

'Burnt, was it?'

Annie felt control of the situation leaking away. She'd expected Lorraine to play at being an innocent witness at the very least. 'You must know it was or you wouldn't ask.'

Lorraine turned to her with a smile and leant forward. 'Does it matter, Annie?' Her blue eyes stared deep into Annie's as though they saw inside her soul. 'Remember, Annie. Remember?' Lorraine leant closer.

Annie heard her own voice say 'Yes...' She felt emotions stir. Recognition, deep inside. 'Yes, it's...' She could reach out for ... something ... It was there, within reach. One more second and she would see her mother's face.

'No!' Shocked, Annie drew back and stared at Lorraine.

'Yes, Annie. Remember the chants. So beautiful.' Lorraine's voice was faraway now, not trying to capture Annie any more, talking to herself. What was she saying? Why did it resonate?

Then Annie saw it in the deep colour of her eyes, in the shape of her head. 'My God, the Doll Makers! You're Beth's mother. You're Ellie.'

And something more powerful overwhelmed her. A presence seemed to stand by Lorraine, a laughing figure that almost turned its head her way. 'My mother!' she cried out. 'What happened to my mother?'

This woman sitting near her held the key to her memories, but showed no emotion at Annie's outburst, no sign she even heard it. If her mother were alive, Annie knew she'd be here next to this woman. Next to Lorraine, not Annie, but Annie would see her face.

'My name is Elora.' Lorraine spoke with a smile and head held high, saying the name proudly. 'I took Lorraine just to create a distance, but I never changed my face, only my label. Wouldn't you have done the same? We didn't want to be the mad children of the mad old man forever.'

That's just what you are, thought Annie. The mad child of the mad old man. Lorraine was completely off her head. No reaction at all to the mention of her daughter. Just pride in her name.

And Annie sat here allowing herself to be pulled in.

'Elora? That's an unusual name.' She softened her voice, tried to find a connection with Lorraine that she could use.

Lorraine's face relaxed into a smile. 'It's a beautiful name, Annie, and it was a beautiful life. I didn't spoil it. He was never the mad old man, you know. You do know that, don't you, Annie?'

'Yes, of course I know.' Annie made her voice drip with understanding, with a secret shared. Lorraine was off with the fairies. She hadn't a clue how to handle her, she could only try to steer and hope for the best.

'And he never had three mad children, whatever they say.' Lorraine laughed. 'Only one. He shouldn't have done it. Remember the chants, Annie?'

'Elora?' she said gently. 'Why did you go to the edge of the forest the day you met Julia Lee?'

'I went to meet her. She asked.'

'Why did she ask for you?'

'She said she trusted me because I got away.' Lorraine laughed and threw her head back so the red hair bounced around her face. 'She boasted to me what she knew, what she'd seen.'

'What had she seen, Elora?'

Lorraine looked up, her eyes focused beyond Annie as though she'd stopped listening. Annie tried again, placing her words carefully, trying to catch Lorraine's mood. 'But when, Elora? Julia wasn't important enough to see anything.'

'She was in the van when they had to run and hide.'

'The van?'

'They should have left her in it when they burnt it.'

'The van the police were after? Julia was involved in that? But who did she try to blackmail and why did you go to meet her, Elora?'

'He made me.'

'Who made you, Elora?'

'I was the only one she'd trust. She told me I wouldn't betray her. She had no right to tell me what to do. The silly girl had a plan. When I gave her the money she said she'd get a car and push it off the top of Hell's Glen to make out she'd died.'

'Whose body did she intend to put in the car?'

'No one's. I told you it was a silly plan. She didn't even have a car.'

Without knowing the detail, Annie could feel the shape coming together. She could feel sorry for the wreck who had been Julia Lee, who'd fallen over something she thought she could use for blackmail, maybe to set up her and her sister for life. Instead, they'd both died.

'But Julia didn't get off the hill, did she, Elora?'

'I didn't know he'd kill her. Not there and then.' Lorraine shuddered. 'So messy! He would have killed me too. Me! He had no right.'

'He thought you'd just walk away, didn't he? He didn't know you'd come back and see what he'd done.'

'He had no right. I go where I choose.'

'You ended up in the hospital, didn't you, Elora?'

'I didn't talk to anyone.'

'Not even Charlotte?'

'She came to see me. Just like you. And he'll kill you just like he killed them.'

'Why didn't he kill you later, Elora? He found you again, didn't he?'

'Of course he wouldn't kill me.'

'Who was it, Elora?'

Lorraine gave a deep chuckle as though they shared a joke. 'The supplanter, of course.'

Annie stifled a sigh. She must keep a grip on what was important. Forget the rest. Lorraine knew the killer. Annie must get her away from here.

'You do remember the chant, don't you, Annie?'

Annie smiled, her priority to humour the mad woman. 'Yes, of course.' A tendril of fear snaked round her as she spoke. She *did* remember the chant. Lorraine meant the building-with-eyes. 'Crowds,' she whispered. 'I hated the crowds. They scared me silly.'

'You didn't see the crowds,' Lorraine snapped. 'You were too young.'

'But I remember...'

'You don't.'

Annie pulled herself up. 'Please come with me now, Elora.'

'Where, Annie? We can't go back. It's all gone. Ruined. The chant was sacred. He had no right. It's all rotten. Of course it is. What did you expect?'

'Then it's time to put it right.'

Time pressed on her. She didn't want to try to force Lorraine, though with Mike's help she might be able to.

'OK,' Lorraine stood up. 'Let's go.'

Annie jumped to her feet to get Lorraine out of the house before she changed her mind.

They left through the front door. Annie saw Mike across the road and jerked her head to beckon him over.

'Elora and I are old friends.' She took Lorraine's arm and gave Mike a warning look over the mad woman's head. 'Just walk along behind us. We're going down to the station and we'll pick up a cab.'

Lorraine walked beside her, serene. Annie was on edge, wanting more distance between them and the house.

'There,' said Lorraine's voice, laden with self-righteousness. 'I told you...'

Before the speech was half over, instinct had Annie throw herself towards the ground, trying to say something, anything, to warn Mike. She pulled in a breath that seemed never to end, as she turned and ducked ... not knowing what was coming ... where from...

Mike's face was briefly in her line of sight. Shock drained the colour from him. He jerked forward convulsively. She saw the white of his shirt as his jacket billowed open. A red stain erupted.

No!

'Mike! Oh God, Mike...'

She half reached for him. 'Go ... Annie ... They don't know...'

He'd been behind them. He hadn't been the target. If she attached herself to him, she invited the killer to finish him off. She had to run, to get away. But what if he were dying?

Get clear, draw the killer away.

She half ran, half scrambled to the nearest gate and crashed through it, sprinting for the side of another of the big houses. Praying her way wouldn't be barred by gates and unscalable walls, she clambered through bushes, over fences, feeling her clothes tear, the blood run as something sharp scraped down the side of her face.

She reached another road and ran along it, scrabbling her phone from her pocket as she went, diving down the first side street she came to, risking a fraction of a second as she turned the corner to glance at the numbers, to get her finger to stab out 999. Off the road again and forcing her way through back yards and between rusted carcasses of cars.

The voice in her ear was painfully slow, asking questions. 'Ambulance. Police,' she panted out as loudly as she dare.

The voice wanted her name, her number. 'No time. Just listen...' She saw the dead-end up ahead, saw which wall she must climb. It was high.

'A man's been shot.' She gabbled out the name of Lorraine's street. 'Hurry, please. He's badly injured.' Please God that wasn't true. She had to shove the phone back in her pocket, no time even to close the call.

The wall was hard to climb, high and exposed at its summit. She dropped to the ground and ran. More streets, more dusty yards. The light was fading now. The darkness came in to hide her. In the corner of a narrow alleyway, she allowed herself to stop.

She'd heard no screams, no shouting, no sounds of pursuit, but there'd be screams from her right now if she didn't stop thinking about Mike.

'I had to leave you,' she whispered. 'Please understand.'

The police would be out in force, even without her call. No one could fire shots in an area like that and not have the law out. Was it confidence or insanity to risk trying to shoot her like that? Or was it desperation?

Had she got away?

Keep moving. Don't risk him catching up with her. She'd have left a visible trail of broken branches and outraged householders behind her. She must find her way to the lock-up and get her car. She daren't go anywhere near the flat.

Her clothes were filthy and ripped. The people she passed looked away, changed direction to avoid coming close.

If she could only reach the safety of the lock-up, she could let her guard down enough to think. Whoever was behind her, couldn't allow her to live, not now she'd talked to mad Lorraine. But until she got to her father and told him what she knew, she mustn't trust anyone. Even he would have trouble with it, but he'd believe her. He'd mobilize the right teams, find Mike for her. Tears threatened as she replayed the ashen disbelief on Mike's face, the convulsive forward jerk, the sudden eruption of blood that soaked his shirt front.

'I had to leave you.'

Hours later, she made it to the familiar row of garages. An uncontrollable tremble jangled the keys in her hand. She had to hold one hand with the other to get the key in the lock, then grunted with the effort of lifting the door. She slipped inside where the darkness engulfed her as she squeezed down beside the car as far from the world as possible. It didn't matter she couldn't see. The light on her phone was all she needed.

She reached into her jacket pocket. Other pocket ... trouser pockets ... The slow fall into the relief of safety became a frantic scramble. She pushed back past the car, wrenched the door wide, pulled pockets inside out. On hands and knees she searched the floor. Where was her phone? She thought back to the way she'd rammed it into her pocket as she'd thrown herself at that high wall. Wherever she'd dropped it, it was out of reach now.

No. Not her phone. Tears splashed down. She looked at the backs of the houses that edged the alley. Could she walk up to someone's door at this time of night and ask to use the phone? Emergency. It's an emergency, she'd say. She leant back into the garage and looked at her reflection in the car window. Even the blurred and indistinct image looked hopelessly disreputable. She might find someone who'd let her in, but for every one she found, there'd be others who'd slam the door on her and ring the police. How close was her pursuer? No one must find her before she got to her father.

She pulled herself upright, wouldn't give in. No one knew where she was. If she couldn't contact him from here, she'd go and find a pay phone, find him if necessary.

What chance the car? She got in, pushed the key home and turned it. The engine wheezed, but turned. She'd heard worse from it on cold mornings. She tried again and it fired. The machinery coughed, and so did Annie as fumes filled the tiny space. Mustn't gas herself now, that would be giving it to them on a plate. She got out and opened up the door properly. The engine behind her rattled, but kept ticking over. If the car could still function, so could she.

Run fast and far, that was the rule when you'd almost been caught. She wouldn't try to make it all the way home, but she'd get as far as she dared, put at least a couple of hours driving between her and the madman.

She avoided the main routes out of the city, but joined the motorway as soon as she could. Fastest route out.

Disordered images kaleidoscoped through her head. One face showed a grinning assassin, staring right at her. The grin fragmented as the kaleidoscope turned. It became Aunt Marian waggling a finger, 'You know, dear, it was very silly of you.' Spin to Mike. Now it was Mike who fragmented not the image. Blood gushed from Julia Lee's chest. A hand pulled a knife. A face she couldn't see. Her mother approached her from behind, held out the doll.

'Concentrate!' she told herself, feeling a desperation to be back home with her father where all this had started, the only place she could lay the ghosts to rest. *Dad, it's bad news.* And then to Mike, 'I had to leave. He'd have finished you off and got me too. If I could have stayed to help you, I would. If I've lost you forever, please understand...'

It was almost 5 a.m. when she pulled into Tibshelf services. Even at this hour, there were enough people about to hide her, and payphones to take her to her father. Phone first, then coffee to keep her awake as she completed the journey.

She listened to the ringing of her father's phone and braced herself to speak calmly when he answered. Tears threatened. She was afraid she wouldn't be able to stop them when she heard his voice.

The phone rang ... and rang ... and eventually the answer-phone cut in.

She hadn't expected this. She needed him to be there. How could he sleep so deeply? She put the phone down and rang again. Again it rang itself through to the machine. How did she begin to tell him what had happened in an answer phone message?

'Hi Dad, it's Annie. I need to speak to you. I'll ring later. It's ... uh ... it's urgent.' Of course it was urgent at this hour.

Next, she rang the flat, praying her call would be answered, that she'd hear Mike's voice. If he picked up, nothing would stop the tears, but he didn't. She rang again and hit the button for remote access to the answer-phone.

One new message. Mike! Please let it be Mike ringing to say he was OK.

'Annie? You there, Annie?' Jak! She was so surprised, she almost dropped the handset.

His voice slurred, drunk. 'The bastards came after me, Annie. I thought it was you at first. They'll have gone for you too. I got away. Did you get away, Annie? Cos if you did, I've got something for you. You won't believe how close we got. Call me, Annie. I'll show you.'

Pause. Don't hang up, Jak, her mind screamed. Leave a number. She couldn't do 1471 remotely.

'Uh ... call me on...' The number came out in fits and starts as though he read from small print in a badly lit room.

She'd lost Lorraine, but fate had given her Jak. Now she was running with real purpose, a real goal. Mustn't do anything rash. She must deliver Jak to her father. But where was he? She had to find him first.

The phone was answered at the second ring. 'Yeah?'

'Jak? Is that you?'

'Annie! Where are you?' She heard panic in his voice. He was terrified and desperate for her help.

'My God, Jak, I thought you must be dead.'

'Where are you, Annie?'

beep beep beep

Christ! It wanted more money already. She scrabbled for change. 'Hang on, Jak, I'm in a payphone. There ... right. Tell me quick. What have you found?'

'Annie, where are you?'

'Never mind that, Jak. I haven't got much change left. Just tell me. Quickly.' His total bewilderment leaked down the line.

'Come and meet me, Annie. Can you get to Dish's? How quick can you be there?'

beep beep beep

She agonized as she pushed more coins into the slot. What to do? Dish's? No, she wouldn't meet him at that sordid basement but the suggestion had lifted a weight. He was still north of the border. Near her father's. She'd collect him on the way home.

'Not Dish's, Jak. Meet me off the ferry. I'll be there in ... about ... I'll be on the nine-thirty ferry. Meet me at Hunter's Quay.' It was automatic to stretch the time, to make out she wouldn't be in Glasgow before nine. Play for time. She'd be there by eight, but someone might be watching Jak. They'd tried to get him once. 'Is that OK, Jak? You'll be there, won't you? I've no more change when this runs out.'

She felt slightly sick at the thought of introducing Jak to her father.

CHAPTER TWENTY FOUR

When the car juddered and stalled at a red traffic light in the centre of Glasgow, it took Annie whole minutes to realize it had coughed its last. Continued tries with the key produced a dry whine with no glimmer of a spark. She became a temporary island in a flow of moving traffic.

She jumped out, put her shoulder to the door pillar and heaved the car across to a gravelled square of waste ground.

It wasn't far to the ferry docks. She set off at a jog. At just after eight on Sunday morning, the city had a relaxed feel. Cars sped past her, just another early morning jogger. The city absorbed her as one of its own, but the smell of the sea air deceived her. It blew a long way into the city, and mixed with the sickly tang of unburnt fuel. This wasn't a route she'd done on foot before and it was further than she realized. She had to slow to a walk long before the Caledonian MacBrayne dock came in reach. In the car, she'd have driven past and gone on to the Western terminal, but why bother? The first Sunday run was due out. If anyone had outflanked her and got this far, they'd watch for her on a Western ferry. Anyone watching Jak would expect her the other side at ten-ish. This way, she'd be there first, on the wrong boat, and watching for them.

An hour later found her the other side of the estuary, puffing for breath as she climbed the steep hill above Hunter's Quay. There was no point in side-stepping the trap only to walk back into it from behind. The air blew fresher this side. She would sit well out of the way and watch for Jak, sure that he'd come strolling along, hands in pockets just before ten, without a thought for discretion. Annie wouldn't approach him until sure he hadn't a trail of hidden followers.

Her legs protested the climb so soon after her jog through Glasgow and on top of a night without sleep.

She stopped abruptly, and drew back into the shade of a house wall. There was Jak leaning over a wall further along. He had binoculars to his eyes and was watching the ferry terminal. He'd been frightened out of his own sense of self to be this cautious, an hour early and well back from the action.

The outline of his slim profile roused uncomfortable memories, but now Jak was the chance she'd let slip when Lorraine got away. If Mike were ... if he were dead ... it mustn't be for nothing. She must get Jak to her father.

Something held Jak's attention down by the water. Annie moved nearer.

His binoculars were trained on a car down by the dock parked back from the designated parking. Without the benefit of a magnified view, she could see no detail, but didn't need it. A shock ran through her. Someone was down there waiting for her.

Thank God Jak had spotted them and she had found him. They were within touching distance of safety. Just one last short journey across the mountain. She was prepared to steal a car to do it. And they must move now, before the next ferry came in and planted a seed of suspicion.

She walked down towards Jak and spoke his name as she approached. He whirled round to face her, his expression first blank, then shocked. He half-pointed with the binoculars, then laughed. It was close to hysteria.

'Jak.' Annie put her hand on his arm. 'Come on. We've got to get away from here.'

'They're waiting for you, Annie. D'you want to nip down and say hello?'

'Don't even joke about it. Come on. We have to go to my father's. We'll need a car.'

'Where's your car?'

'Broke down in Glasgow.'

'How did you get across?'

'Cal-Mac. Foot-passenger.'

210

He laughed 'I thought I'd no chance when I saw that lot waiting. Come on, Annie.' He reached back and took her arm to help her along. 'You look knackered.'

'I am. I couldn't make it on foot, Jak. We really need to get a car. I suppose if we make our way round, we can get a taxi from—'

'No need. I've got a car.'

'You've got a car?'

'Sure. Borrowed it off Dish. It's on the top road.'

'Dish has a car?'

'You hungry? Thirsty? Don't collapse now, Annie.'

'Starving, but it can wait. It can all wait till we get across the mountain. Got enough petrol?'

'Sure. There's cake and stuff in the car. Bottle of cola. You look wiped out.'

The elderly two-litre saloon sat on the grass at the side of the top road. Annie knew as she looked at it, it wasn't credible. Dish wouldn't have a car. It must be stolen. She didn't care. If it would take them across the mountain, nothing else mattered. She fell on to the passenger seat, as Jak climbed behind the wheel. 'In there.' He pointed to the glove compartment. Annie pulled out a crumpled paper bag and a plastic bottle. The bag contained the crushed remains of what had been cake. 'It's OK,' Jak told her. 'Just got mashed a bit in there.'

It tasted stale and dry, cheap cake he'd picked up from a bargain basement. She was hungry enough to eat it, but it dried her mouth like sawdust.

'What's this?' She held the plastic bottle up.

He twisted the key in the ignition and bumped the car back on to the road. 'Some sorta cola.'

She took a sip, and grimaced at the oversweet syrupy texture. It cleared her mouth of the powdery crumbs, but left a bitter aftertaste. 'C'mon, Jak. Tell me what you found. What did you mean we'd got close?'

'I'll do better than that: I'll show you.'

'No, Jak!' Impatience made her snap at him. 'No detours. Just tell me, then take me home.'

Suddenly, she felt too tired to fight about it, but it hardly mattered. The car sped in the right direction. They drove up into the forest where the trees surrounded them. The dark poles of the trunks blurred until they danced round the car. It was she and Jak who were still, the forest spun round and round. She'd just close her eyes, wouldn't sleep.

'Straight to my father's, Jak. No pissing about.'

'Don't pass out, Annie. Have some more of that.'

She reacted to the alarm in his voice, tried to say, it's OK, I'm only tired. The words wouldn't come. He pushed the bottle at her. The car swerved as he took his eyes off the road. She put the bottle to her lips and tipped her head back. A globule of syrupy slop caught in her throat, made her gag. She thought she'd throw the whole lot up again. The bottle slipped through her fingers and bounced on to the floor. She slumped back into the seat.

Jak's voice droned on at the edge of consciousness, telling her what he'd found, what he'd show her. *No, Jak. Take me home.* Tiredness hit like a shroud thrown over her head. She slept.

Annie woke into a new time of day, a different environment. She lay still and calm. Trees all around. Motionless now. Tall legs growing up to a rainbow awning. She could see every line and contour. Those who didn't know called it empty forest. Annie pitied them. They thought you could see all there was to see because the trees stood apart from each other. Of course, they couldn't. No one could see into the heart of the forest. Only Annie. Nothing could hide from her. She lay back on the seat and watched the world through the side window of the car. The trees nearest stood indifferent to her presence. Their barks leached colour back into the depths of the forest, snaking vines that carried the pictures of aliens in the wood to the scurrying wildlife that drew away. Straggly shrubs, imprisoned in the earth, had to stay and watch the people in the car, so cloaked themselves in invisibility.

I can see you all.

She pointed a finger and a small rodent scuttled away, trailing a rainbow wake of disturbance through the forest floor.

Annie knew one of the car doors was open, a blue-green draught curled round to tell her. She made a conscious decision to turn her head. Jak sat with his back to her, his legs outside the car. A bland grey presence, he hunched over cupped hands trying to light a match. A flame blazed, spearing crimson darts out into space. Acrid smoke floated in.

He glanced round at her, his silhouette leaving a grey ghost like the tail of a comet. She watched the cigarette at his lips, saw him draw deeply on it. 'You want to see this, Annie? Or d'you want to go straight on to your father's?'

Such a feeble, unimportant question, it was hardly worth her while to remember what it was all about. The leg in the loch. The bodies burnt to ash. Her mind ran lazily over the things he'd told her as she'd sunk into sleep on the climb into the mountain. Beyond him in the wood, the colours blended and flowed, parting so she could see inside the souls of every living thing. He was the least important of them all. She reached out and clicked the car door open, saw worry swirl in his eyes. What a fool. He hadn't a clue.

'Christ, you're not used to this are you, Annie?' The concern flowed from his voice. 'I only wanted to wake you up. Get you on the ball a bit more. You looked all in. We'll wait a bit. It won't be too late.'

She laughed at him. How pathetic with his silly panics and fears. She didn't need him. She hadn't needed the mad woman. What she needed to know was inside her, and the colours of the forest would tell her the rest. The life spirit of the trees snaked up to the canopy above, and down into the earth below her feet. All she need do was follow, use the power. She pulled herself out of the car. The uneven carpet of twigs and leaf mould tipped beneath her, made her stagger.

She heard him laugh at her. 'Annie, give over. A piss-up in a brewery's the only party you could join and not be noticed.'

He thought she didn't know where they were or what she had to do. Of course she knew. He'd driven up off the road above the Doll Makers' house, up into a clearing under the trees. Yes, she knew exactly where to go.

Her legs became steadier as she climbed towards the small brow. Jak climbed with her, his voice nagging all the way. 'Annie, you can't ... Annie, I can't help you if ... If they see you, Annie...'

As if she needed his help. As if she didn't know how to hide herself.

She reached the crest of the small hill and stopped. *Observe.* Time slowed. She held the branch of a tree and swayed with its rhythm. To anyone who watched, she'd be indistinguishable from the forest itself.

A knot of people, maybe half a dozen, made their way up the track, heads bowed, dark cloaks obscuring their features. In their wake the ground ripped and bled. Ahead of them the doors of the building-with-eyes stood open a crack, spilling darkness into the forest. Annie moved forward, steps panther-like, so in tune with the earth that no one could stop her. Now she could do whatever she wanted.

Jak's exasperated exclamation from beside her was an irritant to ignore. She was aware that he turned and headed back to the car. Fine.

She slid down on to the track, picked a short length of fallen branch from the ground and floated silently to the wall of the building-with-eyes. She blended into the noise of the forest. The people up ahead didn't turn. One of them dawdled, fell behind, fiddling with the material of the cloak. Annie moved on her panther legs. Silent sprint, grasp, twist, strike. The figure slumped with barely a huff of surprise. She dragged it round the back of the building, pulled off its cloak.

Hesitate. She felt a disapproving gaze. *Dad? Why are you watching me?*

She arranged the unconscious bundle in the recovery position and checked its vital signs. Sound asleep, but a good strong pulse.

See, Dad, I know what to do. Why didn't you see me when I was here before?

The cloak covered her. The mad woman was right. She remembered it all. Jak knew nothing. He'd have blundered in wearing a makeshift cape, not knowing that they counted.

The chant. Beautiful beyond dreaming. Terrifying. She slipped through the gap between the doors.

The chant was soft. Not enough people here yet. No crowd. She floated down the centre aisle, felt contempt for some cloaked figure off to the side feeling for the edges of the pews. The trick was not to look directly at the tiny bursts of light from the candles. They put darkness in the soul. Somewhere behind her a door banged. The darkness was complete.

It was good to be back.

CHAPTER TWENTY FIVE

Annie sauntered past indistinct silhouettes who sat still, heads bowed, cloaks rippling as a breeze crept in from outside. The chant, just a background hum now, would swell as the crowd added its voices one by one. It would rise to a wall of sound that ripped her off her feet, sent her screaming back into the shadows. *Mummy! Help me! Mummy!*

No Mummy to help her now. She was on her own.

Pictures grew as the fragments of memory came together. Elora ... head high, feet floating over the stone floor, the burnt smell of incense swirling around her. *I see the spirit of the earth.*

Look at her eyes, Mummy. Eyes like monsters' eyes?

Quiet, Annie!

I want to see the spirit of the earth, too, Mummy.

And so you shall ... drink this ... ... eat this ... ... breathe in deep, Annie.

Mummy! Help me! Mummy! Monsters chasing me.

Annie spun round, stared into the darkness to where the fiends would burst through with their claws and red eyes. Silence. No chant. Anger rose inside her, mushrooming suddenly out of the black earth, rearing up like a childhood monster. A feeble background hum. Was this all they could manage from the packed pews?

She marched to the nearest and grabbed the bowed figure by the shoulder to shake it out of its stupor. The shoulder she grabbed was so insubstantial, it collapsed under her grasp. A cloud of dust billowed up, something fell at her feet with a dull clatter. This abomination would produce nothing to swell the sound. She grabbed the next one. A broom handle propped scarecrow-like at the seat fell and a length of dark material slid to the floor with a whump that puffed more dust into Annie's face. It must have been there years. What right, Elora? What right had anyone to desecrate the chant with an old scarecrow.

'What right!' Annie shouted into the body of the hall. Her words thundered to the high roof, bounced back, echoed all around. Her gaze darted back and forth, looking for movement in the bowed heads. Nothing. White heat flared inside her. No one used the memory of her mother this way.

'What right!' she shrieked, swinging out at the wooden props in the pews. Dust rose in thick clouds around her, as dark fabric and cobwebs fluttered to the floor. She tasted age and decay as she coughed it out.

'What right? What right?' The filth stole her voice bit by bit, dragged it down into a gravel pit that seared her throat and suppressed it to a whisper.

A sound from the darkness behind her. Someone tried to hold back a reflex cough as the dust billowed. Annie spun round and stalked the length of the aisle. For a second she didn't recognize the crouching figure. Then a tiny voice said, 'Annie Raymond.'

Beth cowered and held out stick-like arms to shield one of the abominations from Annie's attack. Annie stared, then grasped Beth and spun her away. She peered closer at the bowed figure, fingered the cloth that shrouded it. No dust. There was a substantial mass under this cloak. And a voice. A tinny, off-key rendering of the chant. Annie leant closer, lifted the cloak. Beth was at her side, voice fearful, staring from Annie to the gently crooning figure. 'It's Grandmother. She don't hear nothing with her mind no more. She don't know what they've done.'

Annie hummed the chant in time to the old woman's meanderings. This wasn't where she wanted to be. The decay inside the big hall brought a sadness down on her, a malaise that grew from her feet and rose to the top of her head. Tears ran down her cheeks and fell into the dust. She turned her back on Beth and the old woman, and headed for the side of the hall. The hidden stairs. She knew where to go to find her mother. At last. After all these years. Round the corner of the pillar and down the shallow stairway. Her feet took her without hesitation. Annie slipped between the stones as a voice erupted from the far side of the hall.

'Beth, what in hell's the racket?'

'Grandmother got excited. She's quiet now,' said Beth's voice as the old woman crooned on.

Annie marched down the rough stone steps, footsteps sure in the pitch black, as the uneven stone carried her down. The rock swallowed all sound, all sense, it pressed down on her. She reached out a hand. Nothing there. *Mummy, wait for me.*

Relief to push through into the underground cavern, the real hall where the promise of the ritual above was fulfilled. Lights blazed. Harsh neon strips burnt her eyes.

A voice snapped, 'Take your fucking time, why don't you?'

She jumped, startled. A hooded figure was at her elbow. She heard the glare in his voice, though couldn't see the face. He'd waited to count them all in. She thought of the figure she'd ambushed, then watched a paper stuffed in a pocket, heard something slam shut.

The harsh neon had no place in her memory. It scorched her eyes here and now, forced some part of her to wake up. A level of new awareness sliced through, made her turn away, rather than blast the blasphemer with her tongue.

A tendril of doubt snaked in. Wasn't she invincible ... invisible? Awareness slammed into her mind. She was Annie, tumbling down from a high. Jak! *Jak, what did you do?*

She knew what he'd done. She remembered his words. *I only wanted to wake you up. Get you up on the ball a bit more.*

The cake or the cola? Why hadn't he tried harder to stop her? They were in reach of home and he'd let her barge in here to have the Doll-Makers' secret laid bare before her. The colours that swirled were sickly sweet and brought nausea. She edged away. The entrance was barred now, but the shock had cleared her mind. She struggled against an overwhelming desire to hide her face in her hands, to curl into a foetal ball and scream for her mother. This wasn't remembered fear, it was real, here-and-now terror. *Mummy ... don't leave me...*

She backed away, step by step from the irritable figure with the clipboard. Nothing to fight with. Shadows were her only allies. No way out. The door had slammed shut behind her as she'd made her way in.

No way out ... Except ... Except no one knew she was here. Until the person she'd attacked was found, she *was* invisible. And she had her memories, if only she could force them to the surface. The ritual ... the chant ... her mother. Trapped in the labyrinth. No, not trapped. There were other exits that avoided the building-with-eyes. A grass track down by a rocky beach. Miles from here. A broken-down hut by a blank cliff face. Flashbacks of real memory.

This vast space under the building-with-eyes was a tiny corner of a winding labyrinth, that spread tentacles out towards the sea.

One of those tentacles had provided a bolthole for people desperate to hide long enough to shake off their followers, to dispose of whatever they carried, to get their van to one of the high passes where it could be fired and pushed over.

It's mountain tracks they're interested in now, not smugglers' trails. Her father's words. So they'd known the van must have disappeared in the old smuggler's routes. And then later mountain tracks? They'd been looking for Julia's body by then. Had she been a mole or just a weak link taken advantage of by both sides? Annie wondered if they'd found enough to be able to match Julia's body to the leg in the loch. They'd all been so close to laying bare this secret.

There were other ways out and she must remember how to find them.

This was the abomination mad Lorraine had railed against. Harsh neon where there should be candlelight. Drugs processed and packed for efficient distribution where there should be plant extracts painstakingly teased out and distilled for use by the chosen few. Annie's memory walked her towards a space where senses were heightened, where she could fly with the birds in the forest.

Mummy, I want some too.

Here you are, Annie. Fly away with the fairies...

She backed to the side of the cavern. No one took any notice of her. She let her feet glide her silently along the wall, as she willed her memory to tell her where to go. Not even local legend knew anything about the labyrinth beneath the mountain. Childhood Annie knew it all, every step, because coming back into the middle of it put her ahead of the home-time sweetie.

Eat this sweetie, Annie.

I don't want it. It takes stuff out of my head.

Eat!

She had eaten and the memory drained away. No wonder her childhood recollections were so fractured. She'd been stuffed with pills to keep her quiet, out of the way, and pills to make sure she forgot what she saw and couldn't report back.

Tell me about the picture you saw at the cinema, Annie.

Monsters, Daddy. I didn't like it.

But I thought it was a Walt Disney.

Oh, you know what the child's like with her nightmares. Come on, Annie. I'll make you cocoa. Mummy could always make cocoa to make it better. White powder sprinkled on and mixed in. She slept well when Mummy made cocoa. A sharp memory. *I want it like Mummy makes it!* Mrs Latimer had no idea, but she'd hated Annie's mother all the same. All these years, Mrs Latimer had cursed the right person for the wrong reasons, and Annie could only resent her for doing it.

She held herself upright as she headed for the far side of the cavern, looked neither to right nor left; felt the tremble deep inside her; felt the tear trickle down her face. She was back beside her mother's coffin. At last, the memory was whole.

I didn't want her at all. I just wanted to get at the pills in her jacket pocket, as she lay in her coffin. The pills that took memory away, that would make it not have happened.

She let her feet carry her where they would, knowing they'd take her to a half-forgotten exit, and that she'd know the way when she got there.

Recognition hit her peripheral vision. She ducked her head. Mr Caine. The cloak covered his face, but she'd know that fussy walk anywhere. With oily obsequiousness, he engaged a large man in conversation. A small pack was in his hands, a limp straw doll at his feet. He still carried on the family tradition, after a fashion. Annie watched from the corner of her eye as she sidled past.

She remembered the plants. The gateway to the Doll-Makers' world where they were at one with the spirits of the forest. Just a specialist sideline now to keep big brother Caine happy. Someone ... *who?* ... had seen the potential of this forgotten labyrinth.

The other brother? The one no one saw or knew about. The one with the odd name, Kovos. He surely was the one Lorraine called the supplanter; the one who'd spoilt it all, wrecked Lorraine's beautiful existence where potions distilled from exotic plants let her fly with the birds in the forest, sway with the trees, run with the deer. He'd ripped that away and built a modern and efficient drugs-warehousing operation. No mystery now about where a large drugs consignment might disappear for a few hours – into an innocuous looking shed on a remote track, to be swallowed whole by the mountain. As she eased her way across the huge space, her gaze flicked back and forth. Which one was he?

And all the time she kept an eye on Caine. If she recognized him, he might know her. And she remembered Mike and the message from Beth.

He's keen...

All the interest she'd shown in Beth's dolls. The dolls she stuffed with special substances for her Uncle Cain. Beth had tried to tell her who was behind it. Mike had been fooled by her accent. *He's keen ... He's Caine.* Mike. Annie struggled to hold back a sob.

If only Beth had said, *he's Kovos.*

Annie watched Cain/Caine crumple a doll in his hands. It was podgy, a clone of all the dolls that crowded her dreams. He twisted it in his hands and discarded it. Not podgy any more. A limp form fell to the ground, thin, stringy. It was a move Annie had seen a hundred times. Memories reared up, dolls stuffed full, dolls emptied and discarded.

Beyond Caine now, she slipped into the darkness at the edge

of the cavern. Her feet knew the way. Damp hung in the air in a corridor partly hewn from stone, partly shuttered with ancient timber. A gleam of daylight where there should have been no light at all glittered across two decades to show her the way.

Voices. Echoes of running footsteps.

She tried to shake the effects of the drug from her head. Another way out. She had to find another way out.

Memory grabbed her by the arm and pulled her along on feet that skipped over the stones as though they did this every day.

Shouts from ahead. She stopped.

There was a staircase. She knew it led back to the hall, behind the lectern in front of the congregation. Memory told her there'd be a fearsome old man haranguing the crowd, but she knew she'd find no more than an old tape-recorded chant playing to a congregation of posed dummies.

She stepped up quickly, kept low.

Once back in the hall, she crept to the dark edge and ran towards the big door at the back. Shadows were with her, and the pursuit underground. Half an eye on the wooden pews. Nothing came towards her out of the gloom.

Then the pounding of footsteps.

She was at the door now. What held it? She peered into the darkness. A stout plank wedged across held it shut. An old-fashioned but effective lock. She heaved at it ... felt the sweat bead on her brow.

Footsteps drummed louder. Closer.

Wood screeched on metal as she dragged at it. Couldn't stop her grunts of effort as she heaved it inch by inch. The footsteps closed in. It wouldn't come free.

Figures burst out of the blackness all around her.

She threw out her arms to ward them off and opened her mouth to scream for her mother, her father ... for Jak ... for anyone.

Hands grabbed at the cape.

In a starburst of colour and flashing lights, she fell down ... and down ... into a spiral that ended the world.

CHAPTER TWENTY SIX

A dream that came in fragments.

I'm lying here asleep. Where's here?

Nothing for a long time, just a disembodied voice. '... get to her dad...' Small sounds. Rustlings, creakings. Someone moving about. '... Yeah, and Jules too...'

Too soft for a floor. I'm lying in a bed. I don't know what a floor is. Or a bed.

Shadows dance out beyond the reach of sight. Footsteps. People come and go.

Where am I? What happened?

A first stirring of awareness. Annie knew she had eyes and that eyes could see. She tried out the mechanism for opening them. It felt rusted with disuse. Through the bars of a cage she saw a hunched figure.

Am I looking in or looking out? Is Lorraine a bit part in a book I read?

Her eyes closed. The cage door shut.

From a long, long way down, Annie rocketed up. At first, there was relief. Release from limbo. The ascent became a terrifying upward rush. Propelled as high as the clouds, spinning into nausea and dizziness, knowing she must drop like a dead weight to a crashing death far below. Her world exploded. A huge wave broke with a deafening roar, hurling spears of light to hit her senses. She screamed out in terror.

Through the pain she was aware that a hunched figure started up in alarm. 'Fuckin' 'ell!'

Footsteps. Another voice. 'She awake?'

'Iss Caine.' The words slurred, but she heard herself say them. 'Tell 'em iss Caine.'

'Aw, fer crying out loud, Annie! Will you stop saying that?'

No, no. Not Caine. Someone else. Caine isn't important.

Liquid at her lips. She gagged on it.

Wake up, Annie. It's OK. It's just a dream.

Yes, Mummy.

'Wake up, Annie. Wake up.' The voice insisted. She couldn't shut it out.

No, I'm not better yet.

'Wake up, Annie.'

She opened her eyes, tested her power to see, to hear, to feel. The pain hammered dully behind her eyes, the nausea subsided. She tried speech as she looked up at Jak. A gravelly croak she didn't know as her own. 'You saved me?'

'Not yet,' he said. 'Look, Annie, you've got to wake up. We've got to get going. C'mon.'

Two pairs of arms eased her to her feet. Jak to her left with the firmer grip. To her right, a hunched figure it took a moment to identify as Dish. Upright, she was able to see the contours of a small room. Scruffy, paint peeling from the walls. Damp. Progress was slow on feet that were attached but wouldn't do as she told them. A steep wooden staircase pitched in and out of focus. This wasn't possible. She tried to say so.

'Go first,' she heard Jak's voice. 'No room.'

The bundle of rags that was Dish shambled down below her. She wondered who would hurt the most when she fell on him. Jak, behind her, grabbed a handful of clothing, pulling material tight round her neck, pinching her skin. Her feet floundered, useless. She hung awkwardly from his grip, a cub in the mouth of a lion, and felt surprise he was so strong. Jak grunted with the effort of holding her as they went down ... down ... to a cold, damp basement.

Dish, ahead of her, was a hunched head and shoulders above a foreshortened body with no feet.

Somewhere along the way they put her down and left her. She huddled on the stone floor. The cold seeped into her bones. She had no means to gauge time passing, but knew they returned for a while, because the arms were under hers again, moving her. She sat on a heap of rubble propped against something scratchy. Jak talked. She thought she'd remembered how to understand, but it was hard to follow, like listening in a language where she had no fluency.

'Dish ... he'll show you ... wanted to know ... fire ... Jules ... Knows how ... Going to show us ... Pig...'

Pig? She stopped following, tried to interpret. *Wait. I can't hear you yet.* Her mind reached out to feel the space she was in. Cold, and more than that, empty. A space that had forgotten its purpose. A tiny part of it was her, lying up against the detritus of whatever it had once been, her breathing shallow, her body not her own. And a tiny part more was Jak and Dish, but their role shrank as she watched it. They moved away.

Don't leave me. I don't know what's happening.

People are like pigs ... Pigs are like people ... And she could hear snuffling sounds, grunts. A real pig. *A pig of a day ... pig in a bonnet...* And sounds of laughter, some of it her own.

She tried to move, and felt herself slip. The rubble was uncomfortable, and packed with sharp edges that sliced into her skin. The odour of decay rose up as the heap shifted to accommodate her weight. Her head rested for a moment on something deliciously soft. She struggled between disgust at the soggy smell of it and comfort at the feel. Then slid further until there was nowhere left to slide. Jak's face close to hers. He tried to talk to her. The words made sense as disjointed snatches. 'Dish found it all out ... he'll show us how it's done ... he got a pig ... pigs are like people ... burn a pig's carcass ... just like a person ... burn to ash...'

No, Jak. No. Impossible to muster the effort needed to speak. Dusk settled over her and she felt her eyes close.

When she woke it was dark. The only light crept in from high above. It showed silhouettes, shapes not forms. Numbed and part of her surroundings, it was as though the cold had welded her to the floor. She didn't know if she were close to death, but she was whole. Her mind worked again. She made no attempt to move. Just lay still and worked back over the path that led her here.

Jak had tried to keep her going by feeding her something. A crack derivative of sorts by the arrogant rush it produced. They'd crossed the mountain towards her father's house. And they'd had a car. So close ... There was no gain now in agonizing on if onlys. He'd got her free of the building-with-eyes. How? Where was she now? Where was he?

Maybe he hadn't got her free. This malodorous space might be a disused part of the labyrinth. Maybe he'd left her hidden and gone for help. Soon. They'd be back for her soon. She could prepare herself to help the helpers once they arrived. She would remember everything about the building-with-eyes.

The thought buoyed her up, then smashed her down again, as she remembered why she'd been able to infiltrate the place so effectively. She'd broken the spell of the forget-pills, torn through the heavy curtain that shrouded her mother's face. Her mother was there at the heart and the start of it. Joining the rituals, ceremonial eating, drinking, smoking ... a route to find the spirit of the earth. And after all these years, her mother's face slotted back into memory as easily as though it had never been absent. It wasn't the magical face she'd yearned for. It was ordinary, banal. No trace of the loving smile she assumed would be there. Her own face but different, harder, no trace of her father's gentler features, and she knew her mother had never wanted her.

All that pageantry couldn't have survived the old man by long. It had been dragged into the modern world as a lucrative warehousing venture. That Customs operation had been closer than it knew, almost following back to the heart of the lair. Her father couldn't have helped even if he'd known. He didn't know about the labyrinth. The Doll Makers knew and a few outsiders like Annie and her mother and Charlotte's sister, Julia Lee.

Kovos, the one Elora called the supplanter, was the key to it. Caine, an eccentric figure on the periphery, kept up the old traditions, with the traditional plants, with his specialist stock stuffed by Beth into the stomachs of the dolls. Elora was angry even back then. Annie remembered her face, her voice. Elora and her mother together. No wonder the voice had captured her when she'd heard it again.

What had Jak said? Something Dish found out. No, Jak. It's not important. Get word to my father. She'd let Jak down when he needed her, so he'd turned to Dish, his only other ally. She struggled to remember what he'd said that Dish would show her.

Fire ... No, I don't want to know.

How they burn to ash? No, Jak I don't want to know.

She summoned every spark of energy left and pulled herself to her hands and knees to crawl across to the door. Her eyes saw the stone slabs, dirt ingrained into the worn contours, as they swayed in and out of focus too close. The inferno raged in her head. 'No, Jak. Forget it. We've got enough. Take me home. Jak...' Her voice dragged through gravel.

The bottom edge of the door appeared in front of her. A draught sliced through the gap beneath it, cutting across her face. She strained upward and grasped the handle. It turned as she hauled herself upright, but the door didn't budge.

'No, Jak. Tell him we don't need to see.' The words were whispers now between gasps for breath. Glass-encased wire-mesh made a window in the top half of the door. She peered through the filthy glass; felt the smell of dank neglect seep into her nostrils. Another stone-floored space. Another door opposite. Closed. She imagined dragging herself across that other room, hauling herself upright at the next door, looking through on to an infinity of enclosed stone-floored spaces. Trapped in the labyrinth. It was the old nightmare come to life.

The space she looked into was empty but for a fat bundle in the middle of the floor, like a body wrapped in oil cloth.

She grasped the door handle, desperate to stay on her feet. Something caught her gaze. A red stain near one end of the tightly wrapped bundle, almost too small to notice at first. Now as she watched, it spread and oozed through the cloth in thick red gobbits that hung and then eased themselves to the floor. *Pigs are like people ...* Dish had found a real pig and cut its throat, and now ... No, Jak must stop this right now. She pulled in as big a breath as pain would allow, twisted the handle and pulled the door towards her. It didn't even creak.

'Jak!' she put all her effort into it and heard just a thin wail that wouldn't penetrate this one door, never mind the infinity of doors beyond. 'Jak! He's locked me in.'

Her legs began to buckle, giving up the struggle to hold her upright, but while she could still see through the glass panel, the first wisp of smoke rose from the bundle in the next room.

CHAPTER TWENTY SEVEN

Annie lay against the wood of the door until an acrid smell made her flinch. She coughed and retched as the stench hit her. A thick silver blanket oozed under the door, tendrils of smoke snaking up, dissipating as they hit the cooler air.

She dragged herself away from the creeping blanket of death that followed her across the floor. Flashes of light reflected in the glass panel. The fire burnt fiercely now. She could hear the crackle of flames bedding themselves in for a long haul.

As she listened, the sound changed and became the roar of a burner at full power. It startled her into action. There was no escape in this windowless hole no matter how high the ceiling. She had to stop it, to fight back.

She crawled back to the heap of rubbish. The skin tore from her fingers as she scrabbled through bits of brick and concrete. Her hands grasped the slimy black gunge that had once been material. She lay across the heap, pushing the bricks aside, releasing the cloth.

As she dragged it back, she had to stop to lay her face to the floor so she could take a breath of air that would go down into her lungs without choking her. Blinded now by the smoke, she shoved and pushed at the cloth, ramming it into the gap under the door, cramming every last inch home to stop the silver cloud.

The smoke thinned as tendrils spiralled lazily upwards and away.

She reached up to clasp the door handle again to haul herself upright. A workforce of elves and goblins laboured double-speed with knives and hammers in her head, pounding her senses to pulp. She hung, still, against the door until the frenzy subsided.

The oily cloth did its work. A tiny flash of triumph sparked. *I'm still here. Still fighting.*

Her gaze was pulled to the glass panel, the window on her only way out. Smoke of every texture from threadbare black to smooth rounded silver pulled from the tiny furnace at the heart of the blaze. Air currents she couldn't guess at took curling tendrils up beyond where she could see. The bundled-up shape was visible through a flickering film-reel of swirling smoke. At its heart, it burnt fiercely as though it had an acetylene torch planted there, yet cloth was still recognizable at the edges.

Poor pig.

The smell of burning accompanied every memory of her mother's death. The accelerant. She could smell the accelerant. Her father had known. Right from the start when he'd seen Freddie's catch. He'd recognized the heat damage in what she'd seen as decay. He'd known it was the same murderer, all these years later.

As she watched the fire, pieces of the cloth curled in the heat and began to unravel. With that furnace roaring at its centre, it was clear it would burn to ash. But it explained nothing. Was it something in the wrapping, something in the accelerant?

She thought of the care with which leaves and bark were harvested, seeds pressed, oils extracted. Didn't know if she remembered sights from hours or years ago. She could tell him what they used in the fires now. It's a by-product of one of their magic potions, she'd say. It's from the stuff they grow underground.

'Oh God, Jak. We didn't need to see this.' Her voice grated against the roar of the flames. And where was Jak anyway?

'Jak!' She tried to shout, and banged her hands against the door. There was no way to be heard through the roar of the flames.

She stared through the glass as the seat of the fire shifted. A binding gave way and more of the bundle unwrapped. Something broke free and flopped out, as though trying to escape the flames. Annie couldn't break the vice that held her gaze. She stared as the fire blackened and puckered the flesh on what should have been a porcine leg and trotter. But it wasn't.

It was an arm, a man's arm, and at the end of it a hand whose fingers curled in the heat.

Her legs succumbed to a violent shivering and couldn't hold her. She sank down. Now she knew why Jak hadn't come back to get her.

Time didn't matter now. Memories didn't matter. All that mattered was that the only person who knew where she was, lay just beyond that door, crumbling to ash.

Dish was one of them. Had she known him from years ago, had his face nagged at her subconscious all this time? She didn't think so. He was no more than a foot-soldier, but what a good one and what an act.

The only face she couldn't remember now was Kovos's, but when the fire burnt itself out, he'd come for her. And she could do nothing but wait.

Where would Kovos dump her body? In the loch? Would her father be there when it was found? Would he recognize what was left of his only child?

A part of her wanted to hear footsteps, to see the door handle turn, to have just one glimpse of his face to confirm that she knew him. Of course, he couldn't come for her yet. The fire made the only way in and out impassable. It would be hours, and all she could do was wait.

It would be hours. She gave her attention to the door. The only exit. The only entrance. Would he expect her to be conscious after hours in here? Would he even expect her to be alive? She pulled herself half upright and looked round. The movement jarred her senses to awareness of the smell of burning flesh that seeped through. Her stomach churned. She reached a hand up to her head and felt the stickiness of congealed blood in her hair.

No, he wouldn't expect her to be alive when he came to find her, but she was. He certainly wouldn't expect to find any fight left in her.

Still alive. Still fighting.

She pulled herself along the floor to the rubble heap and picked through it. A sharp-edged piece of mortar yielded to her efforts. She hugged it to her breast and curled foetal-like around it, in as comfortable a position as she could find on the hard floor.

Hours yet before anyone could use that door to come in or go out. Time to sleep. If he came back and found her sleeping, he'd finish her off, but if she woke first with energy levels boosted just enough to get behind the door as it opened. Just enough for one good blow before he realized she was capable of it...

It was the thinnest plan she ever staked anything on, but, as she closed her eyes, she gambled her life on it.

Her eyes seemed to open a moment after she shut them. She lay still. Awake. Aware. She moved her hands, felt the scratch of concrete. A brighter light than she remembered filtered through. The air felt damp and heavy with the smell of recent fire. The background noise was different. No roar of flames, just a steady drip of water.

She hadn't woken by chance. Her subconscious had jerked her out of sleep as a new sound filtered in. A soft grunt of effort and the rasp of something scraping on the ground.

She rose to her feet, ignoring the band of pain that tightened round her head, and moved forward. She made herself glide slowly, silently towards the door. The strength was there for one strike.

The handle turned and the door began to open. It stuck on the cloth she'd shoved under it. Another grunt of effort as it was pushed from the other side. She froze in the shadows, waited for her target. A foot appeared first, kicking out at the cloth to get it free of the door. Annie's stare was drawn to it. Red and black. She tensed, gripped the lump of concrete and raised it to strike.

Ellie and Kovos ... Elora and ... the supplanter ... Kovos?

Out of nowhere she remembered the biblical name for the supplanter. Had her mother told her or her aunt? The supplanter. Kovos, short for Iakovos.

Or Jakovos.

234

The door opened and he stepped inside. He looked right at her, took in the stance, the raised weapon. When he spoke, there was amusement as well as exasperation in his tone.

'Chris'sakes, Annie, you're fucking hard to kill,' said Jak, giving her a small back-handed slap to the side of her head that threw her screaming to the ground in agony.

CHAPTER TWENTY EIGHT

It was impossible now to do anything except go where he took her. He held her upper arm and pulled her through the door. The pain was a spear through her head. When he stopped to kick out at the still smouldering remains, she felt only relief that he let her stand still.

She saw a foot in a boot, attached to half a leg. Just like Freddie Pearson's catch. And even now she didn't understand why.

'Dish,' said Jak, as though she'd asked. 'Had his uses, but got a bit sentimental over you. He wanted to take you to your Dad's.'

I remember. I heard him say so.

'You got it now, Annie?' She heard the words but couldn't react while he dragged her on, out of the door she'd watched as the fire started. It didn't lead to an infinity of empty stone-floored rooms, just to a drab corridor. He strode down it, she floundering at his side. It opened to a small space at the end, where there were wooden benches, lockers, cabinets. He sat her down and turned his back to search through a cupboard. So confident he'd subdued her, it was safe to turn his back. He was right. She couldn't move. He repeated his earlier question. 'Have you got it now, Annie?'

'Got what?'

'How they burn to ash.'

'But you were going to burn a pig. You said ... I didn't want you to...' She heard her voice ramble through the irrelevant words. 'I heard it. I heard a pig. You told me...'

He laughed, and snuffled just like the pig noises that had confused her. 'I told you a lot of things, Annie. I told you Charlotte called me. I told you to meet me before you ran home to Daddy. You believed me, Annie. You trusted me. D'you still trust me now?'

He was right. His face and his voice had reached out to her from two decades distant, from beside her mother, and all rational judgement had flown. Too late to remember now.

'I told you I'd burn a pig for you, Annie,' he went on. 'And I did. Like I promised. Tell me, how did it burn to ash?'

'Uh ... accelerant. Some sort of special accelerant.'

He gave her a half-smile over his shoulder. 'Come on, I thought you were smart. You watched it burn, didn't you?'

'It? Dish might have been a loser, but he was a person.'

'No point fighting for losers, Annie. Your mother wouldn't have. What d'you know about the accelerant? Did you smell it?'

'Yes.'

'She told me it was the accelerant, you know. It isn't, but I believed her. That's why she wouldn't burn, but you will.'

Annie flinched.

'The accelerant helps,' Jak went on. 'It lets the flames take hold. It's the wick that's the key, Annie. One match'll do the job, if you have the wick right. Understand now?'

She didn't understand; didn't care. His hands reached out to tip the boxes in the cupboard towards him, so he could see inside. If she hadn't been able to see the likeness in the individual features, she wouldn't recognize him. This wasn't Jak, laid-back, not a care in the world. Nor was it Jak, panicked, vulnerable, unable to cope. Those Jaks never existed except as a desperate ruse to trap her, to find out how much she knew, what Charlotte had told her, where in hell Charlotte had hidden the tapes. And he'd been nearby when she and Charlotte shared confidences in the pub. He'd seen her in the distinctive Margot jacket that sealed Casey's death warrant.

'They know Casey Lane and Julia Lee were killed by the same person.'

'You knew it was Jules, then? When did you find that out?'

'Can't remember.' He didn't know she'd heard the tapes, and she must keep it that way, or he might target Aunt Marian.

Charlotte hadn't lied as much as Annie thought. She'd heard about a leg washed up, didn't want to say anything to wreck her sister's fake death, but was worried sick she couldn't find her. She'd known there was a Doll Maker connection. Annie remembered the questions. And she'd known Jak, in some guise, from somewhere, and walked into his arms just as Annie had.

'I didn't kill the other one, Annie. You killed her when you dressed her up and sent her out into the night. You knew, didn't you? Of course you knew. That's why you sacrificed her. You're one of us really, Annie. You'd be good if you hadn't your father's blood in you.'

He's right on one level, she thought. Her mother had made her part of the pack with all the powders and potions. No wonder it had been like coming home when she found the pill-pushers at school.

'And how did you find my little sister, Annie? How did you find Elora?'

She stared at his back. He'd stopped his rummaging in the cupboard. He'd spoken Elora's name almost reverently.

Would you really have killed your own sister up there on the hill? She couldn't ask because then he'd know she'd heard the tapes, but she knew the answer. If he'd caught her, he'd have killed her. What he hadn't been able to do was kill her later in cold blood. He'd plucked her from the hospital bed and made her tell her story in a protected environment so he could find out exactly what she'd done and who she'd told. It must have panicked him when Charlotte ferreted out the tapes.

And faced with the voice on the tape, Annie had crumbled; not even listened all the way through, because the voice reached out across the years and pulled her back to her childhood nightmares. She'd been just as helpless faced with Jak. Entwined in her past, he'd played her like a prize salmon and she'd never felt the line that snared her, until it dragged her beyond safety.

He turned to face her. 'How did you find her, Annie?'

She stared into his eyes, caught as a rabbit in a spotlight.

His eyes were Elora's, rationality gone. Sanity was a game they played with the world to get what they wanted. Jak ... Kovos ... Iakovos ... the supplanter ... was further gone than any of them, and she'd walked into his arms.

She tumbled back into his world the way she'd fallen into Elora's. 'You must have been so scared when I got away from you, when you knew I'd found Elora. If I hadn't answered your message...'

'But you did, Annie. Sinners always fall. It's how I know I'm right. I can feel the forest better than you ever will. You've never known where I am, have you? Where was I when you rang me?'

'When I rang you? I don't know. At Dish's place.'

'In your flat waiting for you to come home. I had to pull some strings to get to Glasgow ahead of you. You were already on your way, weren't you?'

She nodded.

'How did you find Elora, Annie?' Jak's voice was hard now. She hoped she'd bypassed that question, but now she had to answer.

'I ... uh ... I paid someone to steal some records for me. I got her address.'

'So that was your doing, was it? And he got an address. I was there, you know, near enough to go and see who was meddling. It was only luck that he got away. Someone you paid, eh? I might take the details. He was quite good.'

Annie didn't want to continue down this path, so pulled him back to more recent events. 'What if I hadn't taken that stuff you fed me, if I hadn't been hungry?'

'I'd have made you have it, Annie. I might have had to give you more, might not have had the sport of needling you to go inside. Fun, wasn't it? I didn't know how far you'd get. You got further than I expected.' His tone was friendly, reasonable. Of course, he'd have made her take it. Hadn't she had stuff forced down her all along? Pills from her mother, abuse from Mrs Latimer, and all the time her father with his head turned away. *Dad, you must have seen something...*

Only Aunt Marian had stood rock-solid for her, always doing her best.

In this fractured state, her mind couldn't compete with his. All she could do was avoid dangerous territory. Nothing would keep her from going over this edge, but she mustn't take her aunt this time. Or Beth. Or anyone. Ask him stuff he could boast about, that would divert him. 'How do they burn to ash?'

'You've seen a candle burn, Annie. It just needs a wick. And with the right wick you can get the wax to catch, then it's the devil's job to put it out. Bodies are the same. The fatter the better, but they all burn. With the right wick to direct the fire, the fat catches.'

'It can't be that easy.'

'It isn't easy, Annie. It takes a good while to take hold. People don't sit still and allow themselves to burn. Even if they're out of it, the fire doesn't always catch, but once it does, the body burns itself.'

'But even a crematorium oven...'

'Efficiency, Annie. They take them out before they're done. It'd take too long otherwise.'

'What do you mean, a wick?'

'Down the inside on a candle, down the outside on a body. Works down the outside of a candle too. Try it sometime and see. Well, you won't have a chance, but take my word. Of course, a wick down the outside burns too fast if it's the wrong stuff. I tried all sorts before I got it right. Simplest is usually best, Annie. Ah, here we are.' He pulled a case down from a shelf inside the cupboard and held up a long oilskin coat. 'Oilskin's good, Annie. Just right for a wick. Come on now. Let's try it for size.'

Automatically, she pulled away from his attempt to lift one of her arms into the coat. The movement as she jerked away sent a shaft of fire through her head and she cried out at the pain.

'Poor Annie.' Her skin crawled as he leant close and stroked the side of her face. 'Don't worry. I won't kill you here. I know what's right.'

It was hard to hold back tears of pain and tiredness, but she tried. She didn't care about showing weakness in front of him –

she'd have fallen on her knees and begged if it would have done any good – but he seemed to feed off any emotion. She tried to keep her voice matter-of-fact. Maybe, in his madness, he'd forget who he was, what he was doing

'What do you mean, what's right?'

'You weren't meant to go in an accident. Like Charlie. Or a sordid city murder, head smashed with a hammer.'

Casey died from a hammer blow. Annie wished there was a way to tell Dean she hadn't burnt to death.

'And you aren't even meant to go here. Not even here...'

Annie knew her instinct had been right. They were in some far-flung part of the labyrinth beneath the building-with-eyes. Through the pain of his putting the coat on her, she understood the reprieve. He'd tried to run her car off the road because she'd given him the opportunity and he knew she'd talked to Charlotte, but she'd outrun him and his sleek silver beast in her old Nissan. Then there'd been Casey and now she'd survived injury and smoke despite the locked room. It was unthinkable to him that he'd failed, that she'd been better than him. He had to rationalize it as a higher being telling him she wasn't to die an ordinary death. She was to go with ritual.

She wondered what ritual meant to him, where he would take her, and would the journey there allow her any opportunity to call for help?

'Take these, Annie.' He stood at her side, three white tablets in his hand. He knew she hadn't given up. He'd mocked her up above the building-with-eyes, needled her, knowing what the drug would make her do. What would these tiny pills do?

'No. No, I don't need them.'

'I want you to take them, Annie.'

'No, really. I don't need to take them. Please Jak ... Please Iakovos...'

With no warning, his face pressed close to hers, his hand grasped the material at her throat, choking her. 'You do not know who I am!' he screamed at her.

'No ... no. I don't know...' She rasped out the words through the vice that crushed her head, the twisted material that closed off her windpipe.

He dropped her as quickly as he'd grabbed her. She sat gasping for air, praying for the pounding in her head to subside. She watched him add another two tablets to the ones he still held in his hand, then watched him crush them to powder.

'No ... Jak ... please...'

One hand pinched her nose, and snapped her head backwards. The other was at her mouth, stuffing the bittersweet powder between her lips. She choked and gagged, would have promised to swallow any number of pills if she could have spoken, and begged him to let her go, to let her breathe.

When finally he released her, she pitched forward, retching and trying to cough the powder out of her lungs. She saw the floor swim in and out of focus, knew it was too late. Lead flowed into her limbs and she would have slumped to the ground if he hadn't caught her and lifted her to her feet.

It wasn't like waking up because she was never asleep. She was aware they moved outside; the cold air seeped through her clothes to stroke her body. Forest floor swung into focus and out again. She smelt it. Childhood rambles in the wood, the musty aroma of the undergrowth as small feet kicked through.

Sometime later, he put her on the ground, face in the earth. A sour taste flooded her mouth and her lips felt gritty. The sickly smell of scorched fabric puckered her nostrils. She felt a hand at her back as Jak lifted her to a half-sitting position.

She knew this place.

She looked at Jak as he wandered away from her, inspecting the ground as he went, turning the black earth with the toe of his shoe. He turned and came back to sit facing her. He glanced at his watch. She strained to see but he kept the watch face turned away. The wind gusted through the trees, blowing her hair over her face.

He stared up into the trees. She looked too. Branches waved frantically against a dark sky. The force of the wind grew. The green canopy above rustled in alarm as the wind raced through trying to rip the leaves from their branches. At ground level, an invisible blade sliced through the detritus of the forest floor, throwing flurries of leaves and twigs into the air. It must be late in the day, and a storm was brewing.

The smell of scorched earth rose up again.

Jak eased himself to his feet. He walked over and looked down at her, then dropped to his knees and lifted her hand off the ground, tucking it inside the oilskin coat. He did the same with her other arm and pulled the belt tight so she was in a makeshift straitjacket.

'There, Annie. That's better. Nice and well-wrapped, burns better.'

Her mind had thrown off the chains of the drug, but her body was as limp as one of Beth's straw dolls. She tried to hold down the panic. If she gave in to it, she'd suffocate.

'Wind like this'll really make the flames take hold.' His voice held satisfaction; the weather stormed its approval. At last, he would sacrifice her in a way that would work.

She wanted to ask if he'd kill her first or just set her alight, wanted to know how he'd do it, but couldn't frame a question she could bear to ask.

Beth came to mind. Beth, who knew these woods, who was minus seven years old when Annie's mother died. 'How old were you, Jak?'

'I was twenty one when she went.'

He'd known both the question and the answer, without any pause.

'Did you kill her, Jak?'

'No, Annie. I sacrificed her. She was the first. I told you. I barely scorched her. I doubt she'd have burnt though, whatever I used. She had the devil in her. I wonder if you'll burn.'

The breeze cut cold across Annie's face, where tears tracked down. She couldn't stop them, didn't even know who she cried for. 'Why did you kill her? Why did you kill my mother?'

'Annie, your mother was dangerous. Loose cannon barely scratches the surface. And she was greedy. Where d'you think we'd be now if she'd stayed above ground? With her boasts and her tantrums. She wanted it all at once. It wouldn't work that way. It needed patience. Your mother had no patience, Annie.'

It was true. She could remember that much now, but it wasn't why he'd killed her. He'd killed her because she always had the better of him.

Annie thought of the old man, Kovos and Elora's father, who had died a couple of years before her mother. So Kovos's plans would have been in embryo. Was he sane back then? Elora stuck around for several years afterwards. It had taken a long time to build all this to the efficient operation she'd seen. He must have been sane to get it all off the ground, to keep it going. And now it was in the process of falling apart. Customs sniffing round ... Julia finding things she shouldn't ... and now Annie. He may have been sane once, sane enough to cope, but he was long past that now. So too was Caine. And Elora, who had left them in their small crazy world, and fled to the safety of hers miles away.

Aunt Marian had known him. She'd seen the face of Kovos behind the façade of Jak, but then recognized him as Charlotte's young man and her first impression was chased away. He was *the lad* her aunt meant when she'd talked about Annie's mother taking an unhealthy interest in the Doll Makers.

It was the lad. He nearly led her astray.

Kovos, six or seven years younger than her mother, would have been just a lad to Aunt Marian. There were twenty years between the two sisters. Her mother had been a late baby, spoilt as much by her doting elder sister as her ageing parents.

Now that she unleashed them, memories of Kovos crowded her. The dream where her mother snatched the doll away and scratched her hand had been real.

I want a doll, Mummy.

I said you shouldn't fucking bring her.

No fucking choice, sweetie. She won't say anything.

She's six years old, for Chris'sakes! She'll remember.

Not after the cocktail she had for breakfast.

Loud laughter.

'I remember you from when I was six years old.'

He glanced at her and turned away. The manner of her death was in the hands of a madman. A madman who had killed her mother. And as soon as he'd seen what Freddie pulled from the loch, her father knew it was the same killer. That was what he'd hidden from her all along. She remembered the look on his face. And now his daughter would go to the same man. It would kill him too.

They should all have listened to Aunt Marian. She'd homed in on the tapes, got them out of Charlotte's grasp and hidden them away. She'd recognized Kovos, and she'd known there was more to the straw dolls than the limp oddities Mr Caine sold in his shop.

Your mother bought one ... just a few days before ... I kept it ... always wondered.

And the fat dolls of her own dreams had substance. They were real memories. Her mother, stuffing dolls so their middles bulged ... dolls she wasn't allowed to touch. Dolls that never coincided with memories of her father.

'What are you thinking about, Annie?' The voice from across the clearing caressed her, as though they were lovers, as though he really cared. She looked into his face. It looked back, smiled, almost made her believe in it.

She wouldn't say a word that might take him to her aunt. The trouble with Aunt Marian was that she always had the story sideways. It was the wrong bits she got wrong. Mrs Watson's nephew who'd seen Jak from his bedroom window. It was the alibi that bolstered Annie's misplaced trust in Jak. Hard to believe she'd missed it.

It must have been the holidays.

He wasn't in the school dormitory, he was at home. And that put Jak right on the spot for the night Julia's remains were tossed into the loch.

She'd forgive Aunt Marian because what would she know about school timetables? She'd forgive her aunt anything now. Not that there was anything to forgive. Tears fell from her eyes and dripped down her cheeks.

'Don't be scared, Annie. Nearly time.'

Jak glanced at his watch, then up at the sky. The wind redoubled its efforts to grab the leaves from the trees. If she summoned the energy to scream, the sound would be whipped away and swallowed up.

'Are you worried your dad'll find you? He won't. It'll be Cain. He'll trot up here to see who's lit his bonfire.'

She stared through the fog of the tears that wouldn't stop. He thought that was some sort of consolation. It would kill her father whoever found her, and Aunt Marian too.

She sat in the dolls' graveyard knowing that if her body worked, she could get up and run through the trees. She'd be at her father's door in minutes.

Jak got to his feet. He pulled a knife from his pocket and twisted the blade so it glinted in the light.

So it was to be the knife. She tried to cry out and he gave her a look of surprise. The storm ripped through the trees like a well-intentioned friend coming to the rescue with all the wrong weapons. If it would only be still, she might shout and be heard.

He advanced step by step across the clearing. His footsteps must have crunched in the burnt straw, but all she could hear was the building storm. In a few seconds she would die.

Time slowed to a crawl as an image of her aunt appeared as a ghost somewhere behind Jak. Annie smiled. And there was Mike, a long way behind, searching but looking the wrong way. That was OK. Aunt Marian came first in her thoughts. She wondered if Mike had bled to death on a street hundreds of miles away. How much better to die here within reach of home. Maybe her aunt had died too, and came as a ghost to witness Annie's death. That was good. Far better Aunt Marian was dead than had to bear the news that her niece had died.

There was a third person. Annie almost took her gaze from the glinting blade to try to focus. The small figure didn't come her way, but went off at a tangent. It must be her mother. Jak was very near now with his knife. She sensed his need for her to meet his eye.

The distant figure trailed a cloud of purple. No image of her mother matched that shade. It belonged to a far more recent memory. A long purple scarf. Beth.

Her eyes were forced to meet Jak's, uncomfortably close now. He needed the point of her death to be an intimate moment between them.

She didn't want to look at him, but couldn't look away. She wanted the last thing she saw to be her aunt. The ghost came closer. Annie smiled. Jak smiled back, not knowing she smiled at her aunt. Even in death, Aunt Marian did what she could for her niece, no thought to her own safety.

The ghost of Aunt Marian took a swing at Jak. It was a good sight to die to. Maybe it would dull the pain of the knife.

Jak staggered.

'Oh my God!' The exclamation was torn from her as everything else rushed up at once. Jak felt the blow. It was no ghost. It really was her aunt. She'd seen the knife and hit him without further thought. It hadn't even knocked him off his feet. He'd kill her with one twist of his wrist. But Mike ... Beth...

Thoughts spun as Jak, only slightly off balance, stumbled towards her. She had to stop him. She had to do something ... anything ... to give Aunt Marian the glimmer of a chance to run. But she was in a straitjacket. Mental and physical.

Jak's leg thudded down in front of her, foot planted into the soft ground, already turning...

Her feet were numb, her hands held in a vice she couldn't break. But his leg brushed her face, and even cramped limbs could propel her far enough. She launched herself with every ounce of strength she could muster. She heard his 'Uh!' of surprise as her face pressed into his leg. She bit hard, feeling substance beneath the mouthful of cloth, and she clung on, not knowing if the pain came from the effort of movement or the volley of slaps to her head. She heard an animal shriek of pain, felt her mouth fill with blood.

The flesh between her teeth writhed as a dart of movement showed a dark object – fist or boot – flying towards her. It closed with tremendous speed and at the point of impact, memory stopped.

Chapter Twenty Nine

This light was different. Waking up was a concept Annie strived for and thought she'd never understand. Then it happened, and was ordinary. She lay on her back in a bed with shallow bars at either side and watched a face come into focus.

'Hello, Aunt Marian.'

'Hello, dear,' the placid voice replied, as Annie closed her eyes and went back to sleep.

The next time she woke, the room was crowded. Aunt Marian, her father and ... she stared at the figure standing at the foot of the bed. 'Mike...?'

'Hi, Annie.' He smiled the smile she remembered so well. A real smile, just for her, that melted her inside. Tears streamed.

'But ... Mike...? You're OK?'

'Never mind me.' His voice wasn't quite steady. 'It's you we need to worry about now.'

'I'm fine.'

'No you're not, dear.' Aunt Marian's tone was stern. 'That's a serious head wound and you've fractured your skull. So just lie quietly and rest.'

'But Mike...?'

He flicked open his jacket, showing a shoulder encased in white bandages and arm in a sling. 'I'll be fine. Should get this lot off next week.'

It was later, as the pieces slotted back into sequence that she was able to ask, 'What happened to Lorraine?'

'I'm afraid Lorraine's gone, Annie,' her father told her. 'No trace.'

Under her own steam, Annie wondered, or had someone spirited her away.

'Aunt Marian, how did you find me?'

'I knew at once where you'd be. Your friend here contacted your father and they found this message. Then they found your car.'

'We had someone at the Western terminal most of the day,' her father said. 'We couldn't find anyone who'd seen you, so we didn't know where you were.'

'I came across on a Cal-Mac.'

'But why, dear? We always use the Western ferry on that crossing.'

'I expect Annie had good reason.'

She looked up and met her father's eye. 'Yes,' she said. 'I was hiding from the wrong people.'

If she'd looked through Jak's binoculars, she'd have seen her father's colleagues down there. What would he have done when she tried to run down to them? Used force, made her go with him. It was too late by then, she was in the trap, but she wished she hadn't made things so easy for him.

'Where is he?' It was the question she'd wanted to ask since awareness first crept back. She didn't need a location, just to hear he was behind bars somewhere secure.

An awkward interchange of glances over the bed.

'You didn't get him! He'll come back for me!' For the first time she struggled to rise. Pains shot through her head, an alarm screeched from somewhere behind. It was Mike who was there to push her back to the bed.

She put her hand on Mike's arm but her eyes sought her father.

'He's mad. He might do anything...' She stopped. Did he know what Kovos had done? Yes, he knew. He'd known all along.

'There'll be someone with you night and day until he's caught,' her father said.

'Stop worrying Annie with that sort of talk,' Aunt Marian snapped.

Annie saw her aunt's lips purse in disapproval. It was just the way she'd known it would be. She must get her on her own

250

and talk to her about Mike, explain that much as she liked him nothing could come of the relationship.

'Please tell me what happened. I can't remember. I saw you through the trees, Aunt Marian.'

'We found the message on the answer-phone at the flat,' Mike said.

'I knew who it was at once.' Her aunt's voice held a terse I-told-you-so undercurrent, and Annie remembered it was her aunt who'd been right about Charlotte, right about the tapes. She'd recognized Kovos's voice too, but no one had believed her.

'Someone reported smoke coming from an old shack at the edge of the forest. It led us back into that maze and we found a body,' her father told her.

They didn't know whose remains they'd found – well, she could help them out there – but all that could come later. Annie remembered the way the smoke had curled upwards and away. How insane must Jak be to have played that stunt where he did? Smoke seeping out where there shouldn't be smoke. After all they'd struggled through, he'd given away the secret of the labyrinth himself.

'When I realized what we'd found,' her father said, 'a lot of things fell into place. Caine's involvement for one.' He told how they'd worked their way back to the building-with-eyes. 'We've put a stop to this end of the operation at any rate. And with what we have, and the people we found, we might yet get a handle on a wider network.' Forensics, he told her, were crawling over the post office, the building-with-eyes and the Doll-Makers' house. Annie made a mental note to tell him about Margot's company, the great value-for-money security firm that had inveigled itself to a position from where it had access to all manner of stuff, not least a perfect money-laundering set-up. The betrayal would be uncomfortable but she needn't face it yet. There were more important issues.

'Not Beth. She wasn't part of it. I mean, she was forced. She tried her best to warn me. You mustn't let them put her in care or anything. She'd hate it. It wouldn't be fair.'

'No, it certainly won't come to that. It seems the older ones made some of their contacts the time they were in care. The old man didn't know how right he was when he said they'd come to more harm in care than with him. But no one's after Beth. That child's not a danger to anyone.'

'How did you know where to find me?'

It was Mike who'd remembered her tale of finding the dolls' graveyard, but only Aunt Marian had known where it was, not that they'd taken any notice at first.

'I doubled back,' Mike said, 'when I realized your aunt must be right.' That explained Aunt Marian there on the spot and Mike far behind.

'Was anyone else there?'

'No,' said Mike, 'but I'd called your father so he was on his way.'

Her aunt's gaze shifted from side to side, but she said nothing. 'You were so brave, Aunt Marian, tackling him on your own like that.'

'What else could I do? He had that knife.'

Annie knew she'd seen Beth in her flowing purple scarf. It must have been Beth who'd brought Aunt Marian to the spot. Her aunt hadn't known the dolls' graveyard, but she'd known who to ask. And once she'd led her there, Beth had made off in another direction. She wouldn't want her mad uncle knowing what she'd done. Annie understood that, but was puzzled as her memory watched Beth make off through the trees. It wasn't the direction she'd have expected her to go.

'He saw me coming and he ran.' Mike's voice held some pride. He'd led an exciting life since living with her. 'We didn't try to follow. We stayed to help you.'

'How did he get away?'

'He must have doubled back before we got there,' her father said. 'He may have had a car down on the road, or hitched a lift or something. We haven't found any trace, but we will.'

Annie wanted to believe Jak had run away, but he hadn't. He was nearby. She could feel it in every nerve end.

After her father and aunt left, Annie didn't try to catch the thoughts floating in her head until the sky darkened and the moon came into view, then she let them coalesce. Jak was a killer and mad. He'd come back. He couldn't let her win.

'Five times he tried to kill me.'

'Five!' Mike stared at her, aghast.

She catalogued the incidents to herself. It was five, but Mike didn't know about the night on the pass or the evening at Margot's, and maybe it was best it stayed that way.

She thought about Jak running away. It had happened beyond the point of awareness for her. Why had he run? He'd only had her aunt and Mike to deal with.

'Look, I'm sorry about Aunt Marian. This *your friend* stuff and all the sharp looks. And after all you've done for me.'

'Don't worry about it, Annie. I've weathered worse than that.'

He certainly had while he'd been with her. She reached out to touch the sling on his arm. He must have been strapped up when he came through the forest. Jak, armed with a knife, ran away from Aunt Marian and Mike with his arm in a sling? A prickle ran across her skin that made every nerve end stand to attention. Jak must have assumed her father was close behind with reinforcements. Mad but not foolish, he'd kept one step ahead for years.

'Mike, did they search the forest? Did they find any clue which way he went?'

'It was difficult with the way the storm was blowing, but they assume he doubled back and—'

'No, he didn't. He thought he was trapped. He went straight down the hill towards the loch. You've got to tell my father. Now.'

'Annie, he couldn't have. There's no way down there.'

'He did. Ring my father right now. That's where they'll find any clues to where he went.'

He didn't believe her, but that was fine, as long as he passed the message on. Because she knew exactly what he'd done when he thought he was trapped. He'd run the same way Elora had that day on the moor, the same way she'd outrun him herself on the high pass, and later at Margot's; each time a suicidal sprint.

And because he'd done what they'd done, he'd got away with a head start.

The next morning, Aunt Marian brought a photograph. 'I knew I had one somewhere. That's him, isn't it?'

Annie looked at the couple at the periphery of the crowd. Jak was smartly dressed in a suit. She wouldn't have looked twice without Aunt Marian's words to guide her. 'That's my mother with him, isn't it?'

'Yes, dear. I'm afraid so.'

All these years, Aunt Marian had had a photograph of her mother. She'd never even thought to ask. It didn't matter now; the veil in her head had lifted. She looked at the image of Jak over twenty years ago. He didn't look so very different, hair a more even colour, and prosperous, but that was down to the clothes.

'It's no wonder I didn't recognize him when I saw him with Charlotte,' Aunt Marian said.

'You did recognize him, you know. You told me you thought you knew him from years ago.'

A short time later, her father burst in, a grin across his face. 'Annie, we've found him.'

'Found? You mean arrested, don't you? He's locked up, isn't he?'

'He's dead, Annie. We found him this morning at the bottom of a ravine. Don't know if the fall killed him, or he died later. Blood loss or hypothermia. The post-mortem'll tell us. I won't pretend I'm bothered what caught up with him in the end. It wasn't an easy route down, but you were right about which way he went.'

'What a good job you thought of him going that way, dear. He could have lain there for years.'

'No, he'd have been found. There was a length of scarf caught in the scrub. A flapping purple thing. I don't know if he tripped on it, or if he was wearing it and it caught when he fell, but it marked out the place he went over.'

Annie said nothing. She knew now why Beth had gone in the wrong direction. Beth knew her uncle well enough to know exactly which way he would run. What had happened up there? Maybe it was best that no one would ever know.

In the end, Kovos hadn't managed it. Both she and Elora had outrun him. Annie wondered if he knew that in the second before he died.

Later, when the machines were disconnected and discharge dates were mooted, Annie sat in a chair by the bed and watched Mike fiddle with the TV controls. It occurred to her that he'd been with her every day.

'Shouldn't you be at work?'

'Yeah, should have been, but I decided to stay here.'

'And...?'

He shrugged. 'They sacked me.'

'But the flat ... the bills ... We can't manage...'

'Yup. I might have to call in that loan.'

'But—'

'Joke, Annie. Joke. I can keep us afloat till I get another job. Anyway, your business is going OK now.'

It seemed an age since she'd given it a thought. Pieternel would be spitting feathers having to carry her like this.

Mike looked out of the window. 'Looks like your father's car. He's brought your aunt.'

Annie felt tears roll down her cheeks.

'What's the matter?'

'Aunt Marian tried to attack a madman in the woods. If he'd got hold of her, he'd have pulverized her.'

Mike came and sat on the bed and held her hands. 'Yeah, but he didn't. And he's dead. Now dry your eyes before she gets here.'

'She didn't even think about what would happen to her. She just rushed in. She's done everything for me, Mike. She's been there for me when no one else was.'

Her aunt was the only person who could truly know her and still love her. She'd seen that Mike was too decent a guy to throw himself away on damaged goods. How could she begin to explain any of it?

'She knows me better than anyone. That's why she's like she is with you.'

'I know.' He spoke gently, not understanding. 'You do choose some stupid things to worry about, Annie. Of course she's wary of me. She doesn't think I'm good enough for you. I'll win her round. No one would be good enough for her niece to start with.'

'No, it isn't that.' He'd misread it badly.

'Give it time, Annie. I've hardly had the chance to get to know her.'

She didn't know what to say. He really believed it. And looked at objectively, her aunt's behaviour could be interpreted as the doting aunt protecting her niece. Of course, her aunt always had been there for her, but as to thinking she could do no wrong, or that someone like Mike wasn't good enough, that was laughable.

'I'll nip down and meet them,' Mike said. 'They looked like they'd brought a load of stuff.'

As Mike left the room, Annie thought about the building-with-eyes and how it had unlocked the secrets of her childhood memories. The foundation of her world rocked. *Mummy's bad little girl. So bad that Mummy left her. Then Daddy's bad little girl. He'd had to send her away.*

But she hadn't been Bad Annie at all. Bad Mummy had dragged her little girl into a terrible world. And Daddy hadn't seen, hadn't understood, hadn't coped. Only Aunt Marian had been with her throughout. Not understanding, but closer to the truth than any of them. And always on Annie's side.

She made herself stand back, the way she'd learnt to do with the awkward cases, to look for what was there, not what appeared through the lenses of her own preconceptions.

Mike was right: Aunt Marian loved her and would do anything to protect her. She'd even lay into an armed psychopath. And under it all, she liked the woman her niece had grown into. She judged her a good and decent person. Instinctively, Annie wanted to set aside the judgement as ill-informed, but she stopped herself. This was dangerous territory. She must take things carefully.

The door opened and her father came in. He was alone.

Annie returned his smile. 'Mike said you'd brought Aunt Marian.'

'They've gone to rustle up some coffee. It looks like you'll be out of here soon.'

'Yes, it looks like it.'

'Annie, why don't you come and stay with me for a few days before you go back. Mike can stay too. Mrs Latimer'll have kittens but I'd like you both with me. I'll take leave. We'll have a proper break together. When you came up a few weeks ago, you must have been looking forward to a relaxing few days.'

Hardly that, but she wouldn't say.

'You never got them though, did you? I feel bad about that.'

'Why on earth should you feel bad? None of it was your fault.'

'Looking back, I can see how much you wanted to tell me about your business back in London and I never gave you a chance.'

'What? You mean you knew about it?'

'Not then, of course. I was so wrapped up in all that was going on. But I've spoken to Mike, and I had Pieternel on the phone the other day. She told me how well it's all going. I'm proud of you, Annie.'

For Pieternel to have told her father, it had to be true. It was really going to work out. It was hard to let the thought in, as though she'd chased away too many demons too quickly and needed to hold tight to some to keep her grip on reality.

'I'm just sorry I didn't let you tell me your good news when you wanted to,' her father went on. 'It's a shame for poor Mike though. He's lost his job because of what he's done for you. But don't worry, I'll do whatever it takes to see him through it.'

For a second, Annie wondered if she should feel cheated. Mike was the recipient of the support she'd wanted for herself, but it didn't matter. No point raking over old ground. It had been a rocky path to get this far and now it felt good.

'Yes, it's really coming together now.'

'I always knew you had it in you, Annie.'

Yes, Dad. It's good news.

NEXT TITLE IN THE SERIES

WHERE THERE'S SMOKE

When Annie's arch-critic, Barbara Thompson, goes to extraordinary lengths to get her help, Annie doesn't have to play along, but curiosity wins and she has to know why. It's when someone gets to Barbara first that Annie realises Barbara was playing a dangerous game. And now it's too late to walk away.

She's left with guesswork, supposition and the knowledge that whoever silenced Barbara now thinks Annie herself knows too much.